The Departure Lounge

The Departure Lounge

Stories and a Novella

PAUL EGGERS

THE OHIO STATE UNIVERSITY PRESS • COLUMBUS

Library of Congress Cataloging-in-Publication Data
Eggers, Paul.
The departure lounge / Paul Eggers.
p. cm.
ISBN 978-0-8142-5195-9 (pbk. : alk. paper)
I. Title.
PS3555.G34D47 2009
813.'54—dc22
2008054875

This book is available in the following editions:
Paper (ISBN 978-0-8142-5195-9)
CD-ROM (ISBN 978-0-8142-9195-5)

Cover design by Jason Moore.
Text design and typesetting by Jennifer Shoffey Forsythe.
Type set in Meridien.
Printed by Bookmobile.

∞ The paper used in this publication meets the minimum requirements of the American National Standard for Information Sciences—Permanence of Paper for Printed Library Materials. ANSI Z39.48-1992.

9 8 7 6 5 4 3 2 1

For Ellen,
as always

Contents

Acknowledgments

EARLY VERSIONS of these stories appear in the following periodicals: "This Way, Uncle, into the Palace" in *The Missouri Review;* "Monsieur le Genius" in *Agni;* "Won't You Stay, Please?" in *Prairie Schooner;* "Hey" in *The Santa Monica Review;* and "What's Yours, What's Mine" in *New England Review.*

This Way, Uncle, into the Palace

MY NEPHEW Xuan, now forty and too old for such talk, used an American expression I had never heard before, and after his wife explained it to me in laborious detail I briefly fell deaf. This was at our annual family picnic in Fresno, under a shade tree. When my hearing disappeared I pretended nothing had happened: for months now, whenever I am spoken to insensibly, in a rush of American street slang or media references, I have experienced total silence, lasting up to a minute.

I have not yet told Xuan of my affliction. He sometimes seems to me no longer Vietnamese. His American wife, Janet, and their two mixed-blood sons, and even Janet's parents, whose house we are driving to after the picnic, have transformed him. His family extends me courtesy, but nothing more, and I sense that Xuan, too, no longer holds me dear to his heart. I am the last of my own family's Saigon generation, a dried-out stalk, and one day soon, I know, my nephew will place my portrait on the small altar in his garage and light funeral incense. Until then I have no desire to suffer empty and dismal lamentations from Xuan or his family. Time no longer welcomes my presence. I accept that, even as I accept the betrayal of my adopted language, one I have loved and cultivated for decades. It has now begun to turn its back to me, leaving me bereft, as if standing outside a door, until the door opens again of its own accord. There is nothing that can be done.

We had been at the park, eating picnic food, for perhaps half an hour. Xuan's sons, Peter and Jackson, played nearby in the meadow, throwing a football back and forth. Last week, Xuan told me, a despondent man had been shot dead by the police in their neighborhood. They live in a respectable area, one with many professionals, so of course I was curious. "Suicide by cop," Xuan then said, stuffing potato salad into his mouth. He wore a backwards baseball cap, in imitation of his sons, and he spoke the words so fluently—he still has an accent—I asked him how he came to know such an arcane expression. Then Janet leaned across the picnic table and informed me it was a common phrase. She explained its meaning to me. She must have been worried I'd start to ask for word derivations and such because she then leaned back and tried to expand the conversation. Imagine, she said to us both: imagine making a poor policeman carry around that guilt. What an act of spite, she said. Imagine pulling a stranger into your own darkness. It was like killing two people, yourself and the cop.

That is when my hearing briefly vanished. I nodded politely, and I passed Xuan a hotdog bun when I saw where his eyes were looking. Janet turned toward Peter and Jackson and yelled something, telling them, I think, to hurry up and eat. Soon, before traffic picked up, we would all drive to Janet's parents' house to exclaim over their newly installed hot tub. Peter shouted something back to his mother, but Xuan and Janet simply ignored him. If I had been the parent of either of those two boys, my response would have been much stronger. They had been speaking nonsense all morning, and they both laughed in my face when rude noises came from a mustard container I had squeezed.

I found myself wishing my deafness would continue all day, sparing me from the conversation that would ensue at Janet's parents' house. The last time we had all spent the evening together—it was Christmas dinner, with turkey and pineapple ham—I felt only insult. Xuan, of course, had fitted in quite nicely, raising his glass several times to toast ridiculous things—badminton, the Dallas Cowboys cheerleaders, the benign colon polyp his mother-in-law said doctors had just removed. I was seated at the head of the table, as befits my age, but the evening progressed as though I had been placed under glass. I was faced with disagreeable foods and youth music on the stereo. The conversation was first something about television, then the boys' sports camps, then some funding controversy about widening the freeway. I made an observation to Rick and Donna, Janet's parents, about Vietnamese refugees writing *Cali* on their mailing envelopes instead of *CA*. Why not? I said: in Vietnam that's what people had learned. When I was met with stares, I offered my opinion to Donna about the delicacy of southern Chinese cuisine.

Later, as I was about to return from the hall washroom, I heard Peter talking with Janet outside the door. They must have assumed I was in the main bathroom, off the kitchen, or outside with Xuan and Rick. Mother and son were conversing in low tones, and I placed my ear to the door. I pictured them, conspiratorial and intimate, standing in the narrow hallway leading to what everyone referred to as the Great Room—a dark, carpeted square with a hissing fireplace and dirty sliding glass doors that opened onto a neighbor's fence. Janet, I imagined, was stroking her son's hair, staring with great intensity. What I heard was Peter complaining about me. He told his mother I thought my shit didn't stink. I knew the expression; I recall frowning from surprise. There was silence, then Janet's voice: "You can say *presumptuous,* honey," I heard. "Or you might like *snooty* better. But you have to forgive people, OK? Now let it rest."

I said nothing, of course, and since that time I have even taken up the habit of returning the hugs Xuan's family gives me upon greeting. But as we sat at the picnic table—Peter and Jackson came bounding over, grabbing cookies—I found myself once again trying to comprehend the distance that existed between Xuan's family and me. When my hearing returned after, perhaps, a full minute, the first thing I heard was Xuan apologizing for saying "suicide by cop." He laid his hand on my arm. "It's just an expression on TV, Uncle," he said. "It doesn't mean anything more." He exchanged a glance with Janet, an anxious one, I thought, and though I am not naturally of a suspicious mind I wondered then if he had told his family about my daughter in Vietnam. I wondered how much he recalled from so many years ago, if he told stories that grew out of the air.

"That's fine," I said, and I drew my arm away. Peter and Jackson had returned to throwing their baseball, and the ball made a loud pop when it landed in their big gloves. In the distance, a teenage couple held hands; they stopped to kiss, and the boy put his hand on the girl's hip. Some youth band on a radio nearby played screeching music. Peter shouted out some joking American insult to his brother.

"Xuan," I said. "Nephew." I had no idea how to finish the sentence. I wanted only to say a familiar name and hear it answer.

— — —

During the American war I raised my only child, my daughter Lai, but I never knew her heart. Vietnamese fathers rarely do, which has always been another way of saying our ignorance makes us blameless. But I no longer accept this formulation. I now see in such ignorance an evasion: we Vietnamese of the Saigon generation choose to behave selfishly, then we make ourselves believe that no other behavior is possible. This is how we lost our country to the communists. This is why our own cruelty continues to surprise us. I will say in all truth that Lai does not reside in my memory as one's daughter should, like an ocean forever breaking upon the shore. She exists for me as a smaller thing, like a midnight candle ceremony: a string of bright, hissing illuminations in the night, wisps of flame surrounded by I know not what—striped lemurs asleep on palms, a man with the face of a pelican, giant starving carabao, all the richness and perfume of her life that was held at arm's length from me.

But what is one to do with a stone? She hardly spoke. She spent her days laboring like a dray animal, washing clothes and sewing, over and over. Though I am now familiar with the concepts of autism and neurological disorders, for years I had secretly thought her silence a conscious choice, an act of atonement for her birth: her mother, to whom I had been married only a year, died on the birthing table. Near the end of the American war, I would sometimes in the evening jangle coins in my pocket and stand by the back door to watch my daughter wash clothes by the small well in our washing room. She could not have been more than twelve. The smell that rose from the well was of ammonia, and when Lai paused to rest her elbows on the edge of the well, her skin glistening with water, she breathed deep and long, and she closed her eyes, and at such moments the look on her face seemed to me so distant, so pinched for such a young girl, that her skin in the moonlight turned pale and cold, like the washing floor itself, and I imagined her washing away the smell of her birth.

At the time, such fanciful notions seemed to me the very essence of poetic vision. We lived in the small city of Vinh Loi, northwest of Saigon, where I was a teacher of literature and language at an elite preparatory school for boys. I kept a row of small stones on my table in front of the classroom, and when some dull boy talked stupidly, I threw a stone at him. I was strict but fair, and my shirts were always crisp. In my study was an iron barrel filled with books that Lai would lay out in the sun to kill the earwigs that nibbled the glue. Every evening, after dinner, I put on Moroccan slippers, still trailing the sales tag from a Saigon department store, and walked into my study. I sat in my cane chair and corrected compositions. On weekends I lent my voice to the choir director's demonstrations of musical scales. I was, perhaps, something of a peacock. When the Ministry of Education proposed on blue letterhead that I, a respected man of scholarship and accomplishment, assume the position of headmaster, I exchanged my plastic-rimmed glasses for gold-rimmed glasses to symbolize the richness of my vision. I bought a soft flax cleaning cloth with which to clean my lenses, and at night I sometimes stared up into the sky and whispered poems to the stars about the nocturnal nature of the Vietnamese spirit.

When Lai was very young, I ran an extended household of Saigon relatives who had moved in to eat at my table and raise my daughter. First came Binh, now long dead, my rheumy-eyed aunt from my mother's side. In her wake followed nephew Xuan, who, before arriving in Fresno as an adult, spent a decade in a refugee camp in Malaysia; joining him was his brother Nhu, always plump and scabby. In those days, Xuan was a scrawny and shave-headed tadpole, entirely unremarkable. I had little to do with him or his brother; the boys lived with us only a few weeks out of every year. For reasons unknown to me they arrived by pirate taxi in the middle of the night, squabbled with Aunt Binh, then disappeared back to Saigon for months on end. From my father's side came ancient Uncle Duong, whose mouth snapped like a turtle's when anyone mentioned the Viet Cong. He had been a machinist, and the tips of his fingers were stained black with the oil of his trade.

We all lived, I thought, in harmony, even when Uncle Duong announced one night that diagrams of the Tao implied three, not two, natural forces: *yin, yang,* and the traitorous smaller opposite within each—like infections, he said, like the VC. Mornings, I rose early and threw open the window of my study to smell the canal that flowed, unseen, just past a grove of orange trees across the road in front of our house. I never talked to the vegetable sellers setting up for the day along the canal banks, though I took pleasure in imagining their labors. I pictured them carrying bundles of watercress and radishes and potatoes, then laying them across strips of mottled cardboard that had been soaked in the brown canal water; I imagined the smell of fish and rotting cabbage, and I imagined with much satisfaction their young sons unwinding the knotted twine around their parents' produce. I saw these boys, in my imagination, squatting on the cool cement, then leaping up to whip cockroaches over the canal bank with the twine, pausing long enough to wrap the string in circles and place the loops around their eyes, in imitation of eyeglasses. I was sure, in those days, how peasants thought.

In my mind's eye, in the cool and silence of early morning, I knew, I was absolutely sure, that the boys along the canal believed their string glasses would one day, as if by magic, become real plastic frames and lenses that would let them see the full breasts of American movie starlets painted on the marquees of the downtown streets, high above their heads. Their thoughts, I believed, were crass and even base, and because of that I did not believe our country could fall to an army of peasants.

There was, as well, no fighting in the town, and because of these factors I doubted the government's dire warnings. Our house was built of thick white stone. It seemed a fortress, and the rich appointments of its interior gave an impression of permanence. The corners were filled with vases from Laos and dried lavender, and the tile on the floor of our front room had been constructed of expensive stone from the Choong Tan quarry, in the Delta. We had a Belgian cookstove and two ceramic wash basins; in my study, workmen had installed dark mahogany wainscoting. In back, we looked out a handsome bay window overlooking a small garden, and our tile roof had been streaked by the elements into the color of mangos.

Most impressively, most assuringly, our front door was of thick, burnished teakwood, engraved with swirling dragons and fronted with a wrought-iron accordion guard door with metal guides running along the frame. Its only flaw was also a strength: a cable for the door buzzer had fallen from the metal clasps in the stone, so when you pressed the button, the cable moved as if alive with electricity. I kept the urchin boys from stealing our shoes—we kept them outside, by the door—by telling them a pit viper lived inside the cable. And stories, I knew, reached far, even across the river. Peasants with rifles, with murder on their minds, might race across the road under cover of darkness and sneak to our front steps. But who would raise a hand where a pit viper roamed? Who was to say others did not slither inside the buzzer cable and seek their prey on starless nights?

Yet despite my assurances, despite the confidence with which we undertook our daily tasks, all Lai seemed to do was sit alone, hidden, by the washing room well. Sometimes she hummed baffling little songs to herself; she rocked constantly. I knew, however, I wanted no part of Aunt Binh's explanations about earth essence and water essence. Lai, said Aunt Binh, had a bad wind. "Country talk," I said, and then I walked over to the bookcase to put on my reading glasses. "Great scholar," Aunt Binh said, mocking: "I'm ignorant. You explain it to me." She craned her neck forward like a child, folding her hands in anticipation.

"Lai's a schoolgirl," I said. "We have a saying at school: 'A schoolgirl jumps when chopsticks break.'"

Aunt Binh parted her lips like a fish. "Even the countryside knows that saying." She shook her head at me. "She's not just delicate. It's more."

Later, I poked my head into the kitchen, where my aunt pounded dog meat against the cement. "What's wrong with her is this," I said, and then I recited for her an English phrase I had read in a textbook: "clinical depression." The English words seemed to echo against the sheet metal of the enclosure, and my aunt looked at me as though I had pronounced myself a Viet Cong. When I translated the phrase for her, the Vietnamese words came out "a doctor knows she's sick and sad." Aunt Binh laughed. She lifted the meat high in the air and said it was the brain of an American doctor, and when last it spoke it said woof-woof.

So I withdrew my explanation. I went back into the front room, leafing through back issues of my *Phong-hoa* weeklies, which I sometimes read aloud in English to the family to let them hear the sound of the language. Now even the name of the weeklies didn't sound right in English. "*Manners and Morals,*" I said aloud. It sounded funny. It sounded a bit like country magic. But after dinner that night, Aunt Binh and Uncle Duong told me not to worry about Lai because meekness was, after all, an attractive lure for a husband. I was glad to hear them say this, for at the back of my mind I had begun to wonder if I had rejected the simple interpretations of my family just to demonstrate my sophistication. I accepted their optimism. Lai would grow into whatever flower she was, and I could sleep easily in the knowledge that I raised her with Confucian respect and discipline. So I agreed not to worry. I told them a father's love is absolute. I told them the Americans always talked about their love because they were afraid it would go away. I told them I would show patience. I remember coughing as I spoke; I remember taking my glasses off and rubbing them with my flax cloth and delighting in the knowledge that simply by removing my glasses I could turn my aunt and uncle blurry. *Spectral.* That is perhaps a more accurate word, despite its appeal to magic.

— — —

On those occasions my daughter spoke to me, her words were alarming. Three times a week, at one o'clock, I drove my Citröen to her school to drive her home. There she would be in her white blouse and blue shirt, with a brown satchel lying atop her shoes. The air would be alive with hummingbirds and dragonflies, and the sugar-cane vendors squatted behind their carts, chewing betel nut and spitting.

"Lai," I said one day, honking the horn. "Why the worry face? You look like an old woman."

"It's not a worry face," she said.

I looked at her in surprise. I had trouble recalling her voice. "It's a worry face," I said. "Don't you think it is?" I nodded, encouraging her to talk.

She played with the strap of her satchel and stared long and hard out the window.

"What are you looking at?" I asked. "What's so fascinating?"

"Our roof," she said, and she pointed.

I looked for our house. In the bright sunlight I could hardly see, and when I leaned over to look for it from her angle, I saw only the dull tiles at the end of the road. "What about our roof?" I asked. But the conversation was over. She frowned and rocked a bit, and kept her eyes focused on the same point.

I thought very hard, and I decided upon a meaning. I think for her our roof was a beacon: she always got dizzy in the center of town; it overwhelmed her, made her lose her bearings. Vinh Loi must have been a puzzle to her. I imagined her standing along the road, in the middle of the city, looking past the thatched homes of the lorry drivers and bricklayers. Her eyes would focus on the sooty huge marquee of the Oil and Gas Building, then on the tiny shops filled with mesh bags of raffia string and squirt guns and batteries. She would then look into the middle of the cobblestone street, then past the noodle sellers, the white French tables, the small eruptions of bougainvillea, the mechanics emerging from grease pits. She would be confused and alarmed until at the far end of the road she caught a glimpse of our tile roof, streaked the color of mangos.

For she was just a little girl, and perhaps she was too frail to plug her heart with strength. I'd watch her walk on the long padi dikes near the house, stooping occasionally to pat down dirt on rocks perched close to the water. To me, the rows of padi shined like mirrors, and in the early morning, before the sun burnt through the mist, the blue hills in the distance seemed to ring the town like braided velvet borders. I doubt whether Lai viewed the landscape with such serenity. When she arrived home from school during the rainy season, I was always saddened by her expression, which seemed to me small and fearful. In July when the monsoons came down in thick gray curtains, I pictured her waiting for me to drive up in my Citröen. I pictured her squatting under the eaves of the copra shops, watching men in black shorts heave the matted sheets from one pile to another and snort in the sweet acrid particles that rose from the mats like smoke. The pedicab drivers would cluck rudely to her, nodding to their small carriages, sometimes pointing up the road with bony fingers that popped up from their plastic slickers at impossible angles; and when the sewers began to race, the sweaty cafe waiters, all tattoos and Vo Cam cigarettes, would stand under the eaves with her, hacking onto the sidewalk, grabbing her arm in glee when the sewer water brought forth the small pink bodies of baby rats and plastic wristbands inscribed with Chinese characters.

In the rainy season, she told Aunt Binh, there were only sheets of rain pounding the buildings, only the sound of falling rocks, and when the rain flooded from the gutters it felt warm to the touch, as if it were alive. At night when she looked out the bay window, I saw her stare at the giant black clouds swelling overhead and close her eyes in prayer to the Jade Emperor, who she had heard was the source of beauty and terror.

"I want to learn to swim," she said one day.

I put down my newspaper. "What's so nice about swimming?" I asked.

"What if there's a flood?" she said.

"Then you'll drink so much you'll be too full for dinner."

Aunt Binh put down a pot and grabbed Lai around the waist. "This one won't drink," she said. "She'd be too scared to open her mouth."

Everyone said not to worry about Lai, yet everyone, all of us, tried to help her. In her school pinafore, Lai was called Moonflower because she was thin and brought her arms close to her side, like petals folding, when she was afraid. When Aunt Binh heard the nickname, she passed bracelets over Lai's arms, laughing that it was easier to thread a wooden needle. Then she pinched the bridge of Lai's nose to fatten her up. "That just works for babies," said nephew Xuan, dressed in green school shorts. He and nephew Nhu had arrived the night before; neither had yet changed clothes. Nhu, dressed in a dirty turtleneck, agreed with his brother. Aunt Binh hushed them both by bending her fingers into the shape of a claw and swiping at the air near his face.

"Lai, don't worry so much," said Uncle Duong. He looked down at his niece. "Or I'll throw you to the Viet Cong. You'll be VC stew." He smiled, then snapped his mouth open and shut.

Aunt Binh said the lines on her forehead looked like hair. Lai seemed embarrassed, but even in her sleep the creases stayed, thick as rings on a tree. Mornings, before Lai left for school, Aunt Binh would look up from mincing mulberry leaves and laugh: "Lai! Someone's pasted a leaf across your forehead!" Lai would nod, stopping in her tracks, and draw her hands up to her face to ease the skin back toward her skull; yet minutes later, as she did the morning sweeping, she would be met by cries of exasperation from her uncle. "I could walk to Saigon on roads like that," he'd say, and he'd point to her forehead.

One day Aunt Binh shook her by the shoulder when Lai let out tiny yelps over spilling tea from a metal cup. She wouldn't stop, and the very next day she began yelping again when a rat raced across the dirt patch in front of the house. From the storeroom her uncle's voice rose in irritation: "Lai! Stop that. Right now. Stop."

But she only got worse and worse. Nephews Xuan and Nhu said Lai was afraid of her own shadow, and in the evenings when the kerosene lamp reflected giant images of moths along the wall, they'd giggle to themselves and say Lai was a moth. In the afternoons when Lai bent over the water basin to rinse rice, they sometimes knocked on the corrugated-tin back wall with wooden blocks. She jumped every time. "Lai the hummingbird," they'd say, then they'd laugh very hard and very long. But even they worried for her, though they never said so. On Sundays, after attending Mass with their aunt, the boys would run to the bamboo fence surrounding a neighbor's house, trailing behind them dragonflies tied to strings. They'd set their faces, assuming stern expressions, then twirl around as fast as they could, pretending the dragonflies at the end of their strings were warplanes. "VC," they'd yell. "VC die." They'd twirl faster and faster, and then they'd send their warplanes smashing into the fence to explode on the invisible Viet Cong threatening their cousin. All would die: pilots, planes, enemy. But it made no difference. Day after day, they had to save her all over again.

— — —

When army convoys began to rumble along the cobblestone road in front of our house, Lai made known her distress. In our garden in back she planted tiny nubs of sorghum, sweet potato, and cassava. She planted them, she revealed, for the future.

"Is it as bad as that?" I asked.

In answer she made the sound of an explosion.

Her turn of mind was exasperating. Occasionally I saw silent white bursts from howitzers far away in the mountains to the north, but back in those days the bursts were like shiny carp under a bridge: they opened their wide mouths and said nothing, then they were gone. I revealed to

Aunt Binh one night my discomfort with the implications of disaster suggested by the garden. Uncle Duong raised his beer in agreement. Aunt Binh took a more practical view, arguing that subtle thoughts were never as filling as sweet potatoes and manioc pudding. Still, I took action. "We aren't peasants," I told Lai the following day. "If pork goes to ten *dong*, we'll pay ten *dong*. You see the charcoal in the storeroom? You see the basket of pine resin? We're well stocked."

Lai crinkled her brow at my rebuke, and when I saw the look on her face I felt so tender toward her I dropped to one knee. "An old woman," I said, smiling. "Is that what I see?"

I teased her that night just before the evening meal. I was freshly bathed, dressed in a white shirt, and I stood at the doorway and looked at my watch, then pressed my finger to the door buzzer, calling everyone into the house. It was six o'clock, precisely. Our door buzzer was loud, and because I pressed it at exactly the same time every evening, our neighbors viewed it as a kind of communal clock: parents yelled to their children; old men rose from their chairs to clack down domino tiles. I walked then to my study, and my relatives entered, one by one, kicking off their sandals at the doorway. I had grown so familiar with the different sounds made by their rubber flip-flops I had no need of looking to see who was coming in. Instead, I played a game with myself.

I heard two thumps at the front wall. *Thwack-thwack.* "There's Uncle Duong," I said, aloud.

Tik-tik. "There's Aunt Binh."

Then came the other sounds. Nephew Nhu, fresh from playing, kicked off his sandals and made sounds like spring rain. Xuan ran in after him; he aimed high, hitting the decorative design on the cinders. The sound was of small books falling.

Then I went into the front room and turned my back to the door. I addressed my relatives with a joke. "Where's Lai?" I said. "She hasn't come in yet."

Everyone laughed because Lai had already entered. She was in the kitchen, boiling water.

"Lai the ghost," said Uncle Duong.

"Lai," Aunt Binh called out. "Did you float in?"

But in fact I *had* heard her sandals. That was my joke: I pretended not to hear her, for the sound of her sandals was so slight, like palm leaves dragging in the dirt. *Shush-shush.*

"So you don't hear her when she comes in and out?" I asked. "You truly don't?"

Aunt Binh didn't know what I was talking about.

I asked Uncle Duong and the nephews if they heard. No, they said: Lai walked on mouse paws. So the following night I had Uncle Duong stand at my side, with his back to the door. I told him to listen closely. I told him everyone's sandals made a different sound. *Tik-tik.* "There's Binh," I said. Uncle Duong agreed. There was more noise. "There's Xuan," I said, and he agreed again. Nhu entered next, and Uncle Duong, frowning, shouted out the boy's name. Then I heard Lai's noise: *shush-shush.* "There she is," I said. "Lai's here." Uncle Duong looked at me. He couldn't hear a thing, he said, then he looked over his shoulder and saw her, and yelled in delight.

"Elephant ears," said Uncle Duong, and he waggled his own ears at me in mock tribute. Aunt Binh swore I was hearing air.

And so I began to view the small shuffling sound of Lai's sandals in a different light. I stopped making jokes about it. I was, I decided, privileged: I heard what no one else could. It was as though my daughter were playing music meant only for my ears, though, I had to acknowledge, my ears were not trained to follow with appreciation.

One evening I heard her sandals and turned around and told her that her feet were the noisiest thing about her. I told her she was so small and quiet that she might vanish. She listened solemnly, and at dinner she made a great show of eating two helpings of rice. After eating she threshed rice shoots for hours. Then she washed laundry, pumping the handle of the tiny well over and over, stopping only to slap the shirts and pants against the sides of the giant plastic tub, jiggling the water out in great splashes onto the cement, as if, I thought, she wished me to hear.

— — —

I was at the time intrigued by European ideas, filling the iron barrel in my study with English and French periodicals. I taught Shakespeare to my classes, assigning the highest marks to a student who noted that in disguising themselves as trees, Macbeth's soldiers acted with Taoist virtue. At school, my daughter was an absolute failure. Her exercise booklets were sloppy and she seemed unable to retain details from literature of any sort. Her ineptness embarrassed me, so despite my heavy workload I read aloud to her at night from sentimental Vietnamese classics in order to improve her scores. *The Story of Lady Khieu,* which every schoolgirl was expected to know, was my favorite.

The story told of a maiden, Khieu, promised to a mandarin's son, her first love. The fiancé was called away to war, and during his absence

Khieu was tricked and bullied several times over into a life of prostitution and horror. When she could no longer stand her existence, she threw herself into a river but was lucky to have a priestess pluck her to safety at the last minute. The priestess sent her to a temple, where she was reunited, with much rejoicing, with the mandarin's son, who in her long absence had married her younger sister. So great was the love still between Khieu and the mandarin's son that they agreed to stay together always. With the blessings of Khieu's sister, the two married, and Khieu was established as Wife Number One; yet so pure were their hearts that they restrained their passion and remained forever chaste with each other, lovers only in spirit.

When I read the final scenes my voice quavered with emotion. Lai looked at me curiously, her head tilted to the side. Her eyes scanned my face. She put her fingers to her throat and, sticking out her chin, she began to hum, imitating the quaver of my voice, adjusting the placement of her fingers until she located its source.

"Don't *practice* it," I yelled. I grabbed her hand and thrust it down onto her lap. "You feel it. You don't practice it." I had to restrain myself from slapping her.

That night, as always, Lai positioned a ceramic Buddha at the head of her sleeping mat and touched the photos of dead relatives, lined up like New Year's cards in the corner, just under a painting of Jesus. She drew a crinoline curtain around her mat, and as she sat upright to extinguish her small kerosene lamp, I could see her outline against the cloth. She looked like a small, padded chair.

I had grown comfortable having her in the house, but I had begun to worry over what I now saw as a shadow play of domestic harmony. I knew my daughter as I would know an *amah.* When Lai swept, she teetered forward, on the balls of her feet. She wore her hair in a bun, with stray hairs forever in her face; she sneezed with her eyes shut tight, as though making a wish. In the mornings she woke before dawn, while the air was still sweet from the charcoal fires burning in the neighborhood, and bustled around, shoving the small kerosene stove across the tile to the kitchen. Then I would hear her at the well, filling a pot for my tea and bowl of bananas and rice pudding. Lai kept the house spotless. She swept with a broom of bundled straw, and each week she removed the contents of my bookcase, wiping each book cover with duck feathers. During sunny periods in the rainy season, she laid the books out in the garden on a plastic tarp to drive away insects that might have nested in the bindings. She cooked without error, though with little variation, taking care to remove the stray small pebbles that sometimes accompanied the hard grain. I accepted her work as I would a basket of pine resin for the cookstove, or a table: it was simply part of the house.

But one morning I was lying on a straw mat, resting on one elbow, underlining passages from the class texts with my free hand. I wasn't thinking about Lai at all. Outside, scattering chickens as they went, army convoys began their daily forays out into the countryside. The gears of the trucks growled and whined, and I heard faint strains of laughter as each truck roared by. Then there was pounding at the door. "VC," a voice said harshly. "VC." I sat upright on the mat. The voice set my heart racing, though I recall thinking that surely the Viet Cong would not announce themselves in such a fashion. "VC," I heard again, then what sounded like the stock of a rifle thudded against the door.

I jumped to my feet. Lai came running in from the kitchen. Her face was stricken and pinched, as though she had been shot. Seeing her face so contorted made me think of a photograph I had seen of a Frenchman hugging a young girl, presumably his daughter. I stood to comfort her, sticking out my arms as if measuring for a mat, and walked with my arms outstretched to where she stood. I felt foreign and clumsy, unsure if my heart was pounding so fast from the thumps on the door or the awkward gesture I wished to copy from the Frenchman in the photo. Lai let out a tiny yelp and put one hand to her throat. With the other she flapped like a bird, making my embrace impossible. I returned one of my arms to my side and held her shoulder with the other, stroking her calm, while she looked at me with eyes that seemed not to register the difficulty of my attempt. "Look," I said. "Look." I pointed to the window. Two government soldiers trotted past the window, peering in, grinning hugely. They looked drunk. It was a joke.

When my heart stopped thumping, I reacted not with anger or fear, but by nodding my head where the soldiers had been. This time had been a joke. Yet it was now clear that the war was closing in on us, and the next time the thumps at the door might not be a joke. I thought about dying, and then I thought about Lai. I pictured her as a deep, dry well: death for her would take the shape of workmen coming along and simply boarding her up. I could not get the image out of my head. I walked over to the door and opened it, watching the trucks grow smaller and smaller. The chickens were pecking at the dirt by the road; a pedicab driver sat high in his seat, straining under a load of bricks; mist hung over the padi fields, blowsy and white as steam over a bath.

I realized what I had to do. A husband, I thought: a husband would send her sluggish blood rushing upward, as if from the depths of an underground spring. A husband would peer down, holding a bucket, and she would rise to the surface to meet him, reflecting moonlight, rippling, murmuring water language. I walked outside, barefoot, glad to feel the chill of the patio cement under my feet.

My idea, however, was obviously not without difficulty. I pushed the idea to the back of my mind, and there it stayed until one day shellfire shook the outskirts of the city and brought a soldier trotting down the street in the opposite direction. The man was pushing a wheelbarrow piled with camouflage boots. From the window I saw they were all caked with blood. I then forced myself to act on my idea. I would do it for Lai. I would make sure Lai had a husband. I would do it because I was her father, and I had given her life. I would do it because Lai was my flesh and blood, my moonflower. The next day I sent Lai out to buy a chicken. I then had her dunk it, still squawking, into a scalding pot of water. I called it dinner, but it was a sacrifice, too, an appeasement to the great natural forces. I told no one. I ate in silence, then ordered Lai to gather the plucked feathers and put them in her pillow when they dried.

Days later, not long after the ground had stopped rumbling from the shelling, Le Van Dien, a neighbor's son, came calling. Dien was a sergeant with a Ranger unit, on leave from his base up north in Tuyen Duc province, near the city of Dalat. He was homely, skinny and square-jawed, and though his family was often in dire financial straits, Dien was known to be honest and hardworking. He walked past our stone house, dressed in uniform, sucking sugarcane cubes on a stick. I was inside, reading. Lai, dwarfed by a giant conical hat, was out back, hoeing in the dry soil of the garden.

"*Ong*," I heard. "Sir. Are you here?" Dien stood on the other side of the metal accordion door, which Lai had left half open on her way out. I looked up from my book, and as I did I was conscious of the silence from the back garden. Lai had suddenly stopped hoeing.

I remained silent. It seemed a delicious moment: I, sitting on a straight-back chair; Dien, awkward and stiff on the other side of the door; Lai, her hoe resting on the soil, perhaps arching her back tensely, looking vaguely in the direction of Dien's voice. I pictured us as the three sides of a triangle, connected in blindness.

I heard Lai's hoe clank against the house. She was walking to the front. There was a long silence, then I heard Dien's voice: "Lai, you look like a mushroom." The voice was light and happy. I imagined Dien smiling, pointing to her giant hat.

Lai spoke: "I'm a farmer today. Isn't father inside?" I detected quavering in her voice. I imagined her smiling faintly, blushing like a country girl to hide her nervousness.

"Lai," I heard Dien say, softly.

I heard nothing more. I waited, trying to still my breathing, listening for their voices.

I pictured my triangle again, forcing myself to stay and imagine more. I felt powerful. I wanted Lai to tremble. I wanted her body to ripple with pleasure, with stolen kisses. I imagined Dien's inexperienced hand tracing my daughter's arms. I imagined Dien excited, breathing hard. I imagined the blood rushing through Dien's veins.

I shouldn't think this, I told myself.

Still, I moved my tongue in small circles along my teeth. *Fill the well with water,* I told myself. I opened my mouth slightly, willing Dien to open his own, to let sweet words flow from his lips. I imagined Lai's face, willing her to look him straight in the eye.

Minutes later, I heard Lai's hoe again. *Chop-chop. Chop-chop.* The rhythm was irregular, as if she were distracted. I hoped Dien had touched her. I hoped they had done what I had willed them to do. Later that day I saw Lai smile to herself, and the sight was so beautiful I began to hum a folk song.

— — —

I arranged things between Lai and Dien by driving my Citröen a mile to where Dien's parents lived. His parents' one-room house was made of unpainted wood. Muslin sheets stretched over the window frames where glass should have been, held in place by bricks of dung and straw. Dien and Lai, I said, seemed quite interested in each other, did they not? Would they not make a fine match? His parents smiled with enthusiasm. They told me their son was lonely. They said Dien had described Lai in glowing terms. They offered me tea and betel quid, fussing over my health and drawing attention to their son's military certificates hung on plastic frames by the door.

On the way out I saw Dien squatting by my rear tire. He stood, smiling. We talked awhile, then I drove off; and when I arrived home, I happened to look at the trunk of my Citröen. There, scrawled on the dirty spare tire hub, were the words *Darling Lai.* I could hardly restrain my excitement.

"You should look at my car," I said, when I walked in.

"Were you in an accident?" said Lai.

"No, but you should look. Dien left you a message."

So she went out and looked. When she returned, she said, "*Bố,* I haven't sneaked out at night."

"You're a good daughter!" I said. "Of course you haven't. But what do you think?"

She looked at the floor.

"What a good daughter," I said. "You're such a perfect daughter. His parents think well of you. I talked to them myself."

She was smiling. She hesitated, then she said these words: "If he likes me, then he has to tell me. He has to say it out loud."

We hadn't talked so much to each other in years.

Later she went out to squat by the Citröen. From the window I saw her trace her fingers along the trunk, writing messages in the dirty metal. She stood up, admiring what she had written, then saw me looking out the window. The next thing I knew, she walked to the washing floor and filled a large tub with water, then she walked back to the Citröen and threw the water onto the trunk.

"What are you doing?" I said, as she walked into the house, tapping the tub against her hip.

"*Bố,*" she said. "What if he just points to the car? He has to tell me."

"What a sweet daughter!" I said. The next day I drove back to Dien's parents. They told me their son was going to speak to Lai; they told me he had something to discuss with her.

— — —

Some months before Lai's marriage to Dien, I joined The Association of Fathers of the Republic. Publicly, the Association was a political group. Its members were old men who had sons fighting the communists in the Highlands, or the Chinese Ho-Hoa gangsters in Cholon, or, locally, marauding gangs of young thugs suspected to be orphans. In reality the Association was mostly social. Its monthly meetings were highlighted by drinking warm Bami-Bami beer and playing dominoes on a magnificent porcelain table belonging to one of our members, a Mr. Seng, who, because he was of Chinese descent, was viewed as the logical choice for supplying beer and tiny sweetmeats of glutinous rice in syrup.

Through the Association, I arranged to have my daughter married at the Mary Thu Catholic Church, 40 kilometers from Vinh Loi and untouched by the fighting breaking out all over the district.

The wedding was beautiful. Lai looked so pretty in her lace dress and misty veil and gold tear-shaped jewelry that I dared not speak for fear of crying in joy; and when she placed her hand on mine to guide my fingers over the smooth red plastic fork and knelt at my feet to help me slice a huge square of the gaily colored cake, she told me she was grateful for my happiness because I was her father and had never before eaten a Western cake with icing. When she placed it on my tongue, I chewed with appreciation, delighted that the huge square had shaped itself so quickly to the contours of my mouth while my new son-in-law and his American friends applauded and Aunt Binh wiped at my shirt. The rich paste slid down my throat, and I moaned with pleasure and weepy astonishment that I should be sitting in a white metal chair with my plate on a tablecloth in a room at the best restaurant in the district, where Americans in shiny blue uniforms applauded and Aunt Binh clucked her tongue and fussed with my shirt and columns of light laced through the window and onto the small golden hand of my daughter, who fed me cake with a red plastic fork.

"Friends," I said to the Association members, "we truly live between sky and earth. Our hearts burst like pumpkins with the joy of our land of The Republic of South Vietnam. Yet our spirits soar like orioles when we see the world's bounty. The bounty that is so often invisible . . . the bounty . . . oh, I don't know what." I turned away, overcome with emotion. The Association members applauded, slurping hot tea and throwing rice balls into the air and gulping them down when they descended, demonstrating the link between sky and earth. I continued, but could not find the words to express what I felt: I had led my daughter to happiness, into the world, and she had followed. "When Confucius was asked what he would do if he were given a small kingdom," I concluded, "he replied, 'Correct language.' I feel at this moment the same."

When a month later the body of Lai's husband was brought to Vinh Loi on the back of a Lambretta scooter, the Association was present in force at the funeral and carried Republican banners and patriotic slogans. Lai was inconsolable, one moment flailing her body on the ground, the other heaving herself onto the unpainted coffin. She clawed at her hair and bit her lips and beat her ears until veins as blue as rice shoots appeared on her neck. The Association members gathered around me with concerned looks, and I cleared my throat and threw out my arms, calling to my daughter, but Lai continued to wail, collapsing to the ground. I trotted to her side and leaned down by her ear to whisper comfort, but Lai slapped at me with both hands, contorting her face in such a way as to remind me of the time the soldiers had knocked on the door and she had come running into the room looking as if she had been shot.

I dropped to my knees and closed my eyes, allowing her hands to sting my face, and with each slap I grew more and more surprised at the strength of her blows, for I had not felt her palm to my face since she had stroked it as a child. I heard her grunt with the exertion of striking me, and when I fell on one arm from the force of the blows, I found myself thinking that I should never have given her a husband, for we lived at a time when sky and earth were unstable. "Lai," I said, opening one eye, but then I closed my eye again because her face was a mask that looked like rage. In blindness I held out my hand for her to grasp. I imagined her swollen fingers and wriggled my hand for her to take hold of, feeling in the back of my throat the words that would make her see that I was her father and our hearts were together. I began to paw at the ground, feeling for her fingers, and though I felt nothing, I heard her breath grow fainter and the stiff silk of her dress crinkle along the grass and dirt. I opened my eyes and saw her rolling on the ground like a log, away from me, my flesh and blood, and all I could think to do was to stare at her turning over and over. Two Association members ran to her with confused looks, holding Republican banners to the side, but they let her roll past when they saw me struggle to my feet and walk in silence in her direction.

— — —

For weeks after the funeral Lai did not speak to me. Aunt Binh and Uncle Duong were of little help; they had taken a bus to a nearby town and upon returning related to me the nervousness they felt when passing the burned-out hulks of overturned vehicles along the route, between the government roadblocks. The Americans had almost completely withdrawn, but according to the newspapers our Army of the Republic had killed 70,000 Viet Cong in major battles around An Loc. Uncle Duong's eyes lit up at the figure.

"You look like a Buddhist who just converted a butcher," I said. "I heard 50,000 on the shortwave. Is either one possible? Can you believe anything you hear these days?"

"Hush," said Aunt Binh. "You don't want to upset Lai with your conversation." Aunt Binh looked out toward the half-open door to the washing floor, where Lai was scrubbing clothes.

"She'll just hear it somewhere else," said Uncle Duong. "You can't escape the killing."

"Give her time," said Aunt Binh. "She's still washing her funeral clothes."

"She's been washing all week," I said. I lowered my voice to a whisper. "She's been *making* funeral clothes all week, too. Wash and sew. That's all she does." I pointed to the foot-pedal Singer sticking out from the curtain around her sleeping area.

"Love sickness," said Aunt Binh. "*Tuong tu.*"

"Yes, maybe *tuong tu,*" I said. We all sat silent for a moment, wrapping our fingers around cups of chicory tea and sweetened milk. I started to talk about the stoicism of Dien's parents. They had built a small shrine for him, exhibiting his military certificates and placing oranges and bowls of water under his picture. Still, they had carried on; they went about their work. I did not want to tell Aunt Binh and Uncle Duong that I felt *tuong tu* as well. I knew they would think I could not claim to deserve it. But they had not been shunned by Lai day after day. When I saw her come out from behind her dressing curtain every morning in funeral white, I asked myself if she weren't telling me something about the two of us, as well.

— — —

Aunt Binh and Uncle Duong stayed on, alarmed at the increasing number of travel warnings on the shortwave. Uncle Duong spent hours with his ear pressed to the tiny speaker, listening with great concentration to reports of sudden reversals for the army in the Highlands. Aunt Binh attended to Lai, walking with her arm in arm to the open market for fresh fish. One day she brought back with much gaiety a sparrow in a small bamboo cage. I looked with approval at Lai's response to the bird: she giggled when the bird hopped from bar to bar, and several times she stuck a skewer between the bars of the cage, coaxing the bird onto the stick and bouncing it up and down until the sparrow fluttered its wings.

"It's a beautiful bird, isn't it?" I said to Lai.

"Yes, *bố,*" she replied. "Do you want it for dinner?"

"No!" I said. I drew back. Uncle Duong looked up from the shortwave at the bird, snapping his mouth open and shut.

"No," I said again. I smiled at my daughter. "This is not for dinner. It's so beautiful. I love its song."

"It's just a sparrow," said Lai. She didn't look at me. She left the skewer in the cage, then walked back to her foot-pedal Singer.

"A sparrow has a lovely song," I said to her. I lifted the cage up by the tiny bamboo loop at the top and placed it on top of my bookcase, by my reading glasses, as if to emphasize the bird's permanent place in the household.

"Lai, look," I said, pointing to the bird. My smile was so broad that Uncle Duong whispered under his breath that I should be a politician.

Lai looked and nodded. My action seemed to please her. I was happy with how our exchange had played itself out, and I made hand signals to Aunt Binh that her time with Lai had been well spent. In truth, I found the bird's trilling annoying; in any other circumstances I would have skewered the bird myself. But through the bird I saw an opportunity to influence Lai.

I had lost much sleep over her since the funeral. I had already received solicitous offers of assistance from members of the Association; two, in fact, including vice-president Ly, had come to see me at school, going on and on about the smell from the paper mill, but their real conversation, the one I had anticipated, came as they were leaving. "If you ever have need of this spoon," said Ly, withdrawing the object from his pocket, "it's yours."

He offered it as a medical instrument for use on Lai, a cure for the poisonous wind country people said was the source of most ailments. It was silver, blackened from heating, and bent from much hard scraping along the torsos of those who had undergone its treatments. I was at first embarrassed, then touched by the gesture. I declined the instrument with thanks, then went back to marking essays. I worked for hours until I found myself thinking how my scribbling sounded like the scraping of the heated spoon treatment. I put my pen down on the pile of essays, and my mind wandered to my lectures for the week. I taught my students that the Americans, and before them the French, could not understand the fluid passage between the heavenly and earthly realms. I wondered, looking out onto the dirt campus square, if the limitations of the foreigners were not their appeal, for Lai seemed to me to belong no more to one realm than to the other. It was as though she were not truly alive; and I, in my role as father, could not claim earthly life, either.

I had allowed Lai to ignore me completely for too long. I behaved with restraint even when I had stood outside the crinoline curtain surrounding her sleeping alcove, expressing my admiration of her dead husband, only to be answered by the clanking of her kerosene lamp against the floor. Her pile of newly sewn white funeral clothes continued to grow. Every day when I returned from classes I frowned: she would be hunched over her Singer, surrounded by discarded bobbins and coils of string, too engrossed to even look up.

That night, after dinner, I put on my reading glasses and said to her, "You're making a lot of clothes."

"Yes," she answered. She looked me in the eye. "I'm Widow Lai."

The challenge in her answer so surprised me that I felt she had begun to slap me again, as she had at the funeral. She was by tradition expected to grieve for her dead husband. But the strewn bolts of white silk and cotton by her table spoke of a compliance with tradition that in its excess seemed a mockery of it. She was adamant about her sewing, furrowing her brow in a way I hadn't seen since she was a child. I knew even without asking Aunt Binh that my daughter labored all the hours I was away; I knew because Lai's fingers constantly trembled from fatigue and strain.

"Sew, wash; sew, wash," Aunt Binh told me, later that same night. "*That's* what she does all day." Then Aunt Binh opened the lacquered red box where Lai kept her glass earrings and jade necklace. Inside were uncut betel leaves and a compact case full of crushed limestone. I at first did not understand the significance of the items, but when Aunt Binh bared her own blackened teeth to me, I shut the box in disgust: Lai was now chewing betel, staining her teeth black, making herself as dead to youth as a crone.

"She's got VC inside," said Uncle Duong, pointing to his heart.

I frowned. "Don't say that."

Uncle Duong pressed his finger into his chest. "In here is where she lives. *They* live there too. Their spirit." He made a giant arc with his arm, and as he did I understood that Uncle Duong was referring to the diseased ideas that drove the VC on.

"She has VC eating her heart," he said, emphatically. "Do you understand? They want to change everything. They want to kill everything."

"I *know,*" I said. I looked at him crossly. "Enough. Please."

Uncle Duong apologized, then he and I settled on a plan. We walked to the bookcase, and together we loudly cooed over the sparrow with much enthusiasm. We made trilling sounds to each other, and the bird responded in kind. Aunt Binh laughed theatrically, slapping her hands against her thighs.

Lai entered the room. "Father," she said quietly. She walked over to the cage with a newly sewn white cloth in her hand and quickly slipped the covering over the cage, all the way to the base, and the bird fell silent.

"Why did you do that?" I asked. She mumbled something so quiet that I could not hear, but I was sure I knew the answer anyway.

"Lai, why did you shroud the cage?" I asked again.

"So you won't get hungry," she said.

"No. You know I won't eat it. Why did you shroud the cage?"

She sat down again by her sewing table. Her expression was calm. She brought her hands up and cupped them like a mask over her face.

"Lai," I said sharply.

She did not move.

"Say one thing, do another," Uncle Duong whispered, pointing to his niece. He glanced at me. "Just like VC."

— — —

I began to question the sincerity of Lai's obedience to me, but since I could not make her heart transparent I began to view our relationship as a kind of stalemate. One step forward, one step back. For this reason, perhaps, when I drove my Citröen to campus, I delighted in hurtling myself ahead of the bicyclists and passing the lorries and the ox-driven carts with honks of my horn and daredevil aplomb. It was the hot season, and in early 1975 that meant my students rolled up their long white sleeves, dangling Marlboros from their lips, and dissected news of the latest communist offensive. They huddled in tight circles, taking out their wallets and passing around green military registration cards. Some of the students wore buttons showing the yellow and red flag of the Republic; others wore sandals made of tire rubber, like the Northerners. They swore. They made noises like machine guns when they laughed. They told of relatives in Saigon who had seen American CIA prowl Tu Do Street in pickups, loading the flatbeds with schoolgirls to sell in Thailand. They reported that helicopters flew over the jungle at night, broadcasting ghost noises because the Army of the Republic was running out of bullets. They said the VC had lost so many men that they forded rivers on rafts built from the bodies of their dead. They dog-eared pages from *Paris Match* that showed communist trucks clogging a long jungle road, snaking so far back they appeared to come out of a small hole on the horizon.

On the bulletin board in the dirt campus square they hammered broadsides denouncing the Saigon government over broadsides calling for its support. The next day I heard them sing the national anthem, clapping so hard that passing motorists looked out their windows to check for gunfire. In the late afternoon, sluggish after a plate of rice and pickled eggs, I heard them from my office charging across the dirt with Republican banners, raising huzzahs, waving small branches menacingly over their heads, until the chain-link fence separating the campus from the thoroughfare forced them to stop. Stepping outside, I saw them lower their branches, catching their breath, then regroup into loose ranks and go charging in the opposite direction, yelling at the top of their lungs until the long white wall of the Sciences building stopped their advance; then they charged the other way, then the other, again and again, staining their white shirts with dust and sweat.

"Stop this," I said.

"Don't you love your country?" snapped a student.

I lunged for the boy, but he was elusive, escaping into a large circle of companions.

When I turned on my heels to walk back to my office, I heard a voice shout derisively at my back: "His daughter's a worm wife." I spun around, angry, but I saw only the students' impassive faces. *Worm wife.* Someone married to the dead.

That night Aunt Binh and Uncle Duong squatted on the cool patio cement with me. "You should *tell* her to stop," said Uncle Duong. "She's obedient." He inhaled deeply on a Galoise cigarette.

"No," I said. "That won't do any good." I looked out at the road, hearing the distant whine of truck gears.

I knew Uncle Duong would think that I was worried Lai would say no. But what I could not admit to him—what I did not want to admit to myself—was that I was even more worried she would say yes, then smile behind my back, then cook my dinner, then disobey me and disobey me and disobey me. Say one thing, do another. Perhaps Uncle Duong was right.

— — —

Nephews Xuan and Ngu stopped visiting, and when Aunt Binh and Uncle Duong braved the journey back to Saigon, back to what they thought would be safety, I was left alone with my daughter. There was no one to witness what then occurred between us. I mention this because if nephew Xuan has been telling unflattering remembrances about me to his American family, then his stories would be dishonest: his child's mind back then knew but a thread of the whole cloth; his stories now would paint his memory, not the other way around. Of tadpole Xuan, I recall little. Some months before he and his brother simply disappeared, I cuffed his head roughly; I believe he had entered my study without permission.

My daughter cooked for me, she cleaned, she went to the market, but she began to express herself in ways that seemed not so much distant as dishonest. When she spoke to me at all, her words seemed vile things, floating snakes burrowing into my ears. So I turned to other ways to understand. I listened now to the washroom's rusty pump handle going up and down. Evenings, as I sat with a book in my lap, the sound of the pumping gave me information. When she was content, the pumping was continuous; she would flex the handle up and down until her red plastic washtub was full. When tired, she would pump three times, then sit waiting the length of three more pumps; then she would pump again. I asked her in irritation one night if just for once, just for me, she could pump with a different rhythm. "I know when you're well," I said, "and I know when you're not. Tell me something else." I imagined her pumping erratically, in passion; or slowly, as with a violin, in contemplation. But she looked at me quizzically: "What do you mean, *bố*?" I sighed loudly, swinging the washroom door back and forth, and wondered if she truly did not understand.

When my Association friends dropped by, she made herself scarce. Sometimes she drew the curtain of her sleeping area around her and remained quiet; at other times, she grabbed huge piles of white funeral clothes—clothes I knew were clean—and disappeared into the washing room.

One evening I called to her, wishing to introduce her to an Association colleague. I had thought she was behind her curtain, resting on her sleeping mat. But then I heard water gurgling into the washing room drain. She walked out to front room, sopping wet, the fabric of her blouse sticking to her woman's body, clutching her giant red tub with one hand. Her brassiere was visible. I tried to make light of the situation. "This is my daughter Lai," I said, pointing. "And that's her sister, Red Tub."

Lai set her mouth and gave me a look that in its hardness startled me for a moment. My associate laughed uneasily, and Lai then turned on her heels and returned to the washing room. Afterwards, I walked to the back and opened the washing room door. "Why did you come in like that?" I said.

"I don't understand," she said, looking up. "You told me to come in."

I stared at her face closely. Her expression was wide-eyed and theatrical, and she nodded her head from side to side in what appeared to be exaggerated innocence. I wondered if she were acting. She had meant, I knew now, to mock my authority. It occurred to me that this was her vengeance on the world. I knew that world. I *was* that world, its knowledge and money and power. She would, I feared, lope like a dog if I told her to get something; she would blurt whatever thought was running through her mind if I asked her to speak; she would enter the front room, dripping wet, displaying her body like a bar girl, if I interrupted her washing. She wished to humiliate the world—to humiliate me—and she would do so by obeying.

— — —

When I saw a boy bicycle drunkenly toward me in the morning—was it months later? Weeks? I do not know—when this boy in his white shirt weaved slowly in my direction, the sun had not yet burned off the river mist. Yet I knew even before I saw his stained and mealy face that he had been shot. With one hand he steered his bicycle; with the other he cupped the flap of his cheek. For days, I had heard a chorus of dull gunfire rising from the forest, like axes striking teakwood; silence always followed. Flares lit up the hills at night, and in my dreams enemy soldiers emerged from the river, smelling of lichen and sea slugs; each night they ran into my study, enraged, holding the thick cord of the door buzzer to use as garroting wire. "Where is he?" they'd shout. I knew they meant me.

One morning the ground shook for hours, and the pages of the book on my desk blackened with small tufts of plaster and dust. I began to lose track of time. Through these terrible weeks, I faltered. I moved my chair to the doorway and spent hours watching the military traffic. If we lost, would I be sacked? Considered an undesirable? What would happen to our house? What would become of Lai? I pondered removing my certificates of appreciation from the wall. Every night, my daughter left my dinner on the table and retreated to the washing room. She had become a creature I conjured into being. Without me, I recall thinking, would she have existence? I pictured with such clarity her actions out back, washing and washing, that she became for me a kind of mental furniture, forever stationary and mute, aligned with other furniture in a formal pattern: Lai stretching across her red tub, her face inert, her plain face in counterpoint to the red of a shirt in her hands; Lai lying stiff on her mat, her fingers tracing the straw weave.

We heard a siren one night, and the sound brought her into my study. She smelled, I thought, of eucalyptus and fish; her eyes were wild.

"Are you nervous?" I asked. "Don't be. We're safe."

"It's more of the same," Lai answered, but I could see her hand shaking. Then she walked to the back, opening the sheet-metal door to the washing room, and began pumping the well handle, splashing water into a tub of white clothes.

I followed her. "You're nervous," I said.

"My husband doesn't want me nervous," she said.

I turned around quickly, then walked back to my study and sat down on the wicker chair. I put on my glasses and picked up a book, flipping slowly through the pages. I read, but without meaning. It was one thing to not accept Dien's death at his funeral. It was quite another to invoke him now.

I stood up and yelled toward the washing room. "He's a ghost now," I shouted. "Do you understand?"

I heard only the sound of her scrubbing. Then she stopped. The door to the washing floor was half-open, and I saw her head leaning into the hallway. "Have you heard him, too?" she yelled.

I cursed at her. "Listen," I hissed, making my voice cold. I walked to the front door and with my thumb pressed the button for the buzzer. The buzzer rang out in the night like a claxon, and though I expected to see the police come bicycling down the road to investigate, I pressed with my thumb for so long that I began to feel pain in my elbow. The house across the road suddenly glowed with light, and between its illuminated window slats I could see faces pressed against the panes. "Huy!" I heard, from across the road. Somewhere in the distance there was shouting.

I stopped, then walked quickly to the washing room and stood by the half-open door. Lai was squatting behind her tub of laundry, perfectly still.

"Did you hear that buzzer?" My voice was full of accusation. "Did you? If he can still hear anything, he'll hear *that*," I said. I could not keep the anger from my voice. "If he answers it, he can eat my fish sauce. If he doesn't, then no more of your stupidity." I shook my head in demonstration. "If he comes tonight, then fine. If not, then stop. No more. He's dead." I then slapped my chest. "I am not dead. I am your father, and I am alive, and you are alive. Do you understand?" She looked down at her tub. She did not move.

I avoided her the rest of the night, retiring early, but I could not sleep. Well into the morning I heard her leave the washing room. The door squeaked a little, and when she walked to her sleeping alcove, in the dark, I heard only the tile squishing from the moisture on her feet. From behind her curtain, she called out: "I'm sorry, father." And then I turned on my side. I felt warm with satisfaction.

In the morning, before the roosters started up, the loudspeakers set up by the army crackled to life. They called the Youth Teams to exercises: 4–3–2–1, 4–3–2–2, 4–3–2–3, again and again, to the accompaniment of martial music. The loudspeakers fell silent, and a dog began barking. There was a loud pop, followed by a motor scooter revving its engine. Then the speakers sputtered to life once more and another strain of martial music filled the air. Then they simply stopped.

I heard all the sounds. I listened very closely. My outburst had been successful. I pictured Lai behind her curtain, cupping her hand to her ear during the night. For hours she would have prayed for her dead husband to answer the buzzer, but as dawn approached, she would have stopped. She would have accepted. She would have heard only the crows of roosters break the silence.

Later, she sat out on the cement patio, staring at the convoys lumbering by. I kept an eye on her, first rooting around our storage room for a straw bonnet for her to wear, then weaving a bamboo strip of her basket back into place, then looking out the door to make sure she was still there. I left for coffee with my Association colleagues, and when I arrived back at the house, I could not help smiling when I saw that she hadn't moved from her position on the patio. I called out to her, and she waved. "You're a good daughter," I shouted. "Very good!" I began to walk quickly toward her; the air smelled sweet as figs. If I had owned a victory flag, I would have planted it.

— — —

I assumed then that this chapter of my life had finished. I thought Lai would simply begin to linger at the table after serving my breakfast rice, that she would once again offer to brew my tea; I assumed she would clutch my hand if gunfire filled the forest. And she did. She did all these things, and she even smiled at me one morning, then pointed to a maw-caw perched in a neighbor's tamarind tree.

But it was April of 1975, and the war ended so suddenly we were jolted into chaos once again. When I first heard news of Saigon's collapse, I was sitting perfectly still in a barber chair, receiving ministrations from Mr. Xiep, who was dressed in the oversized white smock of the Heavenly River Barbershop. Mr. Xiep groaned when the news came over the radio and stopped twirling the medicinal cotton-headed toothpick he had inserted into my ear. The shop was filled with the smell of mercurochrome and hair tonics from America, and under the huge screw-in wall mirror in my line of sight were two men covered in dragon tattoos, sleeping on a long bench with steaming towels over their faces, as if on display in a mausoleum. Big Minh, installed as president after Thieu flew off to France, spoke with much dignity and emotion over the radio about communist forces entering the city, and when he did, I found myself wondering what would become of men covered in dragon tattoos, lying as in death on a barbershop bench. My thoughts were not of Lai. She was at home, cleaning; she had just bought a boar-bone comb, and the last I had seen of her that morning she was dragging the comb through her hair; I recall that she rubbed her index finger over her front teeth.

That is the last clear image I have of my daughter. The Northerners marched openly through our city later that afternoon. There was a plume of smoke rising from the forest. Everyone was walking quickly; an old woman selling litchi nuts overturned her cart and began weeping. Newspaper was everywhere, floating down from the clouds. The ground kept shaking; the world seemed about to split. When the loudspeakers called for us all to welcome the liberators, Lai and I stood behind other Association members. There must have been thousands of people by the city hall, and overhead a flock of noisy birds soared over the avenue. No one spoke, but then we all began to shout. I raised my voice with my Association colleagues. We shouted peace—*Hoa binh! Hoa binh!*—at the file of green-shirted boys in pith helmets marching briskly on the cobblestones. Lai stood at my side, clutching lilacs I had thrust into her hands to give to a soldier in case of trouble. I saw her hand wave, but as I waved my own, I noticed her fingers curl into a claw. I continued to chant peace, but I was looking out of the corner of my eye to watch her. Her mouth opened in time with the chants, but her lips were saying something different. She was speaking in a whisper, and at first I could not puzzle out her words, but then I knew: she was chanting the name of her dead husband. Le Van Dien. Le Van Dien. I did nothing; I had no strength in my body. I remember being amazed at how young the soldiers looked. I turned to face my daughter. She looked back at me, without shame, then opened her mouth wide and screamed out Dien's name. I continued to pump my fist in the air, shouting for peace with my Association friends, then I laid my hand upon her shoulder and squeezed it hard to silence her.

She jerked away. She did not look at me, but she threw the lilacs down and they scattered as if a strong wind had blown them to the ground. Then she pushed my colleagues out of the way. She grabbed people by their shoulders and moved them aside, and as I looked on, shouting for her to return, she burst from the crowd and ran onto the cobblestones. She may have tripped. I could not see her momentarily, and then I could. She ran straight at the Northerners and attacked one of the soldiers, hitting him with her fists. The man seemed bewildered; he held his rifle away from his body and shoved back at her with his free hand. Other soldiers fell out of line. They grabbed at Lai's arms. I could see the shock on their faces, their childish confusion. There was a moment of hesitation, then a small circle of men closed in around my daughter and began to stretch, accordion-like, first one way, then another. Through the crowd I caught glimpses of Lai. She was lunging for the rifles on the men's shoulders. One of them raised his weapon high in the air and brought it down swiftly, with force, like a farmer killing a chicken. The blow drove her down hard. Some people in the crowd were screaming, and the soldiers looked back, not unkindly, before jogging to catch up with their marching comrades. When I arrived at my daughter's side, the stones by her head had turned slick and dark. She lifted her hand once, and her eyes opened and shut without reason. She was already beginning to die. And then I couldn't hear anything: not the wails of the crowd, not the prayers of my colleagues. Nothing. Not the loudspeaker, not the screeching birds overhead.

— — —

We drove in the Fresno traffic for nearly an hour. Janet gave up her front seat for me and sat with the boys in back. They were mock arguing, speaking harshly to each other, but also laughing. Peter, apparently, had stolen test answers for his history class; Jackson stored dirty magazines in his gym locker. "Xuan," said Janet, giggling. "They're *your* sons. I don't know these two." Xuan smiled tightly at her in return, but said nothing. He turned to me then. "Uncle," he said, "Rick and Donna said they're looking forward to seeing you again." He learned forward and searched my face.

My nephew's tenderness, I knew, was a continuation of his apology at the picnic. *Suicide by cop:* the expression still hung in the air. I recognized his contrite look. He had always hated to upset me by mentioning the American war. He must have thought the expression reminded me of Lai's death at the hands of the communists. I had told him of that day myself. But he was only half right: I felt again the grief I have carried for years, and I was avoiding Xuan's anxious glances because of that. Yet I had years ago forgiven the communists for what they had done. I had years ago accepted the incompleteness of my life. Riding in the car with my nephew, in the bright sunlight, I felt something within me begin to loosen, somewhere along my spine. The expression Xuan had used had been so casual, so accepting, so crass that it had sailed far from its intended meaning. Even before we began our long drive, Xuan's words, which had seemed so insensible at first, had begun to speak to me, first in a whisper and now powerfully, in a clear voice. It was as though Xuan's American expression had somehow escaped from the well of my deafness. It was as though the strangeness of my adopted language, its perpetual foreignness, kept Xuan's words separate from the world that was deserting me.

So I listened. What I heard were questions I had not asked myself for years, but in different form. Was it not possible that I had been the cop? That I was wrong to deny my daughter her illusion? Was it not possible that her actions that day had been aimed at me, and not at the Northerners? I do not know. Such questions are impossible to answer. They have always been impossible to answer, but in English they seemed once again to beckon. Years ago, when my questions were in Vietnamese, their pattern, their weight, was always the same. Their words always crept along the same familiar pathway, and they led always to where I had started.

By the time we arrived at Janet's parents' house, I was feeling more kindly disposed toward Xuan. I called him a good driver. I turned to Janet and the boys and said I could hardly wait to see the new hot tub. As I spoke, I saw Rick and Donna open the front door. They were smiling and waving. They both have silver hair coifed to look full and youthful. They play tennis, and I heard the boys once remark that their mom's side of the family could still fast-dance like people on TV. Rick, I had been told, had always wanted to be a rock star. He now worked a checkout counter at a department store, where he harbored a raging grudge against the requirement of wearing a red vest. Donna was wearing shorts that revealed purple veins in her legs; every other day she carried padded weights in each hand and jogged to the cul-de-sac a mile away. She liked to tell stories about flirting with repairmen. The boys, I know, admire their American grandparents greatly, and Xuan, who has never expressed any interest in owning a pet, recently bought a spaniel after Donna told him a funny story about a spaniel they had owned when they lived in Bakersfield. The dog, she said, growled whenever she kissed Rick. *Made out,* she had said, laughing, but I think my consternation had been such that she quickly apologized.

As we walked up the driveway, Peter spoke to me. "Do you want to take my hand?" he said, and then he looked away. I doubt if the offer was sincere, but nonetheless I appreciated his politeness. I saw Janet nod to him.

I had never liked Rick and Donna's house. It is small and dark, and its stucco siding is chipped and discolored. The sliding glass doors of the Great Room constantly stick, and the washroom smells of mold; their appliances rumble and squeak, and the walls of their dining room are lined with framed posters of rock bands. Down the hallway are auxiliary rooms I have not entered, but I suspect they are similarly flawed and tasteless.

We walked in a ragged line to the door, and Peter and Jackson both leapt up the front steps and hugged their grandparents. I lingered behind, combing my hair with my hand and taking small, old-man steps. Janet hugged her mother a long time, and Xuan gave Rick a hearty slap on the back. "How are you?" said Rick, addressing me over Xuan's shoulder. I nodded. The others, all of them, stepped into the hallway. "Need some help, partner?" Rick said to me. I waved him off. He stepped back inside, watching me. They were all, I realized, watching. Xuan was whispering something to the boys, and Janet held her mother by the arm. When I reached the door, I smiled my greeting, and Rick beckoned me forward. "Hot tub's out back," he said. I was standing in the archway, swaying a bit, when I saw something to the left of the door that I had never noticed before. There was a large, ornate doorbell buzzer, painted white. I stared briefly at the object; I felt a bit dizzy.

"Well, come on in," said Donna, looking straight at me. "I'll get you some water." I saw her walk to the kitchen sink; I heard water pouring from the spout. I stood there a moment, then stuck out the finger of my right hand and pressed it to the buzzer. I did not wish to take my finger away. It seemed proper to ask for permission to enter. It seemed right that I should put my hand to the bell and stand at the door.

"Uncle," said Xuan. Rick took a step forward, but Janet whispered something to him, and Rick stepped back. Peter and Jackson came out from the kitchen, chewing on something; they stood behind their parents. I cannot say precisely what I wished to accomplish by leaning my finger against the buzzer and not releasing it. I kept my finger on the buzzer and listened to its rich noise, and I felt the expanse of the house reverberate in the sound. I kept my finger there a long time, and Xuan and his family stayed a respectful distance away. No one rushed to grab my hand. No one put their arm around my shoulders. The buzzing seemed never to stop, and I heard in its sharp and loamy bray different modulations. I heard the kitchen faucet running, and the clacking of ice cubes into a glass. I heard the buzzer echo, as in a cavern; I heard an echo and return, over and over, and as I heard these things I grew conscious of the sharp crease in my pants, of the spotless finery of my shirt. I stood straight as I could, pressing hard on the buzzer, my face a question: May I enter? May I enter now, please? For an instant, then, sunlight laced in a column through the sliding glass doors and bathed everyone in brightness, and all the rooms of the house, all its private chambers, the places where secret things lived and rose in the night, seemed to open to me, glowing, and I stepped through the doorway and entered.

Monsieur le Genius

THE JOKE was that Bujumbura's only supermarket, the *Supermarché de Liberté,* ran on the Potemkin Village model: the shelves were full, but only because the rest of the city got the bare bones. In actual fact you could walk through the most desolate neighborhoods and still find vegetable hawkers setting up shop in the alleyways, and lines of gleaming white Mercedes streamed into the interior, even far up Route 1, which emptied into a scrubland valley in neighboring Rwanda. Yet at the American Club the joke persisted. We were all heady, I think, from living in a country at the end of the earth. Airgrams from home asked, "Now where in Africa did you say Burundi was?" and denuding the place over beers helped us maintain equilibrium: the bleaker the country, the brighter our prospects. We were, in our public capacities, like old-fashioned gift bearers, emissaries from a rich and distant realm. We wanted our gifts to be taken.

I had no official embassy or relief-agency connections, but what I had to give was certainly the rarest gift. I was the only chess master, past or present, ever to set foot in Burundi, a fact I used to spread the game's dry magic across the entire country. Chess was about making connections, about seeing patterns; it was about turning disadvantages into advantages—all things the country was eager to learn. My business cards, which I ordered from a Belgian print shop near the national stadium, read "Monsieur le Genius, Grandmaster." It was a ridiculous and even infantile title. I was no genius and no grandmaster, though my recently acquired national master's rating was enough to force grandmasters into long, deep thinks. I regularly played in tournaments back in Seattle, and, thanks to a particularly good performance in the 1992 Washington State Championship, I had finally seen my name mentioned in *Inside Chess.* The issue appeared days before I left for Africa for some relief. My marriage had just fallen apart. My stultifying computer job had dried up and vanished.

But I could perform a dazzling parlor trick. I could play an entire game of chess blindfolded, calling out my moves without sight of the board. Though the same could be said of at least a dozen other chess addicts back in Seattle, my blindfold games had within weeks of my arrival in Burundi created a stir among the locals. They had never seen anything like it. Africans in general cannot read white people, and to the inhabitants of Deepest Darkest—our private term for all the French-speaking massacre countries—a *muzungu* such as myself, an Anglophone at that, was a blank page from a very mysterious book indeed. So I filled in the page for them. The locals took my title seriously, and since none of them could play chess worth a damn, I was for all practical purposes what I claimed. On the street, strangers sometimes greeted me with a solemn "*Ça va,* Monseiur le Genius." In reply, I'd make a cage with my fingers and put the cage to the sides of my head, like a seer receiving a vision.

My chess sponsor, my *patron,* was Jacques Notroyomewa, the Tutsi proprietor of a mail-expediting service. His hooded eyes gave him a sleepy aspect, and he possessed perfect African ears, two small seashells cupping a round, close-cropped skull. He was sharp, and, more important, he was a great fan of chess. He had been schooled in Nigeria, which boasted several players on the international chess circuit, and he often remarked to me, in my capacity as chess genius, how glorious it would be if tiny Burundi could produce its own international-caliber players. "Glor-*ee*us," he'd say, making the word sound bloody, and when he did I encouraged his enthusiasm. Glor-*ee*us. That was how it felt. The locals called to me out of bus windows. The ambassador to Ghana invited me to dinner. Once, a woman in a tight purple dress knocked on my door and had me sleep with her.

So Jacques and I struck a bargain that served us both well, at least at first. He provided me with a modest salary to coach promising players and conduct chess clinics and exhibitions throughout the country. In return, I was to help him put Burundi on the map. I was to help him give the country something to be proud of. "Especially *now,*" he added solemnly. I knew what he meant. It was 1993, and the airwaves were once again electric with Hutu Power speeches; convoys of Tutsi troops had been trucking into the Hutu countryside for weeks.

It was a tidy and beneficial arrangement until Jacques finally concluded I was not a true chess genius. He began to scrutinize my results. In less than a month I had blundered away an easily won game to some functionary smoking a corncob pipe, and a Russian mechanical engineer at the university had held me to a draw in an offhand game of speed chess. "How is this possible?" Jacques asked. "Bobby, are you ill?" I said I was. I claimed that I hadn't slept well for days, that I had been vomiting. But then, on a miserable rainy evening, I missed a simple checkmate against Jacques. I still beat him handily, but afterward he had me reconstruct our game move for move until we came to my mistake. "I have a stomach ailment," I said, putting a hand to my gut and scowling. "I'm not at my best."

Jacques shook his head. He looked heartbroken. I had been his Michelangelo of the chessboard, his artist touched by God, his hope. When we first met, he even thought I might be Bobby Fischer traveling incognito. I did not discourage his error. Fischer had just defeated Spassky in their rematch in Yugoslavia, and his whereabouts were unknown. Photos from the match showed Fischer rumpled and balding; he had high cheekbones and, set back deep under a thick brow, a pair of gunslit eyes, which lent to his expression a certain leonine aspect. We could have been twins. "My name's Robert Wender," I told Jacques, but I let him call me Bobby.

Jacques now drained his bottle of Primus and looked at the ceiling. He may have sighed. "We are bereft," he said at last. His statement alarmed me. I had always thought of his voice as African, spittle-soaked, vaguely promiscuous, but "bereft" seemed to rise from his gut, parched and ashen.

"No, we're not," I said. "We're good. You and me, we're a team." He made no response. He continued to stare at the ceiling.

"I got the big talent, Jacques," I said. "If you're questioning that, I mean." I tapped my forehead. "Do you want me to play you blindfolded again?"

He leaned back in his chair and rested his hands on his paunch. "*We* are bereft," he said quietly. "We Tutsi. We Hutu. Not you *muzungus.* The future is not so much a question for you, is it?"

I couldn't argue the point, but I was happy to see the conversation head in a different direction. The rest of the evening we finished off three more big bottles of Primus and ate Laughing Cow cheese on saltines. The next morning I stopped by his storefront business to make arrangements for an upcoming chess exhibition. I heard him talking loudly on the phone in his office. "Yes," he shouted, in English. The words carried through the thin walls. "That is whom I wish to employ. Yes. A master of chess. Do you understand? Someone who *knows*. A genius of chess. Someone extraordinary. Not like this imposter here."

I left the building as quietly as possible, my head spinning, but Jacques spotted me exiting by the front door. He waved me up to his office, where we spent a few minutes chit-chatting before the conversation turned. He declared that we had some business to discuss. There had to be a safety net, he said, in case I fell sick again, in case my ailments returned. He had to imagine a future without me. "So I have made a decision," Jacques said. "I am flying in an understudy for you shortly. An understudy. You can train this person. You understand? In case your sickness returns. Do you understand?"

I understood: he meant to abandon me. The question was, could he? No grandmaster would leave the tournament circuit to work for peanuts in Central Africa. And African masters were heroes in their own countries. Where would he find one to live in Burundi?

"Understudy," I said sharply. "Do you mean replacement?" I folded my arms.

"Understudy," Jacques said. "I know what word I am using."

He looked at me hard, narrowing his eyes—the glare he reserved for underlings. He had never used that expression on me before. With the sun streaking in through the window slats behind him, his whole body seemed to glow. I tried to summon the peculiar sense of transport I sometimes felt in his presence—as if, lost in our own thoughts, we mimicked a tableau from another century: the African stroking the trinkets placed at his feet, the Crown's minister solemn and watchful, nearby. But I could not summon the image now. My thoughts grew dark, a chorus of taunts. What if he had truly found someone? I had burned too many bridges in the U.S. I would have nothing—no money, no employment documentation. Nothing. I would be bereft.

— — —

A few days later I was sitting at an empty desk in Jacques's business when Gerard sidled up. Despite Gerard's advanced age—his stubble came up gray and pebbly—he worked as Jacques's "boy," a term that lost its haughtiness when Africans used it (he slept in a *boyerie*, a small outbuilding attached to the storeroom). Gerard was a refugee and a cripple. He had crossed the border from Zaire, he once told me, after President Mobutu taxed his left arm and took the right as payment. In its place was a clanking prosthetic, a ghastly salmon-colored reject made in Belgium. Every now and then I caught him whittling old *Zaireois* political slogans into the plastic forearm.

"Mr. Jacques is calling for you," he said in passable English. I didn't look up. First I had been "Monsieur le Genius" to Gerard, then a clipped "Monsieur," and recently, no doubt echoing Jacques's displeasure, a contemptuous "you." But until now I'd had no desire to abuse Gerard. He hovered, then slowly raised his bad arm and pointed his finger-hook to the top of the stairs, toward Jacques's office. He could not bend the elbow, so the arm stuck straight out in a rude gesture of banishment: the white man ordered from his chair.

I jabbed a finger into my documents. "I'll be up in two shakes," I said, then went back to scheduling my chess-exhibition tour dates: a day in Kayanza, perhaps another day in Ngozi, then north up Route 1. Out of the corner of my eye I saw Gerard stare dumbly at my finger. He gave no indication of understanding. The Americanism was unfair, but I wanted him to imagine returning empty-handed up the stairs to his employer's office. I let him stand there, frowning and confused, until he lowered his limb.

"Okay," I said, "Monsieur le Genius will see Mr. Jacques now." Gerard's expression brightened. I slammed my tour book closed, and together we climbed the narrow stairs, Gerard, my herald, scraping his arm along the banister with every step.

The building was dim and poorly ventilated. The second floor, in particular, smelled of the straw mixed into the brick exterior, and after heavy rains the walls turned sweet and pungent. Jacques's office, down the hallway, always smelled wet, though it was brightly lit by columns of sunlight.

I prepared myself for bad news, for an argument I couldn't win. If Jacques had truly found a powerful chess master, I had no way of forcing an eleventh-hour stay of dismissal. For days, I had been reviewing all I knew about Jacques, but nothing suggested itself as a fact I could use. He was buttoned down, presenting himself as a businessman of simple and agreeable tastes. He kept his gray safari suits immaculate, open at the collar, and he used Florida Blackening Cream to cover up the pinkish irritation left on his neck by his necklace's metal amulet. He favored Marlboro over Galoise, local Primus beer over Johnnie Walker, and '70s disco over dance tunes from Zaire; he thought turbaned Sikhs screamingly funny, and he distrusted the national bank, preferring to bind rolls of bills with rubber bands and stuff them into his socks. He led a life of inconsequence and routine. Once a month he treated his family to dinner at the *Cirque Nautique,* where Belgian tourists slathered mayonnaise onto their french fries and watched the hippos yawn out in the mudflats. Every day, he smoked two Legionnaire cigars and watched a bland hour of Channel 1 TV.

Even his rebellions seemed a form of sighing. In the dry season he'd chase off his gardener and strip down to the waist, happily filling plastic buckets with tiny green plantains from his enormous back yard. Invigorated, he'd announce to his wife and children that they were oppressing him, then drive down to the Novotel and pick up a prostitute. All the wealthy Burundians I knew had depressingly similar lapses in public behavior. I think the invisibility of the country—it was only a pinprick in my atlas—lent itself to loud and resentful trumpeting. Even fellow Africans, mostly businessmen stopping over on flights to Europe, stared quizzically at the large *Bienvenu à Bujumbura* sign at the airport.

But thinking along such lines got me nowhere. Jacques's ambitions for the chess future of the country were an extension of his private ambitions. He wished to be taken seriously. He wished to walk down the grand avenues of New York or Paris or London and have it known that he was from Burundi. He wanted to be the man who made a colossus out of a pinprick, and if someone else could assist him better, then my presence was of no importance. I might as well have been Gerard.

Jacques sat frowning at his desk, and after I knocked he motioned for me to sit. He waved Gerard away, then returned to his oversized ledger book, letting his fingers dawdle on a calculator pad. Despite the high ceilings his office seemed cramped. Its walls had been painted hospital green, and streamers of dust and hair rode the rough plaster, trembling at regular intervals from the churning ceiling fan. Over the water-closet door hung a length of butcher paper strung with colored cardboard letters, "J. Notroyemawa, Burundi Import/Export Express," a childish whisper of the imposing wooden sign hanging over the double doors of the streetside entrance.

He looked at me. "I have a task for you, Bobby," he said. "A trip to the airport. Your understudy is due to arrive."

"Can't someone else pick him up?" I asked. But I knew there was no one else. It was understood that Gerard could not be trusted to ferry a new arrival to the office. He would cough messily or clank his arm, a bad first impression.

Jacques cleared his throat. "*He* is actually a *she,*" he said. "In point of fact."

My surprise must have been evident, for Jacques smiled broadly and leaned forward. "A movie-star American girl," he said, which meant nothing, since he called all American women movie stars. He pulled an index card from his shirt pocket, studied it, then announced her name—Annie Polgar. *"Ah-nee,"* he said, as if she were Chinese. "I have been told she is a beautiful brunette," he said. Then he paused dramatically. "A beautiful woman chess master. I have never witnessed such a thing! Can you imagine?"

I looked stupidly around the room. "Well," I said, "this Annie Polgar is coming at a bad time."

Jacques drew himself up in his chair and looked at me crossly. "There is no better time," he said. "Some Hutu students"—he waved his hand vaguely in the direction of the university, miles down the road—"all good chess players—"

"Right. I heard the police questioned them."

He regarded me coolly. "Maybe police. Maybe security. It is impossible to say."

"But nothing happened, right? That's what I heard."

Jacques showed exasperation by clucking. "Do you think such things are chronic with us?" he asked. He shook his head. "This is not normal. There is a beginning to troubles, and there is an end. I do not know which this is."

"I apologize," I said. I raised my hands and showed Jacques two palms, a conciliatory gesture. "I didn't mean to imply anything. I just thought . . . ." I shrugged and stopped talking. The truth was that I did think such things were chronic.

"So time may be important," he said.

"I understand," I said, nodding vigorously. "But I'm making out my exhibition schedule now. Really, I'm swamped."

Jacques smiled. "How long, oh genius, to figure out an exhibition schedule?"

"I've had lots of cancellations," I said. "The Catholic school only scrounged up twenty players."

He laughed. "Bobby, I will *buy* you twenty players. Just go pick her up."

I laughed as well, louder than the joking warranted, but I didn't want Jacques to think me mulish. I was in fact turning something over in my mind. I had never heard of an Annie Polgar. For that matter, I had never heard of a white female chess master in all of Africa. It didn't seem possible.

"Hey," I said then. "Buy me twenty players and I'll drive her around all day." That settled things. We showed teeth and nodded. Jacques looked me up and down, then reached into his desk and tossed me the keys to his old orange Citröen.

"Watch for militia," he said. "And for God's sake," he added, "chat up the place. Make her feel welcome."

So I drove out of the city. Route 5, heading north toward the airport, is a scenic journey, and in the spaces between palm and plantain trees one can catch glimpses of enormous Lake Tanganyika. The road descends quickly, and through some confluence of the rolling hills and haze, the lake appears to tilt toward the viewer, as if the entire body of water is about to be upended. I refused to look at it. I veered to the center of the road, narrowly avoiding bicyclists ferrying loads of firewood; I startled two women carrying cisterns on their heads, honking my horn and whistling at them; I passed a Primus beer truck crawling around a curve; I feathered the accelerator, then closed my eyes on a straightaway and floored it for five exhilarating seconds, in total darkness. I began to feel powerful again.

— — —

A good game of chess is hard to find, but there is no end to the number of bad ones. Nowadays most of the world has access to Staunton-design tournament sets with weighted pieces, and even in the dark, beer-stained shophouses of Kinshasa one can find tournament-quality vinyl roll-up chessboards with green and buff teacup-sized squares; equipment no longer provides a visual clue to the strength of your opponent. For the real player—the aficionado, the master, the addict—games against casual players are not even worth recording. They are dead time, their patterns a form of travel: brief and dizzy arrivals, abrupt leave-takings.

Minutes into the game, even seconds, you see your opponent stare at the queenside when he should be looking at the kingside. Or he clutches his king by its cross and not its stem (there is etiquette involved, after all). Or, doggedly, he lets his gaze linger on a certain square, his eyes no longer mobile or wary. He becomes agitated. He's sure he has you by the fourth move. He thinks he sees something, even when the important pieces are still at slumber and only the faintest outline of the decisive moment has been suggested. You realize that he has not considered the possibilities or, worse, that he thinks he has considered all of them.

For the real player such games are more ritual than struggle, and with each bad game the ritual grows meaner, more like dumb show, tedious and empty. You politely checkmate your opponent, without fanfare or contempt, but you're already miles away. Perhaps tomorrow, you think: perhaps in some near future you will find another real player, an echo of yourself, a necessary someone. You picture your hand circling the board, your fingers coiled and questioning; you picture your opponent's mirroring hand, and together your hands, yours and its mirror, grasp what chessmen they should, and when they should, and precisely. They move a knight or a bishop to exactly the right square, even when time is short, when the flag on the chess clock is teetering, and together your hands swoop down, faster and faster, falling back in release, hovering, then landing again on exactly the right square. One after the other, your hands dive and pause. Together they create a ferocious rhythm, a dizzying and beautiful dance, and sometimes your hands, your own and their mirror, seem no longer to belong to either of you, and at such moments the entire world, all its dark channels of fact, its deep and watery patterns, seem to open themselves to your touch.

I wish I could say this is how I ended up in Burundi. I wish I could say I was the wandering minstrel, the poet-of-the-road seeking glimpses of angels. At one time, years ago, I thought I might be such a person. I carried thousands of chess moves in my head, and I carried them with such care I could not forget them, even decades later. Certain sequences of moves retained the power to thrill me. Certain sequences of moves still made my hands tremble, and sometimes, unbidden, I felt my entire body shaking, eager and burning, as if I were waiting on a wedding bed.

That excitement never left me, not even when I arrived in Bujumbura hung over and slick with sweat. I first set foot in the capital by stumbling out the back of a crowded tourist truck. We had crossed over that morning from Zaire; the truck had canvas webbing behind the cab and wooden benches along the sides, like a troop carrier, and my Belgian truck mates all wore matching shorts and hiking boots. We were stopping for lunch in the city center. I was in bad shape. My throat was swollen, and my loafers were splitting open and lumpy with pebbles. I carried an alligator-hide briefcase covered with chess stickers. Pressed deep into my pockets was enough hashish to last a couple of months. I was feverish, I think, not really sure what country we were in, and all but broke. It wasn't until we began lurching down Bujumbura's main boulevard that I became aware we were in a city.

Early that morning, before the sun burned off the mist, I had been drifting in and out of sleep, and each time I opened my eyes I was startled to find myself in darkness, surrounded by impassive faces. We had just passed a checkpoint near the border. We were on a dirt road in the middle of nowhere, and I had no sense of time. Behind me, the day seemed unnaturally bright. I looked out the back, through what I saw as an enormous, arching hole, and watched a swirling pinkish light drift up and away. It was red dust kicked up from the tires, mountains of it—I think I knew this, I think I understood—but when the pinkish light rose to the top of a line of trees and mingled with leaves and branches, all I could think was that an alien light was blooming. I thought this. I thought exactly this, but at the back of my mind I posed a question. I wondered if what I was seeing was joyous or not. It was such a simple question, yet I could not answer it. I began to cry.

My truck mates all stared past me, and once we reached Bujumbura they began carrying on respectful conversations among themselves. When we finally stopped for good they stared at the floor bed, waiting for the African driver to pull down the latch in back. "Where are we?" I said to no one. "Can you tell me, please?"

The Belgians quietly piled out. They stepped over my legs and excused themselves, and when I was alone I heard the driver speak. "Mister," he said to me. "Oh mister. Mister, please." He climbed aboard and put my briefcase into my hand and folded my fingers around the handle. He lifted me by the armpits and helped me out of the truck. There was a Greek restaurant across the street; tables had been set up on an outside deck. The driver helped me to a table. The menu was all in French, but I recognized *moussaka,* which I had eaten before. I got hold of myself. I waved the driver off and began to feel at ease again. I smelled diesel; a motorcycle roared past. I was once again properly situated: the table had a crisp white tablecloth, and a plastic flower stuck out the top of a decorative bottle. A black waiter gave me his full attention.

I lifted my briefcase onto the table and made a loud show of snapping it open. When I held up my roll-up tournament chessboard, cinched with rubber bands, its green and buff squares announced my presence. Within minutes I heard a voice two tables down: "Are you a chess player?" This was my introduction to Jacques. When he ate he speared his food with sharp thrusts, then jerked his head down to snatch it from the tines. He reminded me of a monstrous pecking bird, and I was weighing my options, wondering whether I should change tables, move closer to some Europeans, when he said, "I love chess. It is my passion."

I withdrew a wooden Jerger chess clock, a flashy, old-fashioned one with two clock faces like the twin portholes of a tiny ship. He nodded in appreciation. "How long are you here?" he asked.

"Depends what there is to stay for," I said. It sounded tough yet sentimental, and therefore reassuring.

He considered this, then took a sip of coffee. "Are you good? A professional?" He nodded toward my chess clock.

I gave him a devastatingly modest smile. "Well," I said, "I better be if I'm going to carry a chess clock around. I better be really good."

He stood and brought his plate over. We played a few quick games, and I defeated him easily. He seemed pleased. Then he asked me what I was hoping to hear.

"Only if you're absolutely sure," I said. "Only if it's convenient. I'd just need a few francs for expenses. But I'd be more than happy to tutor you. Really." We shook on it. A few weeks later Jacques proposed our arrangement.

— — —

At the airport, I had little to go on. I knew only that her name was Annie Polgar and that Jacques had pronounced her dark-haired and pretty. I carried a vague desire that she might reveal herself to be incompetent, exhibiting a kind of drunkenness: the chess addict awkward and bumbling away from the chessboard. I could not help trying to imagine her, even as I heaped abuse on what I imagined.

I waited outside the gate, next to the noisy skycaps, mostly opportunists who wore dirty orange overalls to lend them an official air. The airport terminal smelled of warm beer. It was cramped and musty, and the blue carpeting inside had long ago given way to generations of explosive, wavy stains, like a map of ocean patterns. A line of arrivals from the noon flight filed through the cramped Immigration Hallway. I immediately recognized them as arrivals because they were the only types that ever flew into the country: the continent's businessmen, narrow-shouldered Africans in shiny blue suits, each with a reinforced briefcase and expensive cufflinks; students returning from the Soviet Union or Cuba, bashful in their new eyewear and loose foreign shirts (African tailors insist on a tighter cut); aid workers, mostly agriculturists, hunched and polite, wearing jeans made baggy by months of fever and stomach ailments; Shell engineers blandly ridiculous in all-cotton white outfits with shoulder epaulets and buttons big as sewing bobbins; a few olive-skinned European couples, impatient and haggard, sporting thin watches and aerated shoes with brass eyelets.

That was how, finally, I recognized Annie Polgar. She looked like no one else. I watched her. Her hair was straight and dark, fashionably shoulder length, and she was very pale, which in the African sun made one's skin appear unfinished and creamy, as if the pigment were still wet. Her blue dress, decorated with tiny red and white flowers, accented her paleness. She was young and very thin, boyish even, and her hair hung in damp ropes down the back of her neck. Her body excited me. A motorized trolley cart wheeled the heaped luggage into the waiting area. The air-con wasn't working. I watched her fan herself with her passport, then wander over to where the trolley man was heaving his cargo onto the cement floor. She had the druggy, stunned amble of the newly arrived. The thumping bags echoed rudely, and the skycaps sprinted to the baggage area, where they began yelling pointlessly and lifting suitcases onto their heads like mutinous porters in a Tarzan movie. There weren't enough bags for all the men, and some pushing broke out.

The chaos was intentional, a thuggish ploy to ensure enormous tips from the unwary. She seemed to blanch. She brought one hand protectively to her neck, her fingers resting lightly on her skin. Only then did I rush forward. Waving, I asked her which bags were hers. She pointed dumbly to four green suitcases, and I addressed the porters loudly, shooing away all but four of them, one to a bag. "Monsieur le Genius," one mumbled, loud enough for her to hear. The dismissed skycaps looked at me keenly, then quickly dispersed. I almost shouted from happiness.

"You have to be Robert," she said. Her lips stretched into a wide smile, but her shoulders were still bunched against her collarbone. We exchanged greetings and started toward the exit, followed by our four skycaps, each with a piece of luggage on his head. I didn't like the silence, so I turned to her. "Were you expecting Jacques?"

"No. You. Jacques told me you'd be my welcoming party." Her way of speaking seemed to me peculiar to American women overseas: a small, flat voice more exhaled than spoken, as if one's words simply lay in wait just behind the tongue. We talked a bit more, chitchat about the flight, and when we passed through the terminal doors we heard sunbirds screeching across the road. The sky was so bright the gravel seemed to smolder. All around us, shouting passengers piled into cars and sped off.

I looked slyly at her face, evaluating, excited in a mildly erotic way to be walking a white woman to my car. A thought occurred to me, and I touched her arm. "Just wondering," I said. "How do you know what Robert looks like?" I leaned in close. "I could be anyone."

She shrugged. "Oh, you just look like a chess genius."

I searched her expression for mockery, but she turned abruptly away and began inspecting her luggage. The strap on one of her bags had broken off, and someone had bludgeoned the small combination lock on the zipper.

"Comes with the territory," I said, indicating the lock. "We're over here." I pointed to the car. "So what about you? You going for the killer waif look?" I adopted a chummy tone. "Fresh-faced but still crushing everyone?"

"I'm playing as myself."

It was the sort of awkward assertion that made me doubt her. She was not convincing, and even as I took a mental note to raise my suspicion with Jacques, I heard rattling. One of the skycaps, waiting his turn at the open car trunk, was jiggling his load: the sound was of chess pieces knocking together. She had filled an entire suitcase with chess equipment. It seemed an amateurish thing to do.

We drove off quickly, spewing gravel and dust. "This isn't your car, is it?" Annie asked.

I asked her why she would say such a thing.

"Just being observant. You've got a sprig of mango root tied around the rearview mirror." She tapped the mirror rod. I had never noticed it before, the tribal artifact. Its smell was supposed to keep travelers safe. "My guess," she said, "is that you wouldn't buy into that. In your official capacity, I mean."

"Fair enough," I said.

She slapped me lightly on the shoulder, an intimate gesture. "Just so you know," she said. "I'm aware you're going for a Bobby Fischer look."

I detected a hint of impatience in her tone, the newcomer's anxiety expressing itself as impertinence. She rolled down the window and rested her arm on the door ledge. She looked out at the scenery: rickety wooden tables laden with bundles of green vegetables; small, shaved-head girls walking single file; men on bicycles, carrying stacked columns of plastic buckets. The jungle started at the edge of the blacktop, an enormous wall, and plantain leaves and ferns leaned out over the roadway, nearly touching the car. You could see columns of smoke in the distance.

"You think so?" I asked.

"Robert Wender." Her words came out in a rush. "Robert, as in Bobby? And Wender is Fischer's mother's maiden name. You look just like him."

Her fact-mongering in itself did not alarm me. Yet it had been accompanied by a quavering tremolo, her voice insisting on the importance of her observation. She did not speak like a real player. To a real player, biographical research on grandmasters stank of musty scholarship. It was the province of the camp follower. I searched her face for a sign of intent, but she was staring dully at her hand, wiping at a smudge.

"Well, you got me," I said carefully. "Someone's been doing her homework."

"But that's okay," she added. She folded her arms and spoke with deliberate emphasis. "I think facts are overrated. So what if you aren't using your real name? Show me a fact and I'll show you something more interesting waiting to happen."

I nodded, then shrugged agreeably. Tightening my grasp on the steering wheel, I squinted and hunched forward, exaggerating the danger of not concentrating on the road. We drove in silence for a mile or two, and she stuck her head out the window, a pretty sight. Her waist swiveled; the muscles in her calf contracted, drawing attention to her smooth legs.

I stared at her body until she tired of the wind and sat back in the seat. She turned to me suddenly. "So Jacques doesn't expect an actual genius, right?"

I turned to see if she was joking. "What's your background?" I asked.

She smoothed her hair. "In Uganda they called me the African Queen. I was coaching the university team. I guess Jacques knows the provost there."

I didn't press the issue. There was no need. I would have heard if a white female master was working in Uganda. So I fished a little. I told her that as long as she won, genius or not genius didn't really matter. Her lips seemed to quiver at the ends when I said this—a forced smile—and she turned again to the passenger window. The city was coming into view. Up ahead, gray water sloshed against the harbor wall; a crowd was milling in front of a bakery. In the distance, on three sides, rumpled hills drifted up, smothered with jungle.

"Pawn to queen four," I said.

She looked at me blankly.

"Pawn to queen four," I said again. "Your move."

"Sorry."

"A little blindfold chess. Pawn to queen four. Your move now."

She shook her head.

"Too tired, huh?"

"Yes."

I said nothing for a while. Then I turned to her: "You think I'm testing you."

"Aren't you?" she asked.

"What would you think if I were?"

"I think it wouldn't be very neighborly," she said.

This made me smile. I slowed the car down. "Just tell me what your chess rating is."

"What's yours?"

"First you say."

"Why?" she asked. "Is it important?"

"Just curious."

"What's yours?" she asked again.

"I won't bullshit you, all right? You'll find out soon enough. I'm no genius. But I'm pretty good." I paused. "Low master. Good enough."

She thought about this. "And you've done okay for yourself here, haven't you?"

"Let's say I have," I said gallantly. I noted she wasn't telling me her rating.

"So there aren't any sleepers here? No diamonds in the rough to watch out for?"

"Christ," I said sharply. "Do you know where we are?" I waved my hand at the crumbling buildings around us and spoke with feeling. "It's like playing against your dog here most of the time. The hard part is staying awake. Jesus. The hard part's staying *conscious.*" The passion in my voice surprised me.

I wasn't prepared for her reaction. She leaned back in the seat and her whole face seemed to relax. I backed off.

— — —

Back at the office, Jacques held Annie's hand as he talked. He offered her a chair, then hopped up onto his desktop, dangling his feet like a teenager. "You have come in on Air Zaire," he said. "Ooooh, we call it *Air Peut-Être* here. Air Maybe. Do you understand?" He chuckled, then left his mouth open, and his thick pink tongue quivered. It reminded me of an aquarium slug. "Oooh," he said, bounding down. He was playing Jovial Jack for her, fussing over the broken strap on her luggage. He stood in front of her, reciting the amenities she would find at the Novotel, where he had reserved her a suite for the night. "A swimming pool," he said. "Air-con. Room service. Fresh pastry. Video. Everything a place should have." As he spoke he showed her his palms. White women were excited by them, he had heard: the lighter pigmentation and soft creases reminded them of their own pudenda.

He suggested the three of us have dinner a bit later, after Annie had a chance to get settled in. "You need a good night's sleep tonight," he said. "I have arranged a chess exhibition for the two of you tomorrow morning. In Muramvya. An hour's drive."

He nodded with great enthusiasm, then slapped his forehead. "Where are my manners?" he said theatrically, and guided us over to a wicker chair next to the water closet, where he had placed a plate of brie and crackers. He began cutting into the cheese as if it were cake, thick wedges that he arranged on a platform of crackers.

Gerard walked in, grinning, and Jacques made a show of shoving brie onto some crackers for him too. Then Jacques brought out the chessboard and pieces. He took a big bottle of warm Primus from the bottom drawer of his desk and poured each of us a glass, even Gerard, all the while setting the chessmen onto their initial squares.

"Oh, no chess," said Annie. "I'm really tired."

"Come, come," Jacques said. "Our two geniuses. Let us see you play." He saw we were reluctant, so he reached out and made the first move for me: pawn to king four.

"Oh please, new Annie upon whom so much rests," he said. He gulped from his glass and set it down with a thud. She opened her mouth in protest, then laughed, a trilling, charming sound that made the rest of us laugh as well. She stuck out her hand and let it hover over the chessboard. She answered with the first move of a Sicilian defense.

Jacques sliced another piece of brie. "What brilliance is being played?" he asked, wiping his mouth with a piece of typing paper. We were in a mainline Richter-Rauzer Sicilian, all textbook for six moves. We moved quickly at first, then fell into short thinks. Jacques and Gerard were rapt, watching our hands dart back and forth.

"So?" said Jacques, noting our growing piles of captured chessmen. "Who is winning this battle of titans?"

"Hard to say," I said. But it wasn't. I had already established a strong attack. With each move, it became more and more clear: she could handle casual players, but was no better than middling as a real player. She was always a step behind.

Annie smiled at me, displaying two dazzling rows of teeth. She regarded me studiously. Her legs were crossed, and she was gently stroking her knee with her fingers. She then spoke with an exaggerated Southern accent: "Oh, suh, am ah to rely upon the kindness of strangers?" I had never heard anything sexier.

Jacques looked at her without comprehension.

"Frankly, mah dear," I replied, "ah might give a damn and ah might not."

"Oh, ah would be most grateful, suh," she said. "Most grateful, indeed."

"What are you saying?" Jacques asked. He glanced at Annie, then at me.

"Just chess talk," I said. "Master to master."

Annie nodded vigorously. "The Richter-Rauzer's always given me trouble," she announced.

I told her I hated playing against it myself. I then directed my words to Jacques: even the great Spassky sometimes lost against it, I told him. Even Kasparov and Karpov. Every grandmaster on the planet had his hands full against it. Jacques frowned.

Someone outside started honking a horn. Gerard walked over to the window and banged his prosthetic against the ledge—a demonstration of courtesy, I think, to enforce quiet while a game was in progress. But Jacques scolded him loudly, and as he did, Annie straightened in her chair and exchanged a look with me. She quietly turned her king over, indicating resignation, and reached out to rest her fingers on my hand.

Jacques turned his gaze back toward the chessboard and stared for a long moment at Annie's upturned king. He screwed up his face, then lifted his arm and sent the board and chessmen clattering onto the linoleum.

Annie let out a small cry. Jacques pointed an accusing finger at her; his finger remained erect a long time. He looked so angry I thought he was going to strike her. Instead, he shaped his fingers into a claw and pressed them, hard, to her forehead. "You *muzungus,*" he hissed. He opened his mouth as if to say more, then drew back his hand and walked quickly from the room.

"Don't let him get to you," I whispered, though my thoughts were elsewhere. I was thinking that Jacques would not leave me bereft now. He couldn't. He'd never get a real chess master to come to Burundi. For thousands of miles, I was the closest thing to a future Jacques was going to find.

I put a reassuring hand on Annie's shoulder, and in my mind's eye I saw how things would play out. It was as though someone had handed me a series of photographs and all I had to do was flip through the pictures to learn whatever I wanted to know. I saw what would happen with perfect clarity. Annie would sleep with Jacques in exchange for staying on. And she'd sleep with me because I had the goods on her, because I could make her life hellish or pleasant. She'd sleep with us because that's all she could offer. And more: she'd probably offered up the same thing in Uganda, coaching the university team. They must have tired of her eventually. She had no moorings. She was drifting and unstable, and she found her home in drifting, unstable places. She was drawn to Deepest Darkest, and her white woman's skin made a fine and delicious passport. She'd probably trafficked herself all across the continent.

That was the kind of woman who would come to Burundi at a time like this. A step up from a whore. What she had to offer was not so rare after all.

"Just be ready for tomorrow," I said, and stood to go. "Gerard can walk you to the hotel."

She looked at me anxiously. "Dinner?"

"Sorry," I said, but gave her no explanation. I didn't feel I had to.

— — —

The next morning Jacques drove his Citröen up to the Novotel, with me in the front and Gerard in the back keeping watch over a box of chess clocks and chess sets in drawstring pouches. Annie wore a baseball cap and loose clothing; she clutched a handbag to her stomach. Her expression was sullen and withdrawn, and after we exchanged greetings she sat in the back with Gerard, who kept rubbing his stump, complaining of chafing and tenderness. A small metallic faceplate on his prosthetic was slipping down; it pressed against his shirtsleeve like a shard of bone.

Jacques acted as if nothing had happened the previous day. Driving us to Muramvya, he was Jovial Jack again, shouting over the car's roaring engine. He described the scenery to Annie as if he were a tour guide; he seemed not at all disturbed by her lack of response. He told her that in Bujumbura one could with a great deal of trouble catch a bus going upcountry and in forty minutes climb so high into the mountainous interior that the plantain trees and sorghum fields would give way to firs and barefoot men in Arctic parkas. He told her the ascent to Muramvya was spectacular. It wasn't—the jungly roadsides, I thought, were dull and claustrophobic—but Annie directed her gaze wherever he told her to look.

"See?" he shouted toward the back seat. "Down into the gorges." He drew her attention to the fenced-in huts: they were called *rugos,* he said. Homesteads. The country was full of them, full of isolated homes, not villages. It was a country of *individuals,* he said. There were no Hutus and no Tutsis. There were only Burundians.

I raised my eyebrows at him.

He shouted some more. "However, today you will see mostly Tutsi. There are not so many Hutu in Muramvya."

In fact the army had recently conducted a sweep of the town. I was wondering if he would mention this. When he didn't, I turned to him. "So," I began.

"She is new," he said. He spoke softly now, mumbling under the engine's noise.

I didn't answer.

"I have made a mistake with this girl," he said. "Yes? Okay."

I felt it unwise to press the point, so I shrugged. Jacques began to say something but stopped himself. He wagged his head a bit, as if mulling something over, then caught my eye. I leaned in close.

"Perhaps she can still be of use to us," he said. "To our team. Is that how you phrase it? *Team,* yes? You and me. Our enterprise." He leered at me and gave a hideous smile. "What is past is past. You and I must go forward."

He was smiling so wide I thought he'd start giggling. He told me he had secured her stay for another few nights at the Novotel. We each had our functions, he said, our obligations, and right now his was to make Annie happy. If he did, then she could make *us* happy. Did I understand? Make us happy at the Novotel. On long and lonely nights, he said, nudging my arm: on a big clean bed. He had talked last night to his friend in Uganda. She was okay with such things. She didn't mind. She'd do anything to be thought special.

I nodded, then returned my gaze to the window.

But Jacques wouldn't let it drop. He kept looking over at me, then back at the road. He told me he had seen the way I looked at her. He hoped, he said, that I understood how well he knew me.

"Yes," I said. I wouldn't look at him. "Yes to everything."

"Oh *ho,* oh *ho,*" he sang. "Oh ho, oh ho." He honked the horn, smiling, and I knew then that in revealing my mind to him I had just lost something very valuable.

The farther we drove up into the interior, the more the straining engine overwhelmed our ability to talk. We all fell silent. In Bujumbura the heat had palpable weight, and bloated flies would tumble into your beer; now, forty minutes away, we were all chilled to the bone. It was freezing. I checked the rearview mirror a few times, and once I saw Annie reach into her bag and pull out a plastic squirt bottle of skin cream, which she applied to her face and hands. The thin light was uninspiring, and every few hundred feet we saw small groups of women carrying bright plastic buckets and bulging cloth sacks. Still our car roared upward, past a row of adobe dwellings, and in a clearing by a lonely house, past its battered green door, a swath of frost rimed the ground.

"Burundi!" Jacques shouted to the back seat, for Annie's benefit. "Did you know it is called the Mountains of the Moon? Because of the terrain, you see." In the rearview mirror, I saw her nod in response. She seemed more interested in examining Gerard's prosthetic arm. It was giving him trouble. When she touched it, close to his stump, he winced.

— — —

In Muramvya, Jacques pulled off the asphalt and stopped in front of a gray concrete building. The shophouses were all shuttered; across the street was a raised wooden walkway, but some of the planks were missing. Jacques called over a boy to guard the car. He then had Gerard place the box of chess equipment on his head and led us all down a footpath that wound past a long brick wall. The street behind us was empty, except for a man herding a line of bony dark cattle along the pavement. We passed through a stand of fir and eucalyptus trees, and after a few minutes we emerged at the gate of a walled school compound.

Pandemonium broke out. A small crowd had been awaiting our arrival. *"Muzungu!"* we heard. Most of the crowd looked to be coffee farmers, gangly men without shoes dressed in vaguely military clothes—stained brown slacks, dirty light work shirts—and circling around them were some fidgety boys, all wearing shorts several sizes too big. The school itself was little more than a long series of low-slung concrete rooms, shuttered on one side with frosted window slats, and out of the largest room—our chess venue, judging from the crowd inside—walked a man wearing a powder-blue safari suit. He began talking animatedly to Jacques, then said something to the crowd that I didn't understand. It must have been about Annie and me because everyone exclaimed loudly and looked in our direction.

"I told him today we have two geniuses," Jacques said to us. "Two inspirations. Monsieur le Genius they know. They can all play. They can all use chess clocks. So Annie . . . ." Jacques let his sentence trail off, but his meaning was clear: *Annie, don't let us down.* She removed her baseball cap, then set it back on her head, a gesture of resolve.

Inside, Gerard had already dumped the contents of the box and busied himself emptying the drawstring pouches onto the tables and setting up the chessmen and roll-up boards. Someone had pushed six wooden banquet tables together, three along the window-slat side and three along the opposite wall. Our opponents were already seated in high-backed wooden chairs—ten opponents for each of us. It was to be a simultaneous exhibition: I'd play those along the window slats and

Annie would play those on the other side of the room. We'd each make a move, then go to the next player and make a move, and so on, until all the games were finished.

I took it upon myself to set up the chess clocks on my three tables, while Annie did the same on her side. From the doorway, you could see the compound gate and the dirt courtyard, empty except for a solitary eucalyptus tree in the center. Along the peeling back wall of the classroom stood a line of men and boys, mostly barefoot idlers. There were perhaps forty people inside; overhead, two fluorescent lights flickered, illuminating the chalk dust on the rough blackboard in front. The room smelled of mud, and already the cold was numbing my fingers.

At the doorway, the man in the safari suit raised his voice at a barefoot woman. She wore a coarse gray sweater and held a bundle in her arms. I didn't recognize her, but she shouted to me: "Monsieur le Genius," and continued in the local language. The man in the safari suit laid his hands on her shoulders and pushed her abruptly out the door.

This seemed to agitate Annie. She walked up to Jacques, occupied with instructing Gerard on the proper positioning of chess pieces, and asked what was happening. Jacques had nothing to say, so I tried to help. "Don't worry about it," I told her. "Just a crazy woman. Remember, we're with Jacques. We're just playing chess."

Annie exhaled loudly. "I'm not talking about *us,*" she said. Her tone seemed disrespectful, and I told her so. We were here to promote an enterprise, I said. We had an obligation, I told her, so if she didn't mind, could she please conduct herself accordingly? She looked at the floor.

Take a cue from Gerard, I almost said, but I knew that would have been a pointless escalation. Gerard had set up all the chess sets and clocks, and was now without complaint awaiting his next assignment. It came quickly. Jacques conferred with the man in the safari suit, who subsequently rifled through the teacher's desk and withdrew a short straw broom looped together with wire. Gerard knew what to do. He took the broom with his good hand and walked straightaway to the courtyard, where he began hacking at the packed dirt, sweeping dust toward the eucalyptus tree. Jacques snapped his fingers at him—Gerard was sweeping too hard, bringing dust into the room—but after a brief exchange between the two, Gerard fell into an agreeably languorous rhythm, scraping the cold ground clean.

Jacques signaled to me: it was time. I stood in front of the room and steepled my fingers; Jacques stood to the side, calling for quiet. I smiled pleasantly at Annie, then raised my arms in a dramatic gesture of command. "Let us commence," I said, and we did.

Our opponents straightened in their chairs; some centered their knights more securely on their initial squares. I walked to Board One and set my face with a severe expression: eyes narrowed, lips bunched and tight, a finger to my chin, which gave the appearance of contemplation. I moved the pawn in front of my king forward two squares, then worked my way down the line, making the same first move on all my other boards. Some of my opponents knew enough to reply by pushing their central pawns forward. Others made foolish first moves, pointless pawn pushes that marked them instantly as absolute beginners.

They all moved quickly, but I was even quicker. The cold was getting to me, so I didn't want to stand in one spot for too long. I walked a straight line from one end of the tables to the other, then back again, never pausing more than a couple of seconds for each move. Soon I noticed that one of my opponents had turned away from his board and was staring out the window slats. I was floored: it was his move, and he was letting time tick off his clock. But I followed his gaze and saw two tall men in red berets standing outside, pressing their faces against the window slats. I quickly made out the rest of their outfits. Soldiers. They wore camouflage, and cinched around their waists were thick canvas belts. A black pistol holster hung at the side of the man closest to the entrance. The other carried an enormous automatic weapon, which he casually lowered at that moment, idly tapping the gun's snout against the glass.

Jacques noticed them, too, and so did Annie. I think everyone noticed them. The bystanders continued to chat, and boys who had been milling around the courtyard now drew nearer to the doors of the other classrooms. "Back to business," said Jacques behind me. He said it loudly so that Annie would hear too, and then I saw why: no sooner had the soldiers begun peering in than they drew back and sauntered away, apparently sharing a good joke. One picked up some pebbles and tossed them aimlessly into the courtyard, where Gerard had already swept.

On Board Three I called out "checkmate" and shook my opponent's hand. Five minutes had gone by. After twenty minutes I had won every game. It was as easy as sleeping. Each time one of my opponents turned over his king, Jacques came up behind me and delivered his usual line. Chess, he'd say in the local language, was all about vision.

On her side of the room, Annie had dispatched all but one of her opponents, a plump, middle-aged man with a messy scar stretching from his right eye to his left ear. I pegged him as someone caught up in the '72 massacres. He sat with his arms folded across his stomach.

Jacques motioned me outside. "Will she win?" he asked.

I wasn't sure. She had the advantage, but her opponent was putting up a stout defense. He depressed the plunger of the chess clock with confident ease.

"Monsieur le Genius," I heard then. It was the woman from the doorway. She held out her bundle, wrapped in a plain brown blanket. At the top of the bundle, a baby's head stuck out, eyes staring dully at its mother. She stepped directly in front of me and said something with lots of hanging vowels that I couldn't follow. I frowned. The baby had small scabs on its face; its breathing was labored, like an old man's.

The woman searched my face, then turned her attention to Jacques, who exchanged a few words with her. "She wants you to bless her baby," he said.

"What do you mean?"

"What do you think I mean? I am telling you what she wants." The woman raised her baby to my face. I saw now that her forehead was deeply creased, and I imagined her waiting for me outside all this time, worrying, whispering promises into her baby's ears. She said something that sounded pleading, but Jacques snapped at her and she fell silent.

I lifted my right hand and spread my fingers wide.

"Oh, great *bwana,*" said Jacques to me. His voice was mocking. "Your first blessing." The woman murmured something. She looked at her baby, then brought the bundle to her lips and kissed the baby's forehead. She looked up at me and beamed. "Monsieur le Genius," she said.

"Like Jesus among the lepers, hey, Bobby?" Jacques said. "Do you wish to claim this, too?"

I ignored him. I let my palm hover over the baby's head and made three tight circles in the air. The woman moaned lightly. I then summoned my deepest, most holy voice: "Let this child be safe," I said, and the woman responded with small, encouraging noises.

Jacques snorted. I looked over at him in protest, and for a moment our eyes locked. We stared hard at each other. Without warning, Jacques grabbed my hand and yanked it away from the baby, and when I felt his hand on my skin I reacted instantly, and we began to struggle. His fingers locked around my wrist, and I jerked my arm back and broke free. It took no more than a couple of seconds, but he was not finished. He started whispering rapidly to the woman, a harsh and explosive flurry that I understood to be about me. He held his mouth close to her ear, and then I saw the woman look at me in alarm and shift her baby to her other hip, shielding it with her body.

"Can you two show some decency?" I heard. It was Annie. She was standing in the doorway with her arms folded.

Jacques frowned, but he didn't look at her. "You are the worst of humanity," he said to me.

I wanted to strike him. I wanted to place my hand around his neck and drive him to the ground. But I didn't. I was so furious that I turned from him and stuck my arm straight toward Annie: "Hey," I said to her. I stabbed the air for emphasis. "You can show *us* something later, huh?"

She turned on her heels and went back inside, and I noticed something remarkable: her game was still in progress. She had walked away from her opponent—a breach of etiquette. The man with the scarred face leaned back in his chair, waving his arms around and complaining to some bystanders. And I noticed something else: the two soldiers had returned. They stood by the window slats, looking at Jacques and me expectantly, as if they had happened upon an impromptu piece of street theater. The one with the automatic weapon unbuttoned his fatigues and scratched lazily at his T-shirt. The other one looped his fingers around his canvas belt.

"I apologize," Jacques said to me. He nodded pleasantly to the soldiers.

"I'm sorry, too," I said, and straightened my shirt.

We stood a while, not saying anything. The soldiers didn't move; behind them, Gerard began coughing noisily. "Bobby," Jacques said, "let us think of our obligations."

"I agree. Absolutely."

"So let us comport ourselves," said Jacques. "Please. Bobby, I am sorry." He smiled to some boys watching us from the doorway. He made a show of patting me on the shoulder, and when he did, the soldiers and the boys smiled back.

I was about to point out that Annie had acted high-handed with her opponent, but Jacques was already walking back into the room. He spoke even before he reached her. "Do not leave the board, Annie," he called out in English. "We have an obligation. Please finish," he told her. Please, he said, smiling broadly: please remember why we are here.

The woman with the baby said something to me that sounded disapproving. I shook my head at her and growled, which set the two soldiers to laughing. I laughed along with them, and the woman stopped talking. I laughed like I had never heard anything funnier.

— — —

Ten minutes later, Annie was still playing her last opponent. She had a winning rook-and-pawn ending, but he was hanging tough. Her responses were taking longer and longer.

I had accepted a cigarette from a man in a crisp blue shirt and was beginning to drift off to sleep when Jacques motioned toward the door. "Just ignore," he said in English. Outside, the soldier with the pistol had just barked something at Gerard. Even from where I stood, I could see Gerard's face crinkle with worry. He dropped his broom and jogged over to them, stopping a respectful distance away, but the soldier waved him closer. The man seemed to be consulting with his colleague about something. He grabbed Gerard by his prosthetic and jerked him closer. Gerard yelped. The soldier shook Gerard's bad arm, then twisted it hard; he seemed to be examining the political slogans carved into the plastic. He barked some more at Gerard and yanked again on the prosthetic. Something like a clamp tumbled out of Gerard's sleeve. He cried out in pain.

"Pay no mind," Jacques said to me.

The soldier held the prosthetic close to his face, reading the slogans. Gerard's face contorted; one of his legs seemed to give, and his bad arm jerked for a moment away from the soldier. The soldier with the automatic weapon took a look, and together the two soldiers set out to work on Gerard's bad arm. The one with the pistol read the plastic forearm while the other grasped Gerard by his stump and yanked the prosthetic the opposite way, as if to get a better angle. Gerard was wailing now. With his good arm he clutched the side of his head.

Jacques and I stepped outside for a better view. "They are looking for Hutu," Jacques said. "Agitators. Gerard is only *Zaireois*."

"Not the same, I know," I said. "Just some push-and-shove, right?"

"Yes. It is not serious."

"Do they have to do that here?"

Jacques didn't answer.

Gerard would be okay—a little wear and tear, but he'd be fine in the morning. He had seen worse. But his wails were creating a disturbance in the room, and men began filing out to take a look. Annie was looking, too. She'd stare at the chessboard, then turn and frown in Gerard's direction.

The two soldiers ran their hands along Gerard's plastic arm and fell into a short *tête-à-tête*. The one with the pistol said something and smiled while the other pressed his thumb into Gerard's stump. Gerard fell to his knees, and the soldiers called out, "Okay, okay," to the growing crowd. There was murmuring; somebody began clucking loudly. The soldier with the pistol turned and pointed at the crowd. He straightened his beret, then said something that sounded like a caution.

Jacques responded to him, and some men in the crowd nodded. "I told them everyone is calm," he said in English. A man in a green T-shirt waved to the soldiers. A boy in a parka stuck his head into the open doorway of the schoolroom and said something to Annie's remaining opponent, who was looking out the window, sliding the slats up and down to get a better view. Their chess game was still in progress. I saw Annie next to the board, rummaging through her handbag.

"It is over," Jacques said. "All is fine. It is over." He nudged me. The soldiers were headed out, walking toward the courtyard gate. The soldier with the automatic weapon carried it like a garden tool, dragging the stock along the dirt. Gerard had crawled to the eucalyptus tree. He lay sprawled on the ground, resting his head against the trunk and moaning.

Annie sidled past, clutching her handbag tight, and headed to the tree. She jogged a bit, letting her hair bounce on her shoulders, and when she got to Gerard she squatted down, reaching into the bag. She was on her knees then. My heart started racing. She withdrew her bottle of skin lotion and squirted thick lines of the cream onto her hands and then onto his stump. She put her hands under his armpit and lifted the stump into the air. It was blotchy and engorged, and together she and Gerard fiddled with the prosthetic and let it fall to the ground. What I pictured in my mind thrilled and revolted me: a sexual act, the monstrous stump erect and pulsing. Jacques, too, was looking, and when he caught my eye he smiled, as if acknowledging what I was seeing—as if he, too, saw it.

Annie stayed at Gerard's stump, and her creamy palms made squishing noises as they moved along. She was leaning into him. Some boys joked and gestured, but they quickly quieted down when the man in the safari suit snapped his fingers. Jacques motioned for me, and together we walked across the courtyard. The closer we got, the more I could hear Annie cooing to Gerard, whispering comfort into his ear. "You must go back into the room," Jacques said to Annie, pleasantly. She made no move to stand. "We are not here for this," he said. "You must finish your game. You have an obligation." He clapped his hands, and the sound echoed through the courtyard. "Go back into the room," he said, softly now. "Please. We have an obligation."

She looked up at us—not with anger, I thought, but with a frankness that silenced Jacques and turned the image in my mind watery. She did not budge, and I sensed that behind us the crowd was edging forward. In the cold, our breaths rose like steam and seemed to hang in the air. Annie kept on kneading Gerard's stump, just below his shoulder, and his mangled skin shone with cream. She rubbed so gently and with such precision that I could no longer sustain the picture in my mind. Gerard moaned softly, rocking his head back and forth against the tree trunk, in concert with her caresses. I saw then that her fingers were spotted with his blood. Still she continued. She cupped his stump with one hand and with the other lightly stroked, tracing delicate, glistening circles, and the image in my head dissolved.

Her fingers arched up, then fell, over and over, in a slow and deliberate rhythm. She would not stop. Jacques cleared his throat—a gurgle, I thought, a release—and still she rubbed, greasing Gerard's stump until his face relaxed. What she was doing with her hands reminded me of something from long ago, something I had once known. I could not place it now. For a moment my mind went blank, and I looked without comprehension. I could make no sense of what I was seeing. It was as if I had no frame of reference anymore.

So I turned away, my face burning. I saw that Jacques, too, had turned away. He looked stricken. He lifted his hand as if to touch me, and there it remained, poised and still, for what seemed like forever.

Won't You Stay, Please?

PROFESSOR MUYENZI, head of linguistics, had been so charming in his correspondence—*you will love Burundi, for we are the heart of Africa*—that even at tiny Bujumbura International, with only a handful of people waiting for the arrivals, Neil assumed that the African walking toward him was meeting someone else. The man was short and bug-eyed, with a small, rounded chin and an enormous forehead etched with deep scowl lines. He was not smiling. If not for the tufts of gray hair above his ears, he looked for the world like a sullen child.

The flight to Burundi had been exhausting, three days in total, and when the pinched little man raised an inquiring finger, Neil leaned against the luggage on his cart and closed his eyes. The man wouldn't disappear. It was the professor—he pulled out his card and held it to his lips—but in some ocean-scented region of his brain Neil held out hope that from around the corner some Nelson Mandela look-alike might emerge, someone with a dazzling, I-forgive-you-everything smile, and with a bear hug announce himself to be the charming correspondent. All around the terminal, people were laughing and throwing their arms around each other, and students in tight shirts shouted greetings into their parents' ears. Outside, beyond the huge glass panes, couples walked hand in hand across the gravel to their cars, and a woman in a bright sarong jangled her bracelets at a boy, who grabbed her wrists and pressed them to his cheeks. There was a kind of whoosh in the air, a joyous crackle, but around the professor the sound all but disappeared, as though someone had placed a jar over him. When Neil at last stuck out his hand to shake, he had to fight the urge to say what he had been thinking ever since boarding the flight back in Los Angeles: *I have been deserted.*

"You are the guest linguist?" the professor asked. He sounded bored, and his eyes drifted to Neil's trolley cart. His handshake, Neil thought, was fishy and damp, even less appealing than what he had heard was typical of Africans. "You are not ill, I hope," said the professor. Neil frowned. "Your expression," his host explained. "You looked like you had just eaten something disagreeable."

"Oh no, no, no," Neil said, waving off the suggestion. He made reference to jet lag, then to the tag team of humidity and sun. Who knew? he said: travel was a funny thing, wasn't it? The professor raised his eyebrows—whether the gesture was universal or borrowed from some movie, Neil wasn't sure—then began speaking in French. He was of the opinion that Neil had packed too many bags. One could buy clothes in Burundi, he said. One could even purchase luggage.

Neil laughed in what he hoped was a disarming manner. Of course, he said, he had nothing against the Burundi luggage industry . . . but the professor didn't seem to be listening. His host shooed away some men in dirty orange overalls, one of whom had already laid claim to Neil's biggest suitcase, then abruptly grabbed two of Neil's bags for himself and started toward the exit. "Sorry, sorry," Neil called out, and the professor stopped in his tracks. "Foreigners are expected to spread the wealth," Neil said, motioning to the men in orange. "Give big tips and all that." An Africa scholar back in Los Angeles had told him as much. Over wine, the man had grinned slyly and said, "We all suckle from the same teat." He paused a long time, savoring his earthiness. "But if you've got a bigger mouthful, share it," he continued. "*Noblisse oblige,* my friend. We're all brothers and so on."

The professor remained frozen a moment, then let the suitcases drop. "I am not with you," he said in English. "You are with me." And with that he picked the suitcases back up and continued out the door. Neil followed. What the professor said sounded like a rebuke, but apparently there was to be no standing around to discuss it. Neil's shoulder bag kept slipping, and he quickly fell behind. He hadn't slept for days, and during the layover in Nairobi he had spent an exhausting hour searching for the long-distance phones, tracing and re-tracing his steps, only to discover he had been given the wrong number to the hospital. Not that there was anything he could do now. He was half a world away, passing through a glass door smudged with fingerprints and into the glare and smoking gravel of a foreign parking lot.

People were already pulling away, blaring their horns, then veering sharply onto a ribbon of blacktop walled on both sides by plantain trees and jungly undergrowth. So this was the heart of Africa. Gibbons ate their own young here, and tilapia fish grew to the size of leopards; Hutu boys high on contact cement murdered busloads of Tutsis, then Tutsi soldiers razed entire Hutu villages; witch doctors combed the elephant grass in search of fingernails and molars. And still, Neil marveled, still everyone followed the soccer rankings and blathered away on their cell phones and drank too much over the holidays. Ostriches, as far as the eye could see. Where was the sense of emergency, the busy arms yanking perversion from its hole?

Neil had a million questions for his host. But mostly he wanted to scream at the professor's back. Hey prof, he imagined shouting: how about you learn some manners?

— — —

Five days before boarding at LAX, Neil had disconnected his answering machine. He let the phone ring and ring. I'm gone, he said to the receiver. Like smoke in the wind. Poof. With all that needed attending to—the endless packing, the flight schedule changes, the storage-unit hassles—his sleep had been disturbed, and there was no time for correcting proofs or loading up on Swiss chard at the farmer's market or even for jogging through the park. It was time to disappear.

But the calls kept coming, and when Neil finally answered there was only static, then a sharp intake of breath. "Neil?" he heard. "Is this Neil?" It was an unfamiliar and dismal woman's voice. He didn't at first understand what she was saying. She told him he had to fly up to Tacoma. She told him his father was dying. "Your father, Ray," she said, as if he might not recall the name. For what seemed like an eternity, Neil heard evidence that the end for his father was at hand. "Neil," the woman's voice said, "he's so far gone they can't even operate." Ray's weight had brought on diabetes, then everything failed all at once. He had crusty infections below the knee ("Picture an elephant leg," she said, "then picture it crispy"), a liver stewing in its juices, a droopy and waterlogged pair of lungs, blood clots like little beaver dams in this artery and that.

She ran down a long list of depressing evacuations and abandonments. It was only a matter of days, if not hours.

The woman's tone seemed inappropriately aggressive, and Neil remained silent a long time. "Who did you say you were again?" he finally asked. The voice belonged to Jenny, his younger brother's girlfriend, or so Neil recalled from an old Christmas postcard. Or maybe she was his wife now.

"Can I talk to Pig?" Neil said into the phone. He quickly corrected himself. "Sorry. I don't know where that came from. Can I talk to Peter, please?" Growing up, he had called his brother Pig and his father Hog. They were names you could say and not alarm yourself, cartoon words, not like the doctors' terrifying *morbidly obese* or the schoolyard taunt *feeders*, which gave him nightmares. There was, as well, a quality to the terms used by others that suggested to him even then, as a young boy, the existence of something underneath all the blubber even more grotesque than the blubber itself. All the words except the cartoon words seemed to contain further accusations of personal failings too hazy to be defined with their own words. Ray was, in fact, crazy as a June bug—that had been clear for years—and Peter had followed in his footsteps. They wore their fat like arctic suits, like something purchased, and you got the feeling they kept them on as a kind of insurance, protecting their dodgy, laboring hearts from whatever awaited them outside the door.

"Peter's not here now," Jenny said. There was a pause, then she spoke again: "He's making arrangements. That's why I'm calling."

Of course, Neil thought, of course she would say Peter wasn't there. And of course Peter wasn't the one making the phone call. He had left the task to this woman, this Jenny. Neil shook his head. He pictured his brother sitting across the table from Jenny, grimly waving off her offer of the phone, perhaps stuffing a hoagie or an Eskimo Pie into his mouth as he listened.

Neil agreed to everything Jenny asked of him. He could stay in Tacoma for just a few days, he told her. Yes, he could spell them on the deathwatch. But then he had to leave for Central Africa. He had a research position lined up there, and the gears were already in motion. Did she know he had a Ph.D.? That he was thirty-four? Yes, yes, two years older than Peter. Correct, single again. Correct, two marriages already. Bump and go, yes, if that's how she wanted to phrase it. But did she know he'd had a book proposal accepted? Did she know he was going to spend a year doing field research?

Nothing he said seemed to catch her by surprise. So Peter had been keeping tabs, checking him out on the Internet. At least his brother had shown some initiative. The ironic thing was that the opposite was not required. Ray and Peter had for decades remained true to type, and phone calls or visits or chatty letters produced no more information than settling into his chair and conjuring them up. They were like movie characters, images impervious to time and circumstance, replaying the same scenes over and over. Their *milieu* was the trough, he once said, and surprise or variation had long ago been struck from the menu. He had said that to Karen, his second wife, when she asked, her voice sharp with exasperation, "Can't you tell me *one* thing about your father or brother?" His answer had come across as both thoughtful and cruel, and though he told her cruelty gave him no pleasure, he also noted that honesty was sometimes a brutal mistress.

But privately, he acknowledged he was not being honest. If he were, he would have had to let her know he'd seen them only rarely since he was twelve and that, even then, the occasions lasted only an hour or two. There was shame in that, and, besides, the answer he gave his wife was what she needed. Society was a scold—it criticized but never praised—and for Karen, who phoned her mother twice a week, the fact that he had given her something smart sounding to share was a godsend.

His preference, one he had devoted much time to establishing, was to view his childhood with his father and brother as an exchange-student type of affair. *Hello Mister and Junior, I am friendly youth person.* Sometimes, stoned or woozy drunk after linguistics parties, he could still bring himself to tears with what he could not help thinking of as a modern-day Dickens tale. When he was just a toddler, his mother, Margo, died giving birth to his brother. Outside of a short summer stay with Ray and Peter, at twelve, he had been raised by Aunt Beth, who was already an old woman with tissuey skin when she took him to live with her up in Bellingham.

But Peter stayed with Ray, and together they grew astoundingly fat. Just like Ray, Peter took to wearing suspenders. He developed the same meaty odor, and when Ray lost interest in wearing shoes, he followed suit. Ray made a mess of pronouncing words like *similarly* and *Loyola* ("It's not a tongue for talking," he once said, without irony), and so did Peter. They despised doctors, and neither wanted workmen in the apartment—embarrassment, Neil supposed—so the chair legs cracked one by one, the light switches stopped working, and the pantry door began to sag and wore a groove into the wood flooring. Even when Peter finally moved out, well into his twenties, the move only went as far as down the street. Every once in a while Neil sent them each a holiday card.

Every once in a while he got one in return, signed by both of them.

The next morning Neil flew up to Tacoma. The arrangement was that he would stay with Peter and Jenny in their apartment. "Hope the accommodations are to your liking," Jenny had said before hanging up. On the plane, Neil mulled over her statement. He wasn't certain she intended the comment to imply something about him, but he had noted a certain sass in her tone. Most likely, their apartment was slovenly, even sordid. When the in-flight breakfast arrived, he could not eat the eggs. He told the flight attendant they smelled moldy.

— — —

They drove in silence for several miles—Bujumbura was another thirty minutes away—before the professor turned to Neil and asked about his research project. Neil wagged his head. As head of linguistics, the professor had signed off on his visiting scholar status, though he wasn't the primary sponsor. Still, they had written each other a couple of times, and the professor had spoken glowingly about the linguistics and language instructors in his department, what he called Neil's new African family. So no one had told the head of linguistics a thing about him. That went a long way in explaining the disconnect, exposing the charm of the professor's letters as fraud, as simple careerism masquerading as warmth. The African mask, Neil supposed. Say anything, long as you didn't get sullied.

And, besides, there were plenty of other things Neil would have preferred to talk about right now. That woman carrying the clay cistern: was her head shaved because she had lice? How come no one cut the vegetation back around the highway? And Herr Doctor Professor, yes you, my devious little friend, is there blood on your hands? Are you Hutu, as your height suggests; or are you Tutsi, as your position suggests? What were you doing during the massacres of 1972? How about in '88 or '93? The thrill he had experienced months ago, reading the accounts, felt much different now. Even the interior of the car seemed off-kilter. The professor was one of the elite, for God's sake, educated in modern ways, but the upholstery smelled of sweat and dirt, and the ashtray overflowed with beer caps. The back seats were no better. He had apparently used them recently as a dumping ground for folders, most torn or smudged, and mangled exam booklets.

"No one told you about my project?" Neil asked.

The professor stared at him blankly. Then they rounded a curve, and jagged spaces in the high wall of vegetation suddenly flooded with sunlight. For a moment, the road and the jungle turned white as chalk, and the brightness knifing through the trees mottled the professor's face. Even in the glare Neil saw the professor curl his lips, as if tasting something bitter. The professor brought up his hand as a visor, then muttered something ugly-sounding under his breath. His forehead puckered with angry lines. It was as though the professor now thought himself invisible—as though, all along, the professor had been waiting for kreig lights to blind any witnesses. The moment passed. A driver going the other way tapped his horn, and the professor's expression immediately dropped away. But it was enough: the man had been time traveling, Neil realized, projecting himself back, just for a second, into a scene of ugliness and shock.

So Neil began talking. There was a calming and pleasing quality to research talk, a pattern of thesis and support that suggested all was right with the world: Good morning, ladies and gentlemen, there are no lions on the veranda today, none at all. Let us rejoice. Neil told the professor he was a bit embarrassed to opine about Burundi to a Burundian, especially such a respected and knowledgeable one, but as the professor knew, his beautiful country, unlike neighboring Rwanda, had never employed specialists to remember and relate the goings-on of the royal court. As a result, and as the professor was also aware, Burundi's history was subject to more, should he say, uncertainty than was Rwanda's. And that, he added, was true even in the harsh light of the recent Rwandan genocide.

"You are saying," said the professor, "that we are ignorant of our actual history, *n'est-ce-pas?* That we sometimes use that to—" he paused, searching for the word—"avoid responsibility?"

Oh no, Neil replied, shaking his head, though that was in fact what he meant. That was in fact the supposition driving his project. But the professor had spoken so forcefully, so unexpectedly, that Neil worried his host was trying to pick a fight.

"Would you tell me please what you are here to examine," the professor said, staring straight ahead. It didn't sound like a question.

All he was going to do, Neil told him, speaking evenly, was examine the morphemes in the local Kirundi language used to signify past events. There were of course two such morphemes, Neil said, holding up two fingers. One marked the distant past; the other, the near or very recent past. By examining those morphemes, Neil said, one might find objective data, one way or the other, that Burundians do or do not . . . but he could not find an acceptable way to frame what he wanted to say next. He turned over his palms, a gesture of searching, and looked at a passing truck for inspiration.

The professor spoke: "That we talk about what we did yesterday as if it had already disappeared into history? In regard to certain actions, of course. Yes? And that doing this is equivalent to saying, 'Oh well, nothing can be done'?" He took one hand off the steering wheel and wagged his forefinger in the air. "Even when wrongs can be righted. Even when certain people should be held accountable. Is this what you wish to say?"

Neil exhaled loudly. "Well, no," he said. "That isn't my assumption at all. No. The evidence might very well support the opposite conclusion. But of course the questions have been raised by others."

"Others," the professor said, nodding. "*Muzungus.* You foreigners. There is a saying here. 'The *muzungu* who mocks your clothes sits naked behind his desk.' Do you understand?"

"I get the drift," Neil replied. He placed his hands on the dashboard and turned to his companion. "But I want you to know I'm not that sort of person."

The professor flashed Neil a grim little smile. "We know so much about *muzungus,*" he said. "What do you know about us?"

He spoke with what sounded like pride, but also, Neil thought, with more than a hint of narrow righteousness. Surely the professor understood the geopolitical reasons why Burundians might, out of necessity and self-interest, know more about, say, America than Americans knew about a basket case like Burundi. Outside of peanut butter and beer, the country lacked for everything. There was even that Eddie Izzard routine about having coffee with the President of Burundi. It worked as comedy because geopolitically speaking, there was little difference between the President of Burundi and the King of the Rabbits.

But one could not say such things out loud, not here, and certainly not to this sour African in the driver's seat. Neil found himself waving his hand at the blue mountains in the distance, as if overcome by their beauty. Anything to change the topic. What a tragedy, Neil thought, to be blind to your own circumstances. An amendment occurred to him. Might it be an even greater tragedy to be fully aware? Knowledge like that could eat you up from the inside.

— — —

At Sea-Tac, Neil looked around the baggage claim for Peter and Jenny. He felt clammy and cold, and waiting at the baggage carousel he suddenly doubled over, clutching his stomach. "What the hell?" he whispered, but the pain was so sharp and surprising—how could this be happening? he wondered. *This?*—that he at first did not see the woman—Jenny, he realized—waving at him from of a row of chairs by the windows. Next to her was Peter. His brother's plump and delicate hands were draped across his stomach; he appeared to be dozing. His dark hair was longer than Neil remembered, and the more he allowed his gaze to roam over his brother's body, the more Peter's features seemed to grow flaccid and indistinct, as if receding into his girth.

Jenny walked over. "Good to finally meet you," she said. "I'm just sorry it took this to get us all together." She, too, was squat and heavy, though, Neil was careful to note, not beyond the pale. Maybe fifty pounds over. Put her on an exercise regime, he thought, and she could drop twenty in a month. She wasn't pretty, but he hadn't expected her to be. She wore a brown poncho and black stretch pants—if she thought her outfit hid the pounds, she was mistaken—and her hair was tied back, severely, into a ponytail. She hugged him, then they made their way to the row of chairs.

"Hey," Peter said. He righted himself, all six feet of him, bracing his bulk against the chair. He was breathing noisily through his mouth, and his teeth were still bad, like dull little stumps. Some kind of pimply growth pocked his neck, and under the fluorescent light his skin looked glistening and plastic. His limbs were hairless. Only his eyes, Neil recalled, seemed unaffected. They were still agile and bright, as if transplanted from some alien species. Odd. It was as if they could look right through you, when in fact they registered little that didn't come on a plate.

The sharp pain returned, and Neil pressed his hand to his side and grimaced. "You hurtin' there?" Peter said, pointing.

"Just a side stitch," said Neil. "I don't know. It just came on."

"That's not like *dad's* side stitches, is it?" Peter slurred the words. His flesh, Neil recalled, constricted his windpipe and made his speech sloppy and spittle-filled.

"Whoa," Neil said. He held up his hands in protest. "Don't start, Okay?" His voice was sharper than he had intended.

Jenny watched the exchange. "Well, that's not quite what I imagined for a greeting," she said. She looked first at Peter, then at Neil. "Is there something going on?"

It was an awkward moment, and Neil looked to Peter to see if he'd say anything. But his brother was shaking his head. Then Neil turned to collect his luggage, and when he rejoined them the subject had already changed. Jenny was wiping at something on Peter's shirt. At the automatic door Peter waved his arms in front of him like a magician. "Open says-a-me," he said, fluttering his fingers, and when the door slid open, he laughed.

He had always loved infantile wordplay. When they were teenagers, cousin Jim and his bride Kay had invited the whole extended family to the wedding reception. Neil hadn't seen Peter for a long time, but all Peter wanted to do was go up to people and say, "If you see Kay, tell her not now." No one got the joke, but Peter found it hilarious. "You're supposed to be the smart one," he said to Neil. "If. You. See. Kay. F-U-C-K?" Peter had never learned how to plug his heart, how to make himself presentable, so everyone treated him as if he were a child. "Do you always have to be so embarrassing?" Neil snapped, noticing the bridesmaids' table frowning in their direction. "Can't you grow up? Just for a minute?" Peter flipped him off. They probably would have gotten into a fistfight if Jim hadn't whistled and given them both a nasty look.

On the freeway, Neil sat silent in the back seat of what Peter called their clunkmobile. It was hard to act cheery. The late-afternoon sky was pale blue and washed out, faintly pink near the horizon and completely uninspired. It cast the distant firs in a purple hue, and even with the windows rolled up the long grass along the shoulder filled the car with a dusty, basement smell.

"So you're teaching what?" asked Jenny. "Linguistics, right?" She spoke at the rearview mirror.

"Your job secure?" Peter added.

Neil shifted in his seat. "Yes to the subject matter," he said. "No to job security. I'm not tenure-track."

"A gypsy scholar," said Jenny. "All branches, no roots."

Peter spoke. "Up and out every few years, huh?"

Neil's surprise must have been evident in the rearview mirror. Jenny said, "Did you think we were going to ask what that *ten-year* thing is? I know what tenure is."

"Sorry," Neil said. "Of course you do."

"I went on after high school," Jenny said. "I was just a few credits short of a B.A."

"That's great," said Neil. He slapped the back of her seat in a show of enthusiasm.

But she apparently wasn't ready to acknowledge his gesture. "Tenure," she said. "Let's see. Peter has tenure with his father. I have tenure with Peter."

Neil looked at the rearview mirror to examine Jenny's expression. Her statement seemed unwarranted. He mulled over blurting out something disarming—"I'm innocent of all charges! Case dismissed!"—but the moment seemed to have passed. They'd show him the house, Jenny said, then go in the evening to the hospital. Jenny focused on the road ahead. Then Peter turned the radio to some oldies station and it was too noisy to talk anymore.

— — —

The closer they got to Bujumbura, the more the giant fronds of the plantain trees gave way to scrub and stretches of cracked red clay. The jungle surrounding the narrow highway, Neil realized, had cast everything in shadow until now. It had been like driving in a tunnel, then suddenly emerging into a wide and sky-lit world. Even the air smelled fresher. Small groups of people, walking single-file, now began to appear along the roadside, and in the distance, smoke from cooking fires rose in frayed lines from the city. Now eighteen-wheelers and minivans dotted the road, and scores of frowning men on bicycles seemed to appear out of nowhere, bearing enormous loads of plantains. Despite the traffic, some children were squatting along the roadside, filling plastic buckets with rocks and dirt.

The change of scenery brightened Neil's mood. Even the professor seemed affected. He looked slyly at Neil. "You are hungry?" he asked. Neil said he was. "Good," the professor said, nodding. "There will be many vendors along the road soon."

Up ahead was a slow-moving pickup truck. It took Neil a moment to figure out its cargo, but when he made out the automatic weapons, he knew: two rows of soldiers wearing camouflage and red berets. Tutsi, Neil guessed, judging by their height. They all looked over six feet tall. The truck was taking its time, and as they approached, Neil wondered when the professor was going to slow down. He had been driving at breakneck speed, and for the past few miles he had honked his horn repeatedly at bicyclists. What would happen, Neil wondered, if they got into an accident with the truck? What if, as he suspected, the professor was Hutu?

Neil recalled his conversation with the Africa scholar back in Los Angeles. They had polished off their second bottle before the scholar glanced at his watch and announced he was instituting brass-tacks time. The Hutu-Tutsi conflict, he said, was nearly incomprehensible to outsiders. The two groups shared a common language, religion, culture—nearly everything. Sure, he said, in the bad old days the Belgians documented coarse physical differences—Tutsis were tall and thin, Hutus were short and stocky—but those distinctions were not as dramatic as *muzungus* wanted to believe, and after generations of intermarriage, everyone pretty much looked alike, anyway. The thing was, we *wanted* gross differences. We liked our bloodletting crystal clear. That way, he said, the conflict would make *muzungu*-sense, and, sorry, but that was the sense that counted, now wasn't it?

"It's a strong impulse," the scholar said. "Let me give you an example. Do you know what Americans in Burundi call Hutus and Tutsis? I mean, when they don't want them to understand?" He grinned. "Hamburgers and hotdogs. As in, 'I hear the hotdogs are mad at the hamburgers again.' But in reality it's like saying siblings are only a set of differences." He waved his hand around, as if in apology. "Sorry, but only metaphor seems to clarify this. Truth is, you're never sure if you're talking to a Hutu or a Tutsi, or even what one is anymore."

Neil looked at him quizzically. "But there are differences."

"Jesus," the scholar said. He swished the wine around in his glass. "You and I, we're different. But we're not killing each other, are we?" He leaned forward. "Every jackass and his jackass thinks he's got this stuff figured out." He shook his head. "Think of it like Cain and Abel. We know the story, but not the actual history. So now every *muzungu* with an ax to grind is pushing his own read."

A minivan, its horn wailing, came into view around the corner, headed right toward them. At the same time, the professor pulled into the oncoming lane, passing the pickup. There didn't seem to be enough room. No one slowed down or sped up. No one's expression changed—not the professor's, not the soldiers in the pickup, not the driver of the oncoming van.

Neil turned quickly to the professor. All he could hear was the wail of the van's horn. He saw the driver's eyes: droopy-lidded and calm. In the passenger's seat, and in the back, he made out piles of dead chickens, strung together with wire. They were stacked to the roof. Someone had ripped off their feathers.

Neil lunged at the steering wheel, and his fingers grazed the professor's hand. They struggled briefly, Neil pulling one way, the professor the other. "Do not," the professor shouted. "Do not." Then somehow everything was fine: their car veered back into its lane, now in front of the pickup, and the wailing van sped by without incident.

Neil put his hand to his heart and spoke quickly. "Not my car," he said. "I'm sorry. I shouldn't have done that. Oh, God." He heard the fear linger in his voice. "I thought we were going to die."

The professor turned to Neil and clucked. "We are two in this car," he said, speaking sharply. He stared at Neil a long time. "It is not you alone." Then he did something surprising. He reached over and patted Neil on the shoulder.

— — —

Peter and Jenny's apartment building was in a weedy cul-de-sac. In the parking lot, some shaved-head kid tinkered under the hood of a junker. There were broken empties next to the Dumpster, and a gnawed Big Wheels lay overturned on a pile of weathered plywood.

"Homely sweet home," said Peter. "The neighbors are pretty quiet. You can catch a bus down that way." He pointed a stubby finger at a stand of evergreens behind the building. Cars whizzed by on the other side.

The window air conditioner had been left on, so when they entered, whatever cleanser Peter and Jenny had used had turned disagreeably sweet. Neil stood at the doorway. To his left was a photo display, mounted in expensive-looking frames, the kind of thing shopping malls advertised: Peter and Jenny in model poses, backlit, smiling and bovine in front of a dream-like palette of dark colors. The portraits were ludicrous. But Peter had always been slow to understand that his presence sometimes set people to tittering. He had never learned how to ingratiate himself into a world of complex sensibilities.

They showed Neil around. The counters had been cleaned, but Neil noted what must have been invisible to them: crusted, pebbly bits of food on the cabinets; foggy discolorations in the corners; a stiff patina of burned meals on the stovetop. In the hallway, a washing machine had been shoved against the wall—"there's no laundry room," Peter said, noting Neil's expression—so to get to the bathroom, one would have to squeeze past the washer. The carpet had been recently vacuumed—Neil could see the dark, crisscrossing lines—but there was no way to cover up the generations of spills; they bloomed on top of each other, their outlines distinct as strata, as on a cartographer's map.

Jenny offered to show Neil the bathroom, and as he followed her in, he caught her surreptitiously wiping at something on the sink. The room smelled strongly of disinfectant, but Neil could not help noticing the black hairs wrapped around the shower faucet. The mirror over the sink was spotted with flecks of toothpaste. Jenny told him he had free run of the bathroom, though Peter went to the car wash at nine every morning. "I mean shower," she said quickly, catching Neil's eye. "I just call it the car wash. He takes his shower at nine." She seemed embarrassed.

"Don't sweat it," he said. "Now if you call it a truck wash you might get a call from the word police."

"Peter," Jenny called out. "How about showing your brother your office?" She turned and placed a hand on her husband's arm. "I'll get some coffee going." Peter mumbled something about his labors never ceasing, then led Neil to the bedroom and made reference to what he called, mysteriously, his inventory clearinghouse website. Inside, on the other side of a giant four-poster bed, was an ancient computer and some office supplies—"the storefront," Peter said, somberly—all crammed onto a card table. Nearby was a black leather office chair, missing one arm. All Peter would reveal was that he and Jenny bought figurines and gag gifts wholesale from a catalog, then sold them online. He began shrugging even before he finished.

Neil nodded toward the far corner of the room, where four columns of small, sealed boxes nearly grazed the ceiling. The packaging tape had not yet been removed. "Inventory?" he asked.

Peter looked at the boxes. "Business comes and goes."

"Like the tide, huh?"

"Okay," Peter said, his eyes drifting toward the computer.

"You think the tide's coming in again pretty soon?"

Peter closed his eyes and rocked back and forth for a moment. "Okay," he mumbled. He seemed irritated. "Okay, I'll see you later," he said. "Okay? I gotta track some orders." And with that, he sidestepped some computer cables and settled noisily into the leather chair. So that was it. Tour over. The computer whirred to life, and Neil turned on his heels and left the room.

Later, sitting in the living room, Jenny apologized for her husband's absence. He'd be out soon, she said, handing Neil a cup of decaf. Then she leaned forward. She said she didn't know what the deal was between them, but she wished they'd call a truce.

"Like I said before, nothing's going on," Neil replied.

Oh, but there was, she said.

Neil took a long sip from his cup. Was she maybe, he asked, taking the concept of displacement too far? She folded her arms and waited. It was a linguistic term, he said. It referred to one of the things that marked us as human: the ability to talk about things that weren't present.

"Please don't," she said, closing her eyes.

Don't what? he asked her.

And again: don't what?

She said if he wanted to be an ass then maybe he better figure out where his own asshole was first. Then she said she was sorry. These past few weeks, she said, had been crazy. They had to deal with everything at the hospital, every single day, and it wasn't pleasant. She was just trying to support her husband, that was all. They were family. "You, too," she said, catching Neil's eye: "you're family here, too, you know." She paused. He knew his brother and father were close, right? He knew how that felt? It killed her, she said, to see her husband in such turmoil.

"Peter can't let go," she said suddenly. "He can't say 'bye-bye' like you."

Neil set down his coffee. "I'm sorry. I really am. But that 'like you' sounds a little presumptuous, doesn't it?"

A hissing sound escaped her lips. "Could you stop being superior for just a moment?" she said. She looked at him hard. "You bad-mouth everyone and act like you're the choir boy. Why don't you try turning the evil eye back on yourself?"

"I just want to point out that I came here," he said. "I didn't have to."

"How far gone would you have to be not to?" she said. Then she looked at the floor. Her voice became loud with emotion: "Peter just thinks you cut everyone down and then you cut them out."

"I'm not like that," Neil said quickly. But even as he rose, smiling now, and took one of her hands into his own, demonstrating, she raised her other hand and made snipping motions with her fingers. He took that hand in his own, too, and he felt her fingers thump against his palm. No more, he said. Come on. But she kept on snipping until he released her.

— — —

Just a few more miles, the professor said, and they'd be in Bujumbura. The highway was curvy and mostly downhill, yet the professor continued to drive wildly, swerving around bicyclists, sometimes feathering the accelerator around bends. Was that normal, Neil wondered, even for Burundi? It seemed more likely that his host was still harboring some kind of grudge. Two steps forward, one step back. They had, he thought, ever since he attempted to grab the wheel, reached an unspoken accord of civility. Yet there was a bullying aspect to this part of the journey, like a kidnapping with thank-yous. It was as if the professor were saying *For every kindness, a price.* Couldn't they just arrive?

The professor was only part of his impatience. The landscape they were now hurtling through, the same one that just miles back had filled Neil with reassurance, had been growing steadily richer and more insistent, as in a hallucination, as though the entire country had moved itself here, all at once. Along both sides of the highway stood entire lean-to cities, centers of commerce and hubbub, and even with the car's windows rolled up, Neil swore he heard shouting and music. The women wore gaily colored headscarves. Lines of children sat side by side on planks laid over beer crates, like miniature paratroopers waiting to jump. Vendors squatted behind neat mounds of grains and vegetables, and next to them, in straight-back chairs, old men in skullcaps were inhaling long drags off their cigarettes. Naked infants waddled around everywhere, circled by large, skulking dogs. To the right, the cleared ground slowly gave way to a sloping hillside; to the left, behind everyone, a long, dark outcropping of solid rock—a mountainside, Neil realized, a solid wall—closed in on the crowd, with each passing mile cordoning off more of the lean-to city, squeezing the inhabitants on that side even closer to the traffic speeding by.

There was a time, years ago, when Neil might have encouraged the sensation of encroachment. He had once toyed with joining the Peace Corps. After talking with a recruiter, he had sat through an orientation film in the college auditorium. There, he watched clips of smiling volunteers sitting cross-legged on mats, eating goopy concoctions with their fingers. They were surrounded by a mob of watchful, alien people. Neil couldn't get the mob out of his head. There was no room to breathe, no room to move. They put their hands all over the volunteers. They touched their hair, their limbs, their possessions. Those people, the recruiter said, pointing at the screen—no matter where you go, you'll feel their breath on the back of your neck. People who don't look like you or speak like you or think like you. People who will *always* be there, even when you don't see them. Always.

It was too much. Didn't one always want access to an escape route? Just in case? Who of his own volition would choose a life over which you had so little control? That was the nature of the beast, Neil thought: one always wanted a secret path to some meadow, some nearby open field, some level plot of land you could walk through alone, slow as you please, and not have to return. There was nothing cowardly about wanting that. One didn't wish to become ensnared in impossible situations. One needed to know how to leave.

The professor let out a huge yawn—"I have not been sleeping well," he said—and reminded Neil of his declaration of hunger a few miles back. Oh, that was quite okay, Neil told him: he could wait until they reached the city. But the professor tut-tutted him. His new African family, he told Neil, many of whom had traveled widely, would not hear of their newest member arriving hungry. He smiled. A host had responsibilities, he said. A promise was a promise, and he had promised his guest sustenance.

"Here," the professor said, rounding a bend. Neil saw two boys next to a waterfall. He straightened in his seat while the professor pulled over and braked to a stop. The outcropping had closed the distance to the highway, sealing off the crowds of people and all the noise. There was room for the professor's car, then the space narrowed, leaving only enough room between the rock face and the road for the two boys, selling what looked like vegetables and fruit stacked atop a wooden table. But what made Neil straighten was the waterfall: the outcropping was perhaps a hundred feet high, and over its jagged top flowed clear water in a narrow stream, splashing against imperfections in the rock face, all the way to the ground, where it flowed into a rough gully next to the boys, along the highway's edge.

"That's some tight quarters," Neil said. From his seat, he nodded at one of the boys, who took some red vegetables in both hands and sloshed a few steps through the muddy rivulet until he stood directly behind the waterfall. There was just enough space for him—a pocket between rock and water—and the boy, conscious now of his audience, smiled brightly. He stuck his vegetables, one by one, into the cold water pouring down in front of his face. The sight was mesmerizing: the water was like an envelope, and each time the boy stuck a vegetable into the envelope, an explosion took place, refracting the light, ever so slightly turning parts of the rock face first purple, then green, then shades of red.

Grunting, the professor got out, and in what Neil assumed was Kirundi, the local language, he greeted the boy behind the water. The boy emerged. The two talked with some animation, and for a moment the professor held the boy's hands in his own. Then the professor turned and switched to French. The boy was one of his nephews, he said. Julien. He was twelve, the professor noted, and shy around *muzungus.* The boy regarded Neil coolly.

The professor smiled at Neil. "It is beautiful here, yes?"

Neil agreed. The area was cramped, but spectacular: off to the right, on the other side of the highway, the land had given way, dropping sharply into what Neil now understood to be a terraced tea-plantation field. Below that, a green and tangled valley spread for miles, leading to the outskirts of Bujumbura. There was no traffic noise. There was only the water falling from the top of the rock.

The professor called out for a couple of pineapple skewers, and the other boy—he looked a bit younger than Julien—enthusiastically speared chunks of pineapple with wooden skewers. Neil stepped out of the car and took one, smiling now at the professor, who stuck a skewer into his mouth and held fast to the fruit with his teeth. The action seemed to please him. He smiled back at Neil, then looked at Julien, who had once again gone behind the water, which also seemed to please him. The professor began to move his lips, whispering, and his careful posture—he had clasped his hands together and held them in front of him—reminded Neil of a man in prayer.

"You come here often?" Neil asked, brightly.

"Just this past week," the professor said. "Not before." His posture quickly changed, and he reached into his pocket and pulled out some crumpled Burundi francs, which he waved at the boy behind the table.

"What happened last week?" Neil asked.

But the professor only shrugged, then made a show of handing money over to the boy. He told Neil that the boy and his nephew were friends. "My nephew does not need to work," he said, as if anticipating an objection. "He lives with me now. But he wants to be with his friend." He motioned toward the boy he had just paid, then began moving his lips again.

"Ah," Neil said. The conversation had taken an awkward turn somewhere, and he did not know how to correct it. "A busy recent past," he said. But the professor ignored him.

— — —

Before they drove to see Ray, Neil unpacked his toiletries in the bathroom. He had left the door open—a friendly gesture, he concluded, completely transparent—and out the corner of his eye he saw Peter stumble out of the bedroom-office and walk down the hallway, over to Jenny. Peter was moaning. He bent over in front of her and placed his hands on his knees. Jenny rubbed his back. "Is your gut cramping again?" Neil heard her ask. Peter nuzzled his wife's breasts with his head. "Why are you getting all these stomach pains now? Is it gas?"

So Peter had never told her.

Neil let his fingers linger on the knob. The long hallway, the dray-animal intimacies, the stomach pains: it was all familiar. Like running across a damning photo at the bottom of a shoebox.

Jenny caught Neil staring then, and something about the way she touched her husband must have made Peter aware he was being watched. He jerked his head around. Neil saw panic cross his brother's face, so he nodded curtly at his hosts and closed the door.

— — —

Hadn't Kafka written somewhere that family life required the repression of disgust? Neil, brushing his teeth now for the second time, unsure when to emerge again—he could not hear anything outside the door—was fairly certain he had. But the idea belonged to a different place and time. It was the product of a faded, genteel European poverty, a domesticated life played out in a cramped urban apartment, person after person powerless before the thin walls and rattling, uneven doors, never free of the endless belching and masturbating and tedious, pitying conversations. Would the idea have taken root without the constant, echoing plop and splash of a rusting, pull-chain toilet? Without the thick wool coats always drying over the sill? Without all those bodies leaking their smelly fluids, day after day, onto the furniture and linen?

So no, not disgust.

What then, Neil?

What did you call it when you felt relief because you couldn't hear your brother's voice?

He frowned into the mirror. He threw up his hands and shook his head. What could one do in a cold-war masquerade, after decades of a solemn and silent dance? Open your mouth now, walk straight toward your brother, and you'd stumble around in the dark, a fool in a land of checkpoints and legalities and sand.

There were consequences, of course. No teller, no history. Only invention and blame. But that summer, way back when he was twelve, way back when Aunt Beth dropped him off for a summer stay in Tacoma, *that* was when someone should have spoken. Not now. It was too late.

So at the sink, still thoughtfully brushing, he reassured himself that when he opened the door there would be no clumsy and impossible conversation. There would be no mawkish indulgence, no false embraces. Yet other, troubling thoughts accompanied that certainty. They emerged alien and Sphinx-like, unrecognizable, and he paused in his brushing to contemplate the image in his head, a picture of silence itself as a seed. Silence had a shape, and it was secretive and busy, taking root as you slept, growing while appearing not to grow, year after year, until one morning you awoke and found something ungiving and hard towering over your house, your lover, your dreams. Was that what Peter and Ray saw? Did they sleep in its shade and eat and eat and eat of its gnarled and knuckly fruit?

Aunt Beth had insisted he never blame Peter for their mother's death and never blame Ray for his inadequacies. Margo had died giving birth, and Ray had been unable to cope. Beyond that, no one had any right to make claims. But just a few weeks later after Margo's death, Aunt Beth did stake a claim. She offered to take both him and Peter to live with her up in Bellingham. She had a nice house and lots of money. There was no way, she said, that Ray could raise two young boys by himself. He wasn't able, not in any sense, and he knew it. So Neil went to live with her, with Ray's blessings.

But his youngest, Ray said: Peter was his link to Margo, and he couldn't let that go. Ray was like that, Aunt Beth said. From the beginning, ever since she had known him, Ray had been unusually—that was the word she used, *unusually*—close to his wife. Your father, she told Neil, was his own worst enemy. Then she raised her eyebrows. "All roads don't lead to Rome," she said. "Some just go in a circle. Okay?"

But that summer Aunt Beth thought a visit down to Tacoma might do Neil some good. He hadn't seen his father and brother all year. Ray, she informed him, claimed to be housebound now; and whenever he called his eldest boy long-distance, which was infrequent, he seemed even to Neil distracted and vague, and the chats were never more than how-do-you-do.

His first night back in Tacoma, Neil could not get over how much weight his father and brother had put on. Peter told him that Ray now positioned a stool by the refrigerator, and from every room in the house, you could see him reach into the trays and pull things into his mouth. Peter had always been heavy for his age, mocked by playmates, but Neil could tell the sight bothered him. Why else would he not joke around about it? Of all the things to mention, why would he mention Ray's refrigerator habits?

Neil saw for himself his father's stool in the corner of the kitchen. He heard the effort behind his father's breathing, the noticeable new limp to his walk. He saw, too, his first week, that Ray would without warning sometimes double over, moaning and grabbing at his shirt. Sympathy pains, Ray called them. They got so bad, an ambulance had come for him once, and a nurse pressed cold compresses to his sides and stomach. A doctor gave him some pills, but they didn't do anything except cloud his head. Ever since their mother died, Peter said, the sympathy pains had been growing worse.

"Sympathy pains," Neil said. "That's where the guy feels bad, right? His wife's pregnant?"

Yeah, smart guy, Peter told him. Yeah.

So what the fuck?

You'll see, Peter said. Maybe.

What?

Peter seemed to get angry then, and he shoved Neil hard. Neil shoved him back, and Peter lost his balance and hurt his wrist on the counter.

Later, Ray led Neil and Peter from their morning TV into the living room. He let them know that one day they, too, would be felled by genetics. "Let's say I'm dying," he said. "You two will feel it. Just like I felt it. Just like your mother felt it." He lifted Peter's shirt. Then he lifted Neil's. The pain, he said, would probably begin right *there,* under the right breast pocket, then work its way down. He put a hand to both their stomachs. Count on it, he said. Blood was blood, and there was no getting around it.

So when Neil saw Ray clutch his gut the following week and fall to the floor, he was not surprised. He had been prepared. It was happening now, Peter told him, dragging the coffee table out of the way. Then Ray opened and closed his eyes. He stretched out on his back; he upturned an ashtray, and the ashes coated the carpet.

"Oh, dear God," Ray moaned. A sound like a revving engine came from some place deep inside him.

"Are you okay?" Neil asked, bending down. "Are you all right?"

"Dear God," Ray said. His mouth opened. He clutched his stomach hard. "The baby's coming."

Neil straightened. He looked to Peter, who immediately turned and ran toward the bathroom. His father, sweating now, rolled one way, then the other, and ash stuck to the hairs on his arms. "What?" Neil said, putting his hands to his ears. "What's happening?" But there was only his father writhing on the carpet, his shirt unfurling around his stomach, and the sound of Peter opening and shutting the medicine cabinet.

"What? What?" Neil said when his brother returned. Peter waved around a pink bottle of Pepto-Bismol in his hand, and Ray grabbed the bottle and drank from it deeply, then reached up and pulled Peter down to his knees. "It's time," he said to Peter. Then, to Neil: "Doctor. It's time."

Peter's expression didn't change. He dropped to his knees and curled into a fetal position, in front of his father's bulging stomach, the carpet tickling his ear, and started mewling like a baby. Neil understood: Peter's own birth was being enacted. It was like a play. His father was his mother, dying on the delivery table; Peter was himself, a ten-pound, four-ounce, angel of death, or that was how it seemed to him, that was the only thing that made sense. "Kick," Ray barked at Peter. "Kick and scream."

Peter thumped his feet on the floor and his yells came out muted and polite. Ray closed his eyes, and Peter did, too, and they stayed like that, locked together, their bellies rising and falling until Peter scraped his head against Ray's shirt buttons and bawled in a higher pitch, screeches his tiny assassin's mouth must have made when he was born. Oh God, oh God, oh God, Ray shouted. He drew Peter close, draping his immense hand around Peter's ribs and squeezing hard as he could, squeezing and yelling until Neil sat down on the couch and picked up a magazine.

Holding the shower rod now, Neil was conscious of moving his lips. He pictured the scene clearly. Yes, it had happened exactly like that. That was what Ray and Peter did. Years later, Neil recalled, he heard Aunt Beth speaking sternly into the phone to his father. His youngest had a bruised ribcage, she said into the receiver. She had heard. She kept tabs. Why? she demanded. What was going on? Peter had gone to school and a nurse had asked the same thing, but standing there at the base of the stairs, listening, Neil recalled his brother's calm demeanor that afternoon, his practiced movements, and his father's precise choreography and the way, afterwards, they both simply brushed away the cigarette ash and walked into the kitchen for sodas. *How would I know?* he imagined saying to some inquisitor, though Aunt Beth didn't ask. *I don't live there. They live there. Ask them.*

And it was true, he didn't know what was happening. He had seen something once, that was all, something like a living-room play, and then his father and brother had struggled to their feet and acted like he wasn't even there. They drank 7-Up, he remembered, and when Ray offered him a bottle, he took it without a word. That same evening, Peter walked into Neil's room. He had filled a battered measuring cup with some kind of alcohol. He sat on Neil's bed, and they traded swigs. They said hateful things to each other. Mister I'm So Special, Peter called him. Fat fuck, Neil replied.

Little Lord Fauntleroy.

Blubber boy.

No one wants you here, bitch. You're trash.

Killer.

What did you say?

You heard me.

They let the words hang in the air awhile, they let the words lick their ears, and they sat on Neil's bed and drank from the cup and let the words drift like smoke until the moonlight came through the window just right and they could see the light trying to take shape.

"This is you in here," Peter said, his voice a snarl. He plucked at the air and closed his fist, and his fist shook as if something were trying to escape. "No, this is *you,*" Neil hissed, and he grabbed something invisible in the air and closed his fist around it. He squeezed so hard his fingers turned white. "Gonna fuck you up now," Neil said.

Peter then grabbed a pillow and shook it until the pillow fell out and he was holding only the pillowcase. "Gonna fuck *you* up," Peter said, but even though it was just a game, just blowing off steam, Neil swore he could feel something between his fingers, something soft and alive. Peter said he felt it, too, and then they yelled a little, surprised, and they both closed their fists and grabbed the pillowcase, grabbed it *hard,* and shoved what they pretended was in their hands into the pillowcase, and when all they could hear was the freeway outside they jammed their arms all the way to the bottom of the pillowcase, bone and nail, and they felt a hot, soft thing squirming inside, only when they looked all they saw was their hands and fingers in a jumble, all slick and blotchy.

Aunt Beth came the next day. She stood at the doorway, clutching her purse tightly. Surprise, she said. She had something to discuss with their father, she said, and told them to go outside and play. When they returned, Ray and Aunt Beth were sitting on opposite sides of the couch. Aunt Beth told Neil that a few days were enough: he was coming home with her today. Then she turned to Peter. Who, she asked him, would he like to live with? Would he like to join his brother and live with her? Up in Bellingham there was lots of room for a boy to play, and a really good school, and all sorts of advantages—then she stopped talking. Ray cleared his throat. It was Peter's choice, he said, and his choice alone. Whatever his son decided, he would be loved. They were family, he said, and no bond was stronger than that.

Peter started to cry. There was lots of cooing and hugging. Later in the afternoon, when Neil got in the car with Aunt Beth, he turned around and saw Peter watching them through the window, crying all over again.

"How was it?" Aunt Beth asked.

He looked at her. "They got really fat. They're weird."

"Neil."

"Well, they are."

"That's no way to talk about family," she said.

So he didn't. He thanked her in his head for what she had just told him.

And now when Neil emerged for the second time that day from behind the bathroom door, he saw Peter and Jenny watching TV, the sound low and muted. "Hospital duty," said Jenny, looking up. Peter struggled to his feet. "You ready?" Peter said. His voice was bland and bored. He picked up his jacket, draped over the arm of the couch, and no one said another word until they were on the road.

— — —

The professor closed his eyes and chewed his pineapple slowly, in small bites, then walked calmly to the waterfall, where his nephew Julien was squatting, washing and re-washing some produce. He said a few incomprehensible words to the boy, and Julien again stepped behind the water and stood up straight, a green bell pepper in his hand. The professor stuck out his hand. Slowly, with great precision, he stuck his forefinger into the water. Julien smiled. It seemed to be a game, Julien edging his face as close to the water's surface as possible, the professor sticking his erect finger into the water, stopping just inches from his face nephew's face.

"You know I don't actually speak Kirundi, right?" Neil asked suddenly.

The professor withdrew his hand. "*Bien sûr,*" he said, sharply. "Of course. Speaking a language is not necessary for studying the language. Of course I know this."

"I meant no offense," Neil said. "This is all so new, that's all. But before I meet my new African family, I was hoping to get a leg up. How do you say 'they're dead' in Kirundi? In the distant past? Is there a morpheme change between that and 'they're dead' in the recent past?"

The professor turned his head sideways and looked at Neil out the corner of his eye. "Why do you wish to know this particular phrase?"

"Just curious."

"What is it you are curious about?"

"I'm just asking a question," Neil said.

The professor pursed his lips and stared at Neil a long time. He was frowning. Then he snorted—a refusal, Neil thought, a hostile act—and locked his teeth onto another chunk of pineapple.

Neil had read accounts where butchers neither accepted nor rejected the charges leveled against them. They lived in a purgatory of evasions and half-truths, too mired in justification to come clean, too guilty to deny what had taken place. Had he just witnessed such an event? It was possible. Every step seemed a potential minefield. When, Neil wondered, had even the smallest encounters become so fraught with anxiety? Years ago, he'd experienced moments of pure animal joy, feelings so powerful he'd find himself on the verge on tears: the ecstasy of laughing, the feel of a girl's hand in his, the way she'd flip her hair just so. There was no headlong rush into significance, nothing you couldn't take back. Nothing had to connect with anything else. Had even asking questions now become impossible?

He stared back at the professor. They both stuck their skewers into their mouths and pulled off pieces of fruit. The professor's expression, Neil thought, was contemptuous. Briefly, wildly, he imagined the professor fashioning a knife out of his skewer.

But Julien's companion then approached the professor and began an insistent, nagging monologue in Kirundi. Extraordinary. Since when did African children speak at length to professors? Something was going on. The boy's words sounded whiny, and he diverted his gaze to some distant point. Then there was his timid stance—head bowed, shoulders hunched. Still he talked, and when Neil eyes fell on the francs sticking out of the boy's shirt pocket, he found himself suspecting the professor of not paying enough for the skewers. It had taken his host a while even to offer payment. Was he taking advantage, perhaps, claiming family privilege, cheating this poor boy, bizarrely, out of what he was due? Could he be that depraved? The professor was growing animated now, pressing a hand to his head, then throwing his arms out dramatically. The boy looked at the ground, as if chastised.

Hey, Neil imagined saying. Hey you. Bullyboy. He tossed his skewer aside and took a resolute step forward. This unpleasant man, with all his rudeness and presumption: if push came to shove, if the boy cried out for assistance, he'd protect him. He'd shield him from the professor and take out American dollars and give him a fistful, and when the boy was safe he'd wheel around and make the professor sorry. What a coward the man was, what a son of a bitch. How could you turn on the powerless like that? How could you live with yourself?

But the professor and the boy then switched to French, and the gibberish Neil was hearing—their common tongue seemed a series of nonsense syllables, a make-believe language—the gibberish gave way to familiar, open vowels, and the lolling words fell into line and calmed him.

"My mother," the boy said, gravely, "she sends her sympathies to you."

"Merci."

"She says to tell you," the boy continued, "your father and sister were loved. We are sorry to hear of their passing."

The professor nodded. *"Merci beaucoup,"* he said, and then his voice broke and all he could do was repeat himself. *"Merci beaucoup. Merci beaucoup."*

It seemed to Neil then that the professor's face was about to collapse. The professor stumbled a bit, then righted himself and directed his gaze once again toward Julien, still standing behind the waterfall. He approached the water slowly, and Julien smiled. The professor stuck out his arm and allowed his fingers to once again break the water's surface tension. He stuck his entire hand into the water, his fingers taut and straight, as though trying to touch the face leaning against the rock. He stood there a long time, his arm sticking straight out, allowing his fingers to move up and down. His nephew didn't move. The professor turned distractedly toward Neil, but he wasn't really looking at him. He was lost, Neil understood, in his own thoughts. He moved his hand through the curtain of water, his fingers inches from his nephew's face, hovering. He didn't care anymore that a *muzungu* was watching.

But Neil turned his head anyway. He stared past the road, down into the tea terraces and beyond, into the wide, deep valley, and he felt his body clench and twist, and his hand went to his side, probing, feeling for what Peter had spoken of back at Sea-Tac. He had to make sure. Nothing. No sympathy pains. It was the professor's grief pulling at him, grief so public and absolute it seemed to ride the air and settle onto his skin. That was what nearly felled him, what nearly dropped him to his knees, and now with his back to the sheer rock wall, in full view of any passersby, he put his hands to his knees and breathed deeply, rapidly, so when he stood again his face would be still and calm as a summer waterway.

— — —

On the drive to the hospital, Neil understood Jenny's conversation as manipulation. She was driving, and from his position in the back seat, Neil had a hard time hearing over the roar of the engine. But he heard enough. After this was over, she kept saying to Peter, they could do such and such. After this was all over, they could go to this place and that place and drive around and clear their heads. Once they got onto the freeway, she started telling Peter stories about people she ran into in stores and social-service agencies, usually involving some kind of sharp exchange. She didn't as much tell her stories as relive them, like a defendant on a TV judge show: she gestured wildly; she recited, word for word, the passionate parts of the conversation ("So he said, 'Ma'am, you can't do that.' And I said, 'Oh, you just watch me!'"). In particularly dramatic parts, she turned her head toward the side window, as if addressing the person under discussion.

He saw right through her. She pushed Peter where she wanted him to go, and where she wanted him to go now was far from the hospital. She'd take care of the unpleasantness. She'd ask the hard questions, place the difficult calls. Peter's job was to snap out of his funk.

Neil, kicking away the burger wrappers at his feet, could not fault her for summoning another life into being. Yet, all the same, the content of her imagining—Disneyland, staying up past Letterman, Blizzards at the DQ in Hoquiam—the content revealed her vulgar turn of mind. Peter was just sitting there like a lump, his hands folded across his stomach. His hair had been blown every which way when they left the apartment, but he hadn't bothered to drag a comb through it or pat it down. He was breathing through his mouth, and he hardly moved his eyes. The perpetual child, Neil thought, unwilling and unable. All that lardbutt-ism. And then he found the word he'd been looking for ever since Jenny had attacked him in the living room: she was Peter's caretaker. She petted her husband when he needed petting, she prodded him, she scolded, she ordered, she probably wiped his face when food dribbled down his chin.

And Neil thought something more: was that how Ray had been with their mother? So passive? It seemed likely, and the likelihood made him angry. You had choices. You didn't have to keep all the cards you had been dealt. People like his brother and father: they pulled at your heart, but they'd suck the lifeblood right out of you if you let them. All you could do, really, Neil thought, as a decent and successful person, as the white sheep of the family, was try to guide people like that into accepting a level of dignity.

Neil leaned forward, inches from his brother's ear. Peter was too mopey to notice, and Jenny kept chattering on, jutting her jaw forward like a bulldog when cars tried to pass. He tested. "Peter," he whispered. There was no response, so he opened his lips slightly, as if mumbling. He moved his tongue, he formed words inside the cave of his mouth, but he didn't make a sound. It was like an appeal to magic, he knew, speaking without speaking, pantomiming actual speech. But Peter was so vigilant with him, so ready to take offense . . . so yes, subterfuge was reasonable, even necessary. One had to be a kind of spy sometimes, creeping without creeping, doing without doing, influencing events in subtle and invisible ways.

Peter, Neil mimed in his own mouth, Peter, when you're at the service, when the casket's behind you, Peter, get off your ass and stand up. Do it for yourself and do it for Ray. Stand up and walk to the podium, cough if you want, but look out at all the faces and talk about Ray. But don't talk about his life. Don't you dare. Give him some dignity. Assign him some. Assign it to him and to yourself. No one can know another person's life, but you can at least make something up. You can. Look out at everyone and tell them that a long time ago Ray began to disappear into his body. Tell them he was engulfed and gasping. Tell them his every breath was a hero's act.

"Are you trying to say something?" said Jenny, frowning into the rearview mirror.

Neil leaned back and cleared his throat. "Just talking to myself," he answered. "Passing the time."

No one responded, so Neil leaned to his left, out of range of the mirror. He waited a moment, then continued.

There was nothing anyone could have done for him, right, Peter? Nothing. He must have imagined himself, Peter, as a man drowning from the inside out. That image must have sustained him with the dignity of his own suffering. There's dignity in that, isn't there? Sure there is. Peter, you know there is. Let's say Ray was in a boat before he drowned, even before he got married, Peter. Say he was in a boat and something happened, something no one could see, and then he was in the water. Say that, Peter, tell everyone he was a man treading water, just trying to stay afloat, and the water was a raging ocean, and in the hospital he felt his limbs grow numb and cold, and at the end he opened his mouth and let the water rush in, and when he gurgled and closed his eyes, his arm rose, yes, he lifted his arm off the bed and raised it straight as a mast, for just a moment, for one ferocious and inspired moment, and then it was over, Peter, just like that, and Ray's arm collapsed back onto the mattress and he drifted down and down, and then he was gone, and there was nothing anyone could do.

If his mime-words had any effect, he couldn't tell. Peter blinked a few times, but mostly he seemed focused on turning his head to where Jenny was cursing at some slowpoke driver or other. They were pulling into the hospital parking lot. Were all the parking spaces taken? she complained. Was *everyone* freaking sick? Jesus H in a handbasket, when would their travels ever cease? At the reception desk, she loudly announced their presence, and they all took the elevator to the ICU ward. What a sight, Neil thought, taking up the rear: the fat man and his pudgy boor of a wife, trailed by the professor. No one spoke. It was a short walk, and by the door to what Jenny said was Ray's room, a young nurse was flipping the pages of a clipboard. She looked at Peter and Jenny, Neil thought, with disapproval.

He wouldn't have known it was his father if Peter and Jenny hadn't stood on the side of the bed and stared with recognition at the patient. There was always an aura of theater about hospital rooms, what with their sci-fi tubing and soupy, plastic overhead bags and shiny metal machines that sometimes made noises like people breathing. It was hard for the bedridden not to look already dead. But Ray was only asleep—Neil saw his belly rise and fall—and his saggy arms were pocked with little marks from needles. His mouth was open. One of his front teeth was missing.

Neil took up his position on the other side of the bed. "Ray, Ray," Jenny said. Peter pressed his fingers into the mattress. When Ray opened his eyes, Neil jumped a bit and took a step back. Ray's eyes were fluttering. They were milky and clouded, and as they opened and closed without reason, Neil could not help thinking of cartoon shades going up and down. He pressed his lips together.

Ray said something then. He spoke clearly, though he didn't seem to be talking to anyone in particular. He didn't seem to recognize who was in the room. "What body of water is this?" he said, and Neil straightened.

Jenny leaned in close. "There's no water, Ray," she said. "That's the drugs talking. You're in the hospital. The medication's wearing off and you're waking up in the hospital. There's just a parking lot outside. There's no body of water."

Neil looked first at Jenny, then at Peter. Neither looked at him back.

"Today is Tuesday," Jenny said. "You're nowhere near water, Ray. That's the drugs talking. There's just concrete and cars outside."

Blood rushed to Neil's face. It was too much. He wanted to shove Jenny away from the bed. He could not bear to hear any more. Peter should have been shushing her; he should have been leaning down and whispering into their father's ears that he was quietly drifting in Puget Sound, and the water was endless and warm and clear. He wanted his brother to say that the summer sky was bountiful and clean, far as you could see. The water was everywhere, he wanted him to say, and it was deep and blue and peaceful, and wherever you looked you saw thousands of fishes. He wanted Peter to say it to Ray. He wanted some doctor to rush into the room and say it, some nurse, some orderly, anyone.

How could Peter let his wife speak to their father like that? What was wrong with him?

"What, Neil?" Jenny said. There was irritation in her voice. "Do you have a comment? You're a member of the family. You can talk, you know."

Neil shook his head. He didn't say fanciful words into his father's ears. He didn't say anything to Jenny. He felt hot and thirsty, and he looked over at his brother and caught him with mouth hanging open, stupidly, mute as a piece of furniture. If Peter had been standing next to him, he would have hit him, hard, and dropped him to the floor. "We're a million miles from water, Ray," Jenny said. "You're in a hospital bed, okay?" For all Neil knew, what Jenny was saying might be the last words Ray would ever hear. Yet still his brother allowed this woman to tell their father he was dying in some dingy hospital overlooking a parking lot.

— — —

When the professor was finished, he pulled out a handkerchief and wiped his dripping hand. He was composed now, and he shook the handkerchief vigorously and stuffed it back into his trouser pocket. Neil regarded his host with formality, nodding, and the professor nodded back, and then they stood silent a moment, listening to the falling water. They stared out at the highway, toward the valley, and from around a bend of road they had already traveled they saw the pickup coming their way. It was the truck from before, just a small dot now, but its cargo of soldiers seemed to move in tiny, jerky motions, as if awakened by some commotion. The professor then addressed Neil. It was true, he said: last week, his father and sister both passed away. He wished to apologize now, if his guest would accept it, for his failings as host. He hadn't been himself, he said. The strain of the past week had been too much.

Of course, Neil said, oh of course, and he took a few steps forward and shook the professor's hand. Please, he said to the professor. Please. But he did not know how to finish his sentence. They lingered in their handshake, pressing firmly, their hands like a knot. Yet there was in the gesture an incompleteness, as if by coming clean, the professor had led Neil from a tidy and claustrophobic room into a buzzing, dark field, and in the field were troubling sounds, too faint and rattling to identify. There was courage in what the professor had done in his presence, and because of that it seemed to Neil they had been given a gift of time and opportunity. They would arrive in Bujumbura in a mood of harmony, at least for a while, but all the time and opportunity in the world could not excuse everything, and Neil was conscious now of an overweening smallness and disappointment being held at bay only by their isolation.

The professor, too, seemed to sense it, and he pointed suddenly to Julien and his companion. "You see these two?" he said. The boys were tossing a piece of fruit back and forth, making fancy catches. Julien caught one behind his back, and the other boy whooped. His nephew, the professor said, was Hutu. His friend was Tutsi.

Neil nodded, and then from around the bend the pickup nosed

forward, its gears grinding. The soldiers in back were fiddling with a transistor radio, knocking it sharply against a long metal box, and the weapons at their sides bristled like antennae. Julien and his companion stopped playing catch. They all stood there—Neil, the professor, the two boys—as if in a diorama, a wall of rock at their backs, the truck in front. The driver slowed and with a somber expression looked everyone over. He slapped his hand, hard, against the cab of the truck, and a couple of the soldiers turned their heads. Their expressions revealed nothing. The pickup slowed to a crawl, and Neil heard something metallic and heavy scrape along the truck bed. Then one of the soldiers raised his automatic weapon over his head—in greeting or in warning, it was impossible to say—and the truck suddenly roared to life and disappeared around the bend.

No one said a word for a moment. Then Julien and his friend began chattering loudly and ran to the roadside, watching the truck grow smaller and smaller. They pointed. They held their hands to their hearts and shrieked. They laughed, and they wouldn't stop. The professor followed, slowly walking out to the side of the road, watching the truck. He turned to Neil. "You still accuse me. Us."

For what? Neil asked, throwing out his arms. He wasn't accusing anyone of anything. What did he mean?

The professor resumed following the truck's path, then bent down to wipe something from his nephew's shirt. When he stood again, he told Neil he wanted to tell him something more. His father and sister, he said, had been killed in Paris. On holiday. "Not here," he said, pointing a finger emphatically at the ground. He waved his hand in the air, a shooing gesture, and his arm fell to his side.

"Do you understand why I have told you these things?" the professor asked. He snapped his fingers at the boys, signaling for quiet.

Neil stuck his hands into his pockets. Bujumbura was down there, in the wide valley, climbing up the sides of some mountain off to the north. It was just minutes away now. He would meet his new African family soon, and they would want to know what kind of *muzungu* he was going to be. They would want to know if he thought them brutish.

"I understand," he said.

And then the professor at last began to ask the questions Neil had been expecting ever since he arrived. He talked like a man who had not talked for days. Was Neil married? Had he always lived in California? Where did he receive his doctorate? Had he traveled much before?

When the professor asked him about his family, Neil didn't answer at first. He pictured the hospital room in Tacoma. After Jenny finished speaking to his father, he had stepped out with Peter into the hallway. Jenny went the other way to quiz a nurse about something, then Neil turned to his brother and asked if there was going to be a service before the funeral. Peter shook his head no. "No service," Neil said to him. Neil crossed his arms. "Don't you care?" The words came out too loud, and some passing teenager hunched his shoulders, as if witnessing a collision.

Peter looked stricken. He stared down at his shoes and brought his hands up to cover his face. Then his whole body seemed to sag. His arms flopped to his sides, and he turned and slowly began walking toward the nurse's station. After a few steps, he just stopped. He didn't even seem to be breathing. For a long moment, Neil watched for movement. Was it possible? It happened to horses sometimes. Their legs would lock and they'd die standing up, then fall over. Had his brother just died? It was absurd to think, but had he just killed him? He held his arms out and called Peter's name, loudly, and as he did, Jenny raised her head and motioned for her husband to hurry up. Peter's legs seemed to tremble then, and he let out what sounded like a swallowed sob, then began to shuffle forward again, toward her voice.

When Peter and Jenny dropped him off at the airport the following day, they didn't get out of the car to see him off. Ray was still holding on, so full of drugs he didn't know what was happening. Peter wrote a telephone number on the back of an envelope and shoved it at Neil through the open window. He looked Neil in the eye, and when he spoke his voice was hard and sharp. "We're done," he said. "You want to know anything, call the hospital, not me." Jenny leaned her head out. She said if he wanted a service so bad, maybe he should have stuck around and done it himself.

So Neil told the professor his father was floating around in a boat in Puget Sound, near the Canadian border, where the water was quiet and warm. It wasn't just his father out there, he said, it was his brother, too. He had a father and he had a brother. He told the professor how beautiful the water was, how the summer sky was so clear you could make out a star or two, even in the early afternoon. The water was everywhere, he said, and under the boat you could see thousands of fishes, orange and striped like tigers, and on the shoreline lumbering beasts were emerging from sleep and stretching in the bright and dazzling sunlight.

He said this, and as he spoke he saw the professor looking at him in confusion, a smile frozen onto his face. At some other time, Neil might have said that words do not speak louder than actions. He might have noted, with polite contempt, that it was too easy to use fanciful words with some foreigner, some stranger you had just met. But it was not easy. He was already falling from a dream: he would not walk proudly among the Africans. He would not be admired. This would not be a fresh start. Somewhere behind his smile, the professor was arriving at a decision, and in the weeks to come he would tell a mocking story about Neil to his colleagues, and over lunch or tea Neil would be questioned by his new African family about what he had said to the head of linguistics today, and at year's end no one would mourn his absence. The fish were bright and iridescent, Neil said to the professor, and his father and brother were probably leaning over the boat and jabbering and pointing, having a fine time. All you had to do, he said, if it wasn't asking too much, if you could trouble yourself for just one goddamn minute, was stand on the shore and let them know you were there, that was all, just shout something out and wave your arms around. Do you hear me? Just let them know, and they could stay out there all day and into the evening, and even into the day after that.

Hey

WHEN MY older brother, Rick, left Tacoma for South Vietnam—he was going to be an infantryman in the Delta, a radio operator—I was at nineteen given to understand that people from families such as my own invariably came to a mean and wasteful end. It was January of 1969, a Thursday, and I was poring over chess books, in preparation for the upcoming Washington State Chess Championship. Just that morning I had stood somberly alongside my mother and father at the bus station downtown, saying goodbye to newly minted Pfc. Rick. By evening, joint in hand, I was slightly stoned, still trying to unwind from what I had witnessed earlier. I sat with a *Chess Informant #46* at my elbow, analyzing on my magnetic pocket chess set a brilliant innovation by Bobby Fischer, a move so profound it overturned in a single stroke decades of grandmasterly assumptions.

Stirred, perhaps, by Bobby's improbable victory over communal and ingrained ideas, I saw in my own dogged attention to the move an attempt to renounce the certain outcome of my older brother's tour of duty, the certainty of which had been made clear to me that morning at the bus station. I began nodding. Outcomes, I knew even then, were echoes of their beginnings and middles. The trajectory could be traced, the trace illuminated, sources identified.

It could not be denied that my brother's beginnings and middles under the family roof commingled with my own. There was contamination involved, leaching, a hoary and involuntary exchange of cells and fluids, DNA. Once, maybe twice, I thumped my chess set for emphasis. I found myself suddenly teary. I stretched out my arms then, wriggling my hands around, and by this act gave form to what I had always known but had never before confronted: at the core of our shared history, mine and Rick's, burned only a great empty nothing, a vast and terrible chasm excluding brother Rick from the fate-altering sources of strength and community that family life is intended to promote.

Fact: until he left that morning on the bus, Rick had seemed composed only occasionally of actual physical mass. My older brother's conduct of daily life had occurred just out of my line of vision, like a TV flickering in the corner. Rick was, in effect, the idea of an older brother, not the older brother himself, and, like most things one step removed, Rick had always willingly and without complaint accepted temporary reclassification by others into being the thing itself, aware in some household-pet kind of way that his fortunes rose and fell at the whim of those, such as myself, whose collective will constitutes the social and physical world. That, like it or not, was the nature of things. Right or wrong was not the issue.

Still, I now affirmed that I had never willfully obstructed Rick's forays into a wider, fuller existence; at the same time I could not help admitting in certain synapse-depleted regions of my unconscious mind that I had sometimes offered up Rick's life to unnamed natural deities in exchange for increasingly brutish rewards, concluding during my junior and senior years with sincere prayers for a richly pornographic hour with Annie Hershberger, who lived in the Sorenson Trailer Park and wore hot pants like no one else. For such acts no court of law could have or would have convicted me, true. There was, as well, much to be said for standing up for yourself and for your place in the world. Winters, for example, I joined with neighbors Dan Bacha and Tim Underwood in grinding my brother's face into mounds of dirty snow. Summers, we jabbed Rick's fat gut with a rake handle until rosy welts bloomed on his skin in a lush, garden-like patch. Once, making some point or other about weak chess players, I told some mocking Rick-story in front of Russ Rassmussen, the Tacoma Chess Club ratings-ladder leader and many-times Washington State Chess Champion. "You got your white sheep, you got your black sheep," said Rassmussen, shaking his head. "Then you just got sheep."

I could not have agreed more. Though my mother, Cindy, and father, Marion, had wondered aloud sometimes if the abuse I meted out was intended to punish my dim and flabby elder brother for being unlovable, and though to me the word *unlovable* sounded foreign and hysterical, altogether inappropriate, I had never been able to restrain from noting, publicly and defiantly, a mewling *lack* in my older brother. This lack, this absence, was of concern not only to me but, I believed, to the entire community. By proximity and parasitic contact, Rick posed the threat of infection. He was a corruption, a distortion, a shrinkage, even, of the rigorous and unforgiving larger order.

There was much evidence. Rick was large-hipped, questionably muscled, possessed of soft pouty lips and luxurious brown hair; he wore thick, black horn-rims and blushed easily; when the sun slanted just so, flooding between pine branches, his cheeks sometimes turned so pink you had to wonder if had applied a layer of rouge. He couldn't fight, and in personality he was grimly unimaginative, once pissing his pants in the hallway when the cylinder on the bathroom doorknob snapped, barring his entry, rather than risking discovery by relieving himself into a glass tumbler or a bucket from the garage. So when out of nowhere Rick would cry—and he cried all the time, a regular baby boo-hoo—I did not ask what was wrong. When we argued, I simply hit him, then watched in silence as Rick fell to the floor and spouted outrage, too slow to fend off blows, too stupid to shut up. We shared nothing, not friends, bikes, smokes, ways to steal change from vending machines.

But now in Vietnam Rick was going to get the top of his head blown off, and when he lay dying in the elephant grass he would think to himself how loud the flies were buzzing today and how muggy the air had grown and how dizzy he felt, and maybe even how the voices of his platoon buddies hovering overhead brought him comfort and joy. He would not think of Tacoma or his mother or father, and he would certainly not think of his younger brother, who, that night, pausing after Bobby Fischer's brilliant new move, found himself weepy with shock and self-recrimination that all he could think to do at the bus station earlier was to shake his older brother's hand and say, stupidly, "Take care of yourself."

At such moments young men sometimes feel their spirits push out against their skin, held in check only by welling goose bumps and electrified hairs. And, in fact, at that moment of goodbye inside the bus station I had very nearly left my body. The station smelled of diesel and rank toilet water. The green paint of the pillars had been inscribed with racial epithets, and on the pavement lay a naked plastic doll, beheaded and dirty. Behind our family, a greasy man in a trench coat, some lunatic, kept up a feverish banging on a trash can, then lifted the lid by its broken handle and spun the lid around, as if to make it fly. Rick was already gone, his face a failed mask of warrior calm. Cindy and Marion bore the look of children receiving punishment for crimes they did not understand, stunned and distant, not up to acknowledging what had come to pass. A million thoughts went through my head, but they all seemed to circle like bees, busy and confused, as if trucked through the night and presented in the bright morning with a new and uncharted field. My hand went up, bye, then Rick's paunchy form boarded the idling bus, settling deeply into the crinkly brown seat.

That settling, viewed from below, outside, nearly caused me to cry out in alarm. The window framed the image: Rick frowning and frizzy-haired in the heat; Rick's head suddenly sinking back—I swore I could hear the bus seat exhale—as if into the wrinkled palm of some malevolent and fantastical creature. The sight was so unexpected, so jolting, as to seem removed from normal space and time. I did not experience a premonition, exactly, or even the moment of clarity I had heard visited those blessed with higher orders of intelligence and observation. It was a moment commonly experienced, yet little discussed, that lit-from-within passage of time in which you sense that another you is present, another you who knows all the ways in which this moment is a beginning to some things and an end to others. My other me knew, and thus I knew, that brother Rick, burying his sad-sack head deeper into the seat, receding from sight bit by bit, was by this act meekly surrendering to a monstrous, hurrying machinery of which real machinery was but a part. The bus would race him to the airport, a jet would sling him across the Pacific, then a shuddering chopper would dump him onto some flat, boring field—quick now, double quick!—so that someone, some hurrying alien stranger, could shear off the top of his head clean as an onion.

Surely Columbus, centuries ago, had experienced such a moment of awareness: months of muscular, rude waves and empty, gaping horizons, enormous and mushrooming heavens. Sky above, water below. The cosmos growing, day by day. Then out of nowhere: a strip of island, a black smudge. *India,* Columbus reported wrongly, but that couldn't have been his most immediate or most significant thought. The smudge surely did not inspire in him the objective contemplation of his commercial and scientific idea, the verifiable end of a long train of inquisitive thought. The most immediate, and meaningful, response aboard his stinking and unhappy ship must surely have been of awe, of helpless, fearful praise in the presence of something strange and powerful. What that smudge actually was made little difference, at least at first. Any number of images would have sufficed: mermaids, an orange and purple circle of jutting rocks, a phalanx of futuristic skyscrapers, even apparitions, the guardians of the mystic Spanish universe. All would have burned into his mind with the intensity of a clapping, bubbling emotion, the unprovoked kiss of a girl you just met, the curious, burrowing muzzle of an animal you didn't know was creeping up from behind. *I am small,* one thinks at such moments. *The story is in progress and cannot be stopped.*

That was how I felt on the way home. Shaken, invigorated, vaguely embarrassed, I thought, If that's true . . . well, if that's how the world turns, then what difference does anything . . . what chance do I . . .

I threw myself into preparation for the state championship. My *Informants*, of course, but also *Chess Life, Schachmanty Bulletin, Modern Chess Openings* (5th edition), even *The Dynamic Caro-Kann Defense: A Monograph*—I searched their pages for blunders, traps, sacrifices, for secrets. I didn't want to think about Rick anymore. I didn't want to think about what was unfolding in front of my eyes.

— — —

The following week, Russ Rassmussen (Washington State Chess Champion, 1960, '62–'65, '67) phoned our house and invited me to be his training partner for the state championship, less than a month away. "I want you to be ready for some work," said Rassmussen. "No screwing around. Anything that's not chess, put on hold." I jumped at the chance.

Rassmussen appeared to be in his late thirties, compact and dark-haired, with small pitted holes on one cheek that had grown so smooth over the years they appeared to have been scooped by a tiny spoon. When he walked into the club, heads turned, and when his fine-looking girlfriend (Rassmussen never revealed her name) strolled in occasionally to say hi, she sent electricity up everyone's spine. Regardless of the weather, Rassmussen always wore a nice long-sleeved, button-down shirt and a brown sport coat, an attractive and even necessary wardrobe, I thought, if you spent weekends hunched over a chessboard, alongside rows of the grossly ugly and fearful and inept, who also, bafflingly and unexpectedly—they are nothing like *me,* one thinks, they are aberrations—filled those nearby rows of tables and chairs, and said hello to you and made howlingly stupid moves with their chessmen. An instructor of English at the community college, Rassmussen smoked Dunhills housed in a small, narrow cardboard box and claimed not to understand that a *tenny runner* was what kids in Tacoma called a sneaker, all of which gave him an air of rigor and sophistication, especially when viewed in the context of his polite but distancing lack of interaction with the aforementioned patzers and woodpushers—"fish," in chess parlance, the bottom-dwellers blind to the tricks being played upon them by the strong players above.

The club itself was in a small building downtown. It smelled of pipe tobacco and urine, and its rows of chess sets were said to have been specially constructed by a Pakistani craftsman for the 1960 Seattle World's Fair. The club's plate-glass window, notable for its professionally painted giant knight and pawn, suggested an older time. So, too, did the giant ratings-ladder board, a green-felted expanse of plywood, bolted to the wall, on which members' names and chess rating had been written on white cards, in Magic Marker, and affixed by sewing pins in order of chess rating; so did the heavy chairs and tables, made of fine burnished dark wood, and so did the long line of framed black-and-white photos, along both walls, of deceased and still-living world chess champions. There were, as well, bulky onyx ashtrays, purchased and donated, the treasurer said, by retired master sergeant Jim "Ju-Ju" Bowen at an airbase in Guam, and a stainless-steel coffee urn that seemed forever to be percolating; and the linoleum floor, installed for free by immediate past vice-president D. Dzironky ("I am Dee," he said, in thickly accented English), was of a serendipitous and pleasing rust and cream chessboard pattern.

The club was a home away from home, lovingly tended by the city's small but committed cadre, and sometimes late in the evening, fresh from a victory, I would rub my thumb on the glass of the picture frames, searching for resemblances between me and the former champions, whose likenesses seemed to stare back with a severe and regal sympathy. There was an air of calm and easy familiarity. On the giant ratings board you saw your name and rating, and everyone else did, too. There were no secrets, no withholdings, and you spent your evenings knowing all you needed to know about the fish sitting across from you, or about the fish grimacing by the coffeepot, or about the fish striking the plunger of the chess clock too hard.

Even a cursory glance at the giant ratings board told you something very clear and important: Russ Rassmussen had been at the top forever. His card, occupying the first spot on the board, had turned yellow with age, and it still had no creases, no thumbprints, as if never touched by human hands. Rassmussen had been profiled twice in the *Tribune;* he had once received a complimentary handwritten note from a visiting

Latvian champion; he had been elected unanimously to the Washington State Chess Hall of Fame. Recently, though, not all the talk was of Rassmussen. As any visitor in the past six months would have clearly seen, the ratings board had begun to reveal something new, something equally clear and important: below Rassmussen, in the second spot but well above the depressingly but unsurprisingly vast ocean of fish ("The poor, sayeth Jesus, shall always be among you," said Rassmussen), was my bright, well-creased card, the card of the whiz-kid rising so fast some fish once asked me if I was getting the bends.

Now, Tuesdays and Thursday evenings, and on weekends, I trained with chessmaster Russ Rassmussen. We played five-minute chess for quarters. We reviewed mating attacks with bishop and knight versus king, contemplated rook and pawn endings, studied variations and subvariations of the King's Indian, the Sicilian, and the Ruy Lopez. "Pay attention," said Rassmussen, snapping his fingers. "You've got to be *here*, not floating around." So I straightened in my chair. I watched Rassmussen take apart my Nimzo-Indian. Then I showed Rassmussen a gambit line in the French Defense; Rassmussen found a flaw immediately. We stayed until the buses stopped running.

Through it all, through the bitter coffee in Styrofoam cups that Rassmussen brought along, I could not still my mind long enough to stop thinking about that awful morning at the bus station. I thought about it in roundabout ways. I thought, for example, about our family's living situation. We lived in a small, boxy house in the south part of the city, at its farthest point, in unincorporated Tacoma. The house stood on a crumbling unpaved street where neighbors were set far apart, separated by mole mounds, patches of foxglove, and spindly firs that grew heavy with moisture and sometimes dropped sodden branches onto cars. I had pulled a 3.0 GPA in high school without ever doing homework, and friends called me Brainiac (I had won the state high-school chess championship my junior year), but I had no plans, and money was tight so I lived in my parents' attached garage, despite the wolf spiders in the shag rug by my bed and, especially during dry months, the bloated snakeflies that rose in the night to burrow into my mattress and deposit larvae.

I had never been sure how, in a legal sense, the unincorporated part of Tacoma differed from the incorporated part. I knew only that the houses around me were dark and peeling, and everyone's yard was treacherously soft, rotting underfoot from the seepage of decaying septic tanks. It rained a lot in Tacoma, and in the aftermath of storms or drizzles, grey, still pools appeared on our swayback roof and out in the rough terrain of the unincorporated gravel road, and everything got muddy and smelled like moss. Late into the evening, after the air turned chilly, insects walked the water, their pinprick ripples the only movement, and you got the sense that you were not in Tacoma at all, but in some place ancient and recurring, one full of drain water and holes, like a stretch of battleground.

Certainly the only time you saw couples at the threshold of their houses was when one was shoving the other out the door. I had witnessed such an event in the neighborhood three times. The man would be standing outside on the steps, the woman would be inside, half-exposed, grasping the knob, opening and closing the door quickly. *You give me nothing,* she'd yell, something like that. The man, silent and fuming, would turn and see me staring, then shout something equally loud toward the door, *bitch, cunt,* words to that effect, and walk quickly to the car and spray gravel into the sewage drain and go roaring down the road. The woman would then appear behind the living-room window, veins ballooning on her face, hands pressed white against the pane, shouting something I couldn't hear.

Why should such an event occur right in front of me three times? It defied statistics. How was it that, a few blocks down, in incorporated Tacoma, life proceeded along lines of generosity and fullness? It seemed a conspiracy of great natural forces, and from what I could tell, the city planners seemed to go to great lengths to reinforce the distinctions between incorporated and unincorporated Tacoma. Two blocks north of us, the vague and beaten unincorporated gravel road transformed into a thickly tarred street, one smooth and wide as a private waterway, marking entry into the incorporated sections of the city. There, a good rain made the houses shine, and the dew hung from shrubs like the sheer cloth you sometimes see on women in religious paintings. The tucking in the brickwork was fresh, the windows clean, and the gutters were straight and cleared of birds' nests. Evenings, you could see middle-aged couples inspecting their marigolds and roses, bending plumply at the knees, their iced teas held at arm's length, like the tiny, pole-borne weights carried by high-wire walkers.

Invariably Cindy would say, "Look at all this." My mother would be cornering, turning the steering wheel of our rusting Buick by tiny increments, keeping her hands in a ten-and-two position. "Everything's so nice," she'd say, sharply. Then she'd stomp on the gas pedal and speed home dangerously, running stop signs sometimes, once driving a girl on a bike into the curb. Had she always acted so crazy? I wasn't sure. I listened intently now from the passenger seat. I analyzed. She worked in a dry cleaners and smelled of dyes and wet wool. Most of the time she spoke in the swallowed monotone of someone used to being ignored.

"All the little Cornish hens nice in a row," she said, roaring down the incorporated street. "*Look* at these houses." She had a thing about Cornish hens. For years she had prepared dinners of Cornish hens, four whole birds on four plates, and even when the family stopped having dinners together, sometimes I saw her at the table, sawing with a plastic knife and fork through the innards of a freshly cooked Cornish hen. They were perfect, she'd always said: complete, separate, an entire creature in miniature. And it was true, you felt important when you ate one, like a giant. In a few quick bites you could swallow everything, limbs and breasts and neck.

Maybe, really, that's what she wanted to do. Every day she had to drive home in the Buick, down Marigold Avenue, then onto 70th, past all that perfection. Maybe she wanted to stride down those sparkling blacktop streets and devour tree and shrub and house, and maybe the fact that she couldn't made her tempt the laws of statistics. Maybe, when I thought about it, she saw in the line between incorporated and unincorporated Tacoma evidence of a hurrying, hateful machinery. Quick now! As fast as you can go. Double quick, out, out! In photographs I had seen, black-and-white shots with wavy edges, she looked pretty and dark-haired. Now she wore a clear plastic cap around her head. Her face and arms looked drained of blood. She hardly ever seemed to move her eyes.

— — —

I had been blessed with certain attributes—a fine head of blond hair, a pleasant face, a compressed stomach. Rick, who had not been blessed with certain attributes, had always been blubbery, even after basic training, as were so many of the fish at the chess club. The club was always full of stinky fat men, and they moved as slowly as dray animals. There were cripples, too, men in wheelchairs, and quiet, doughy boys who didn't like the sun; and there were blotchy alcoholics and bearded men who apparently didn't bathe. Occasionally, unkempt souls in dirty pants wandered in and helped themselves to coffee. Months ago, I had looked on with approval when Mr. Finnegan walked in, Mr. Finnegan looking like Burt Lancaster, tall and athletic, well-groomed, Mr. Finnegan, who might as well have punched me in the face when he told Russ Rassmussen he was a machinist and out of a job.

Now these men filled me with rage. Now I wanted them dead. "Quiet," I barked at a chatty newcomer. I picked up a pawn and cocked my arm, as if to hurl it at the offender's head.

"Oh, my," whispered Rassmussen. He reached into his pants pocket and much to my surprise pulled out a folded Swiss army knife. "You'll be using this next if you're not careful." He quickly put the knife back into his pocket, then reached across the chessboard and placed a hand on my arm. "Focus," he said, gently. "Just let them be. We all play the hand we're dealt."

Rassmussen's fingers weighed a ton. They seemed to burn into my skin. I looked Rassmussen in the eye. What if, I wondered, the hand I had been dealt was in fact Rassmussen's hand? There were sources, traces, trajectories binding us together. I had known Rassmussen for more than a year. We were at the top, the lion and the cub. Rassmussen had *chosen* me, for Christ's sake. Rassmussen had the big talent, and maybe I did, too. I told my friends Dan Bacha and Tim Underwood I won money in tournaments—local ones, to be sure, but officially sanctioned tournaments, nonetheless—and they called me a professional. I never bothered to correct them. I had cash in my pocket; I had trophies on a bookshelf and an inscribed certificate from the United States Chess Federation.

With Rassmussen as tutor, I thought I might even win the state championship, might get my photo in the paper. At some distant point I might even *be* another Rassmussen, a man with a white-collar job, with neatly pressed clothes, a man with a presentable face and body, a fine-looking girlfriend, a sense of humor appreciated by others, a ready fund of knowledge about the world outside (coming in late one evening, Rassmussen had excused himself, saying he'd been working on the McGovern campaign). Once, I had smelled alcohol on Rassmussen's breath, but it had been late in the evening and near Christmas. The man presented a wonderful picture, and that night I had a flying dream. In the morning, I swore I would cut back on weed and the occasional chaser of speed, and cease masturbating altogether, at least until after the state championship.

But other days, walking in the front yard, I passed through patches of tall wet grass and felt the heavy moisture clinging to the blades. Tropical, I concluded. I squatted and ran my fingers through the foliage. I stared long and hard into the tree line down the block. It would be scary, sure, but wouldn't it be something to walk up behind Rick in some rice padi and stick out my hand and tap Rick on the shoulder and say Hey. Wouldn't it be something? *Hey,* I whispered, and I stuck out my hand, shoulder-height, tapping air. Hey. Hey, Rick.

In the house, my father, Marion, was always watching TV. "One boy in Vietnam, one boy here," Marion would say, tipping back a Schlitz.

"One fights a war, other plays chess. What you gonna do, sir? What you gonna do?"

Marion had always done that, had always mumbled to himself like an actor memorizing a script, but his question—*what you gonna do?*—soon became a mantra, at least when I was around. The mantra was hypnotic and for that reason powerful, especially when intoned, increasingly now, in front of my friend Tim Underwood, who tromped through the living room with a folding chessboard and plastic pieces, intent on finally beating me in an offhand game, before we went down to the Sorenson Trailer Park, where we'd drive around, smoke grass, maybe scare some kids, see if Annie Hershberger was in her hot pants and wanted a ride somewhere. "You win the state championship," said Tim Underwood, "Hershberger'll do it with you. I bet you she will. Win that title, Brainiac."

"Oh, I will," I said, capturing another of my friend's chess pieces. "I'm on a mission."

Marion calmly wheezed, talking loudly from a chair in the kitchen. Cindy sat across the table, watching Walter Cronkite on their small black-and-white TV. "Sir, what you gonna do?" said Marion to no one in particular. "You sir, that's right, you." He stared glumly at some point on the wall.

Looking up from the chessboard (I was already killing Tim), I saw in Marion's narrow, blinking eyes the strain of a man struggling to hold back something. A judgment, perhaps. A summing up. Marion's words took on a menacing aspect, grazing my ear like scattershot. This man, this father, bunched on the chair, working swing shift at the warehouse, sleeping through the day: had he always looked so weary and so baffled?

I captured another of Tim's chessmen and shouted out to Marion: "If I ever saw a gook here, I wouldn't want to be in his shoes." I then shook my head for a long time, signaling that what I'd do to the trespasser was too terrible to tell.

Marion, sighing, got up and walked toward the refrigerator.

"Do you want another beer?" Cindy said, turning from the TV.

"Yes ma'am," Marion said. "I want another beer."

She watched him pull out a Schlitz. "Well, you know where they are."

Marion walked back to his chair.

"You know what I'd do?" I said. I looked up from the chessboard at Marion, then at Cindy. "I'd beat the shit out of the gook, that's what I'd do."

Marion got up and opened the door to the utility room. He rolled the cold can across his forehead and proceeded down the stairs.

Cindy shook her head and looked at me. "No swear words in the house," she said. She balled up a fist, raised her arm slightly, then splayed her fingers, as if discarding something.

There's no trash like white trash, Cindy was fond of saying. Of late, she had begun to let her tossing motion say the words for her.

— — —

We live implausibly but admit to only the plainest of sins. The two parts of that sentence are as close to making sense of my past I have ever found. The soaring of the first part is forever shackled to the mutters of the second: *soar mutter, soar mutter, soar mutter,* over and over so fast and so hard the oppositions threaten to break the middle. Things began to happen quickly, and for me time took on a fantastical, herky-jerky quality, though one with a pattern, with a movement forward, like when you're swimming, the water thunking against you, your face shining and clean, and you suddenly plunge upside-down, driven for reasons you cannot say toward the sea grasses and sand, down into a strong-arming current that bullies you along wherever it wants to go.

Rick was killed in action October 12, 1969, outside the village of Quang Ngu, known locally for its excellent rice wine. Cindy and Marion did not weep, at least not in front of me or the neighbors, trying hard, I heard them say on the phone, to be strong for their boy still there. It was that language—*we're being strong for our boy here*—that I remember most clearly, that I understood as proof of what had happened, words treadworn and wrong, and, because treadworn and wrong, terrifying. Cindy brought home dinners of Kentucky Fried Chicken; Marion mowed the grass three days in a row. There was a shopping trip: a new tie, dress-up black shoes. Then I sat quietly in the back of the Buick. Lots of cars were parked in front of the church. Marion addressed Ken or Mike, some barking kind of name, and let hands rest on his shoulder. "We lost one boy . . . ," Marion said, miserably, vaguely biblically. His face seemed to collapse. "And we found the other." Cindy turned away and her shoulders began to tremble.

It was as though Marion had opened the wrong book, was quoting from the wrong pages. *What does that mean?* I wanted to ask, but didn't. *What are you saying?* On the car ride back, we all looked out the windows. Cindy baked some cherry brownies—for the smell, she said; the smell always cheered her up—and Marion stood with her in the kitchen and put his hand around her waist whenever she was still.

Evening, I was still lying in my bed in the garage, stroking my new tie, which I declared to Cindy and Marion was my new favorite. My room had always been a mess, and now the mess and the poor light and the smell seemed an accusation. Behind my bed, on top of a dented ice cooler, were paper plates crusted with mustard and bits of pizza. Clothes lay in detergent boxes piled atop older, crushed boxes from which leaked glimpses of rags and garden gloves and oddly affecting objects—a miniature stirrup, a plastic battleship, a clock reading *Sprite,* a baseball glove without webbing, mementos I could no longer associate with the person who owned them. My bookshelves, lines of planks and concrete blocks, had been stacked with dog-eared books and papers and journals with vaguely thrilling titles, *Der Schachspeiler, 64, The Blackmar-Deimer, Pawn Power, D'Echecs Europa #23.* In front of me was a Dutch Masters cigar box containing my chess notes and tournament games; on the cement floor, croutons, a dirty glass, a mysterious white button, a few tooth-marked plastic pens, and floor stains of indeterminate origin and color spreading toward the door. My chessboard lay at an angle in one corner; my chessmen, greasy and dull, were scattered in another.

So I rolled up the garage door. I walked to the end of the driveway and wrestled the metal garbage can into my room. I swept with a push broom. I poured motor-oil cleanser onto a small space on the floor, the area in front of my bed, and I scrubbed the surface clean. I tightened the screws on a folded card table near the door and dragged it to the cleared space, then I wiped the table clean and, with architectural precision, placed my board and pieces in the exact center of the table. The pieces and board I wiped clean, too, rubbing until they gleamed, and on one corner of the table I carefully placed a new black pen, and on the other I placed a new booklet of chess score sheets. I brought in a small wooden chair from the kitchen and aligned it in front of the table. The result was so perfect I found myself shy in touching the arrangement. When I finally sat down, straightening my tie, my heart was racing, and I nodded to myself, pleased at the bright, uniform chessmen and board, the clean surface of the table and floor. There was something comforting about it all, something quiet and powerful in the way the table and board and chessmen stood out from the rest of the room.

When Cindy saw what I had done she folded her arms. She nodded toward the table, toward the shiny chessmen and board. "It looks like a religious icon," she said, and I thought how strange it was to hear those words come from her—*religious icon*—words she had never spoken before. Leaving, she brushed against my arm, and I nearly jumped. I hadn't felt my mother's skin in years. And more: she was of the womanly flesh I desired, though she herself did not possess that flesh. Her flesh disgusted me, and I was aware in a vague way of something I hadn't thought about in years: that I had wanted a sister, someone sexy and cooing, but also distant; a girl with breasts I could savor only from afar, a beautiful girl with long hair and bright lips, a narrow waist, long, slim fingers hanging a polka-dot dress from the shower rod.

Early the next day Cindy knocked on the garage door and gave me a letter from a Pfc. Jerome Witte. "When you have a moment," she said, nodding toward the letter. She left for work. Pfc. Witte had been in Rick's platoon. He painted a strange, hagiographic picture of Rick, called him a hero, let us know that Rick had uttered brave and decisive final words.

He said It don't mean nothing, Pfc. Witte wrote. *He was as tough as they come. Then he was take* [sic] *by the Lord. I loved him like a brother.* I imagined the scene, Rick lying in the tall grass, his glasses probably bent at some odd angle, heaving. He would have said those tough words because he would have heard them somewhere, from his buddies, a movie or two. He wouldn't have known what was happening. *It don't mean nothing.* As if some kind of bartering had taken place. As if all reasonable offers had been considered.

Later, after Tim Underwood and I smoked a few joints, we drove in Tim's pickup to the Sorenson Trailer Park and slapped around some black kid until he got on his knees and confessed he was a nigger. We waved around our nickel bag, and we got Annie Hershberger to go for a ride, and later Tim tried to fuck her hard, before she was moist, and made her yell Stop it, stop it *now.* Then we all drove back to the trailer park in silence and dropped her off and waved and made plans to have a picnic together up at Snoqualmie Falls one of these days.

— — —

"Something wrong?" Rassmussen asked me at the club. I was losing every training game, and the state championship was in two days. I was missing simple combinations, easy threats.

"No," I said. I looked around the room, at all the patient, sweaty men, all their mulish failure. "Just tired, that's all."

"Things OK at home?"

I nodded. When Rassmussen had asked where the hell I had been the past week, I had shrugged and said sorry. I didn't mention Rick. Rassmussen, smiling, had made a joke of it: "So buck up, boy," he said. I smiled back.

Every moment now, it seemed, I thought of my brother lurching through booby-trapped jungle trails. A picture formed in my head, and the picture wouldn't go away. Rick would be lying flat on a muddy field, and Marines would be kneeling around him, saying soothing words. The top of Rick's head would be gone, only Rick wouldn't know it, and no matter how hard I tried to change the picture, I could see only loose meaty things bunched around my brother's skull, and not the spirits or inscriptions of a holy nature I knew were etched onto his bones.

When I played Rassmussen now, my fingers lingered over the wooden tops of the chessmen. I held up the chessmen to the light and looked closely, squinting like a jeweler.

— — —

The state championship, held over two consecutive weekends, was played in the back room of the Arby's on Pacific Avenue. It was an eight-man round-robin. Rassmussen was the first seed; I was the eighth. I lost quickly in Round 1. In Round 2, Lawrence Dorfner, an awful player, a man of no consequence, beat me. "Good game," I kept saying, afterwards. "Good game." When Rassmussen walked up, inquiring, we all chatted a while, then we moved the conversation to the tournament director's table and stood looking at the other game results, taped on large sheets onto the wall. Rassmussen did some calculating, and Dorfner nodded and wondered aloud about who would make the best matchups for Round 3.

There was a pause. Then I said, "My brother just got killed. I couldn't concentrate, man."

Rassmussen and Dorfner looked at me blankly. Rassmussen then opened his mouth as if to speak, but only frowned. At the bus stop later, I saw two men in leather jackets and black pants. They were boisterous, swinging their arms expansively; one was swearing. It was chilly and drizzling, and their hair was plastered like helmets to their skulls. The men seemed far away as the moon, and for a moment nothing made sense, there was no sound, no substance to the bench I was sitting on, no smell, and all I could do was rise and address them: *motherfucking cocksuckers fuck off go fuck yourself buttfucks.* I said the words so loud I closed my eyes and felt the spit run down my chin, and I stuck out my face. One of the men punched me hard, then they pushed me around some before walking away.

— — —

By Sunday of the first weekend, the halfway point, I was 0–4, no wins and four losses. Rassmussen approached me. He stuck a Dunhill in his mouth.

"What'dya say?" said Rassmussen, lighting up. "Nasty bruise."

"We still got next weekend," I said. "I'm just having trouble concentrating."

Rassmussen smiled. He talked about cabins up by Snoqualmie Falls, about how beautiful the scenery was, how relaxing the pines. It was all the rainfall in the woods, he said. The entire Cascade Peninsula was in a rainshadow, or, as the botanists and ecologists termed it, a *saaniche*. "Good for what ails you," he said, and he put his hand on my shoulder. He told me he was going up there tomorrow night with his girlfriend. Just to look around, relax. There was a cabin with separate rooms. If I was free . . .

I shrugged. "I should bone up on my rook and pawn endings."

"A trip to the Falls," said Rassmussen. "It's on me. All expenses paid. It'd do you good to get away for a while. There shouldn't be too much rain. Plus you'll get to meet my lady. What do you say?"

I stuck my hands in my pocket. "OK," I said, sounding less enthusiastic than I intended. I pictured myself throwing my arms around Rassmussen. *Now,* I wanted to say. Let's go now.

— — —

The next morning we left in Rassmussen's car to the cabin near Snoqualmie Falls. Rassmussen's girlfriend introduced herself as Tina. She was a pretty brunette. Her voice was surprisingly loud; she had a tinkling laugh. She, too, was an instructor—"just artsy fartsy stuff," she said—at the community college.

The air turned cold almost immediately, and Tina, fiddling up front with the heater, said she felt like an explorer to the North Pole. I agreed. I pulled up the collar of my jean jacket. It had been a wet fall in Tacoma, and moss was growing thick as honeycomb and creeping in wide sheets under everyone's shingles. Even in incorporated Tacoma, the earth stuck to your shoes wherever you walked, and for weeks on end you'd track wet clumps onto the linoleum. The leaves were everywhere, and cars left thin trails of mealy debris on the roadways, and sometimes the drivers couldn't stop because their tire treads were clogged. The car was like an icebreaker, said Tina, and they were sluicing through the icecaps. The *H.M.S. Bullpucky,* said Rassmussen, and Tina punched him lightly on the shoulder.

But it was true, driving out of the city, ghostly Mount Rainier floating high in the sky, soggy branches and earth and leaves everywhere, giant pines around you, there was a sense of racing toward something, not away, and the more all the familiar objects and machines and landscape fell away, the more you felt like driving farther. Up we went, the radio on loud, me in the back seat munching on tuna sandwiches prepared by Tina. We passed giant white puffballs splitting open along the roadside, spores floating in the wind. We smelled basswood, saw fields of white, glowing birches. We roared past moccasin flowers, a swarm of moths, stands of pine and Bigtooth Aspen, a sheet of drowned squirrel corn on the pavement.

"Nice," I said, happily. "Nice." There was much to look at. At the falls, we stared for a long time at the thin white thread of water plunging down dramatically from the rock face. Rassmussen pulled out a pocket flask and took a few swigs. Tina gave him a disapproving look. "My keeper," he said, and they giggled and hugged each other. At Tina's request, we all played cards on a visitors' center bench, then we each went for a long, solitary walk in the mushy woods. At the Falls Restaurant, we lingered in the souvenir shop. Rassmussen and Tina held hands. Rassmussen held up a postcard showing a dog smiling at a fire hydrant. "Now who would buy something like that?" he asked, and I said I didn't know, but it sure wouldn't be me. "Give me a blank card, any day," Rassmussen added. "Just a white sheet of paper."

That evening we ate cheeseburgers and fries, and Rassmussen built a crackling fire in the brick fireplace. Tina pulled out a bottle of red wine from her travel bag, and Rassmussen, laughing, excused himself and returned with two more bottles. "Russ," said Tina, darkly. "A jug o' wine, a loaf o' bread, and thou," said Rassmussen. They kissed.

It was warm by the fireplace, and I removed my jacket. "Aren't you hot?" I asked, noting Rassmussen's long-sleeved shirt. Rassmussen shook his head. "What's hot," he said, "is me beating you in speed chess." He then ran back to the bedroom and returned with a chessboard and chess clock. Tina rolled her eyes and excused herself—she'd read in the bedroom, she said—so Rassmussen, winking, set up the chessmen and play began. Rassmussen poured himself a glass of wine. He was expansive, more solemn as well as funnier than I had ever seen him; he was playing brilliant speed chess, all the while keeping up a stream of banter.

"You're going through a rough time," said Rassmussen, offering some wine. I declined. "I don't want to intrude," said Rassmussen. He captured one of my chessmen. "So I won't. Chess is easy compared to the world." But no sooner did he utter the words than he started clowning around. He sang:

Burzy Wurzy was a bear,
Burzy Wurzy had no hair.
Burzy Wurzy wasn't very burzy,
Wurzy?

"Those lyrics right?" I asked.

"They're as right as the other version, aren't they?" said Rassmussen. "Who makes the rules? Checkmate in three, by the way."

We started laughing, it was great fun, and the time passed agreeably, speed chess game after speed chess game, glass after glass. Rassmussen, calling himself a klutz, licked up some wine that had dropped onto his hand.

"Oh, my," Rassmussen said. I had launched an attack.

"Got you now," I said, sending my chessmen rampaging around Rassmussen's king.

Rassmussen shook his head. "I think you're painting your dick red and calling it a charlie pole."

It didn't make any sense, but I laughed anyway. I was shaking a little, I felt so good.

"Chess is like war," said Rassmussen. He opened another bottle. "But I guess you've heard that one. I guess that's not news." He seemed about to say something more when Tina reappeared, looking spectacular in a red sweater and slacks.

"Russ," she said, "I forgot to tell you. I got a letter from a magazine last week. A rejection, but a good one."

"She's a poet," said Rassmussen. He raised his hand over the chessboard, signaling we should stop.

"Don't make it sound so dramatic," she said, turning to me. "I write poems and sometimes they get published. Sometimes not." She reached into her pocket and pulled out a folded piece of paper. "Here's my latest," she said, and she waved it near Rassmussen's lips.

"Let's hear," Rassmussen said.

"I'm a little shy," she said. She looked at me.

"I like poetry," I said. "I want to hear."

So she sat in a chair and cleared her throat. *My fingers are eight lies about darkness,* she read. Her voice was shaky.

"Sounds persnickety," said Rassmussen. He was drinking straight from the bottle. "Thumbs don't count?"

"Let me finish. You can't complain before the last line."

"I'm not complaining. I'm just pointing something out."

"Are you on the second bottle?" she asked.

"Depends. So what's the lie about darkness?"

"There are eight of them."

"Exactly eight lies about darkness," he said, pleasantly. He turned to me. "Imagine that."

"Sweetie, I don't want to read the rest," she said, standing. She put the paper back in her pocket and sat down next to Rassmussen. "I'm interrupting your game." She draped her arm around his neck.

The trouble was, Rassmussen said, pouring Tina a glass, in chess all facts were equally true, or equally false or equally neutral, however you wanted to put it. There were no lies—not eight, not seven, not six—but there wasn't any truth, either. Nothing about chess amounted to a hill of beans.

In real life, he said, taking a swig from the bottle, some facts were truer than others. Some facts burrowed deep into your chest and balled up tight as a fist and made you bolt upright in your bed in the middle of the night. Some facts passed right through you and some set up shop inside your chest.

So what was he saying? I asked. What facts?

Rassmussen stood, a bit unsteady, and, turning his free hand into a scythe, swept aside some chessmen on the board. The action seemed consciously theatrical, as if rehearsed, but Rassmussen's face was hard and red. My shoulders tensed up. "I'm saying chess don't mean shit," said Rassmussen, "that's what I mean. All those years . . . might as well go spit in the Grand Canyon. Doesn't make a goddamn bit of difference."

I looked away.

"Russ, please," said Tina. I wasn't sure what happened next. I heard Tina cry out, and when I looked up I saw that Rassmussen had lost his balance and fallen against the coffee table. There was a thud. Rassmussen was on the floor, clutching his head and rocking.

I leaped up to get a towel from the bathroom. "They're all dirty," Tina shouted. She told me to get some from the back of the car. I grabbed the keys on the counter and ran out.

When I returned, Rassmussen and Tina were squatting in front of the fireplace. It was dark—the fire was barely flickering—but I saw a rumpled quilt next to them. Rassmussen's shirt had been removed; Tina was dabbing his face with her sleeve. "Here are some towels," I said. I saw dark lines on Rassmussen's arms, then on his chest and stomach. I squinted. Rassmussen's eyes were closed; he was still clutching his head. Rassmussen's body was nearly hairless, and on his chest, I saw the outline of a knight, then a bishop. Tina was rubbing one of the knights, by his left nipple. There was the outline of a pawn on Rassmussen's shoulder. I saw two rooks on his right forearm; his shoulders and arms had scars forming the outline of pawns and kings.

"Russ," said Tina, in a warning voice. Rassmussen opened his eyes. She hurriedly grabbed the quilt and placed it like a curtain in front of him.

"Skin etchings," said Rassmussen. There was a dark patch on his scalp. He looked straight at me. "Like tattoos, OK?" He sounded angry. "I do them myself. That OK with you? You ever see Michelangelo's men in stone?" He let the quilt drop, then grabbed loose skin on his stomach. He pulled the skin taut. "See this stuff?" A network of jagged scars ran across his torso. The top of one of the knights seemed to be bleeding. "That's a whole lot of nothing trying to get *out,* man. You hear me? *Nothing,* man."

Tina walked over to me, a never-mind smile on her face. "Time to turn in," she said in a sing-songy voice. "Thank you for the towels." Her back was to Rassmussen. Drawing close, she caught my eye, then stuck out her forefinger and made a quick slicing motion across her breasts, then across her arms. She leaned in and whispered: "Sometimes he gets carried away. He cuts himself. You know?" I exhaled loudly, then turned and headed toward my room. I closed the door and quietly locked it. All night I heard noises—whispered conversations, some thumps, a scrapping like sandpaper; a heavy bottle clinked against something metallic. In the morning, I heard snores coming from their room; underwear lay bunched outside their door. Wine in a drying red pool covered part of the floor.

On the drive home, Tina slept in the front seat. I sat in the back. We stopped for a quick breakfast at the Great Northwoods Café, eggs and toast, lots of coffee, but mostly we were quiet, pointing every now and then at drivers in cowboy hats, once passing a solitary cow in a field. The silence was unbearable. It was as though time had ceased, as though everything would remain in a perpetual present tense until someone spoke. Rassmussen felt it, too, I thought, and Tina. Pulling up to our driveway, Rassmussen got out and helped me rummage through the trunk for my jacket. I thanked him for the trip.

"I hope I didn't scare you away," Rassmussen said.

"That's OK," I answered. I didn't know what else to say.

Rassmussen surprised me by grabbing my hand and shaking it, as if we'd just met.

"I'm dropping out of the tournament," I said then.

Rassmussen looked at the ground for a moment. "Well," he said. "I'm sorry to hear that. I really am." He knew what I was saying. He knew it would be a long time, if ever, before we saw each other again. Then he was back in the car, waving bye with Tina, and they were gone, turning left on Marigold, toward incorporated Tacoma.

Inside the garage, I heard Cindy and Marion in the living room, watching TV. It was almost noon. Through the wall I heard the hollow sound of Cindy placing a coffee cup on the table, the squeaks of the couch when Marion sat. I wasn't sure when, but after listening for a while, I picked up the board and chessmen from the card table and shoved it on top of a case of soft drinks. Some of the pawns fell off, and I left them there. I dragged the card table back to a dark corner, pushing it against the cleaning materials and air filters. I walked back to my bed, then heard *The Dick Van Dyke Show* come on. I stood, brushed off my pants, and walked through the door, past the kitchen, then into the living room, where Cindy and Marion sat listening to the theme song.

We are born in a caul of sin, and the world is a wicked place. But if you had said that to me then, I would have called you an asshole. The words were no revelation. They were not news. No clutter: that's what I was thinking. Back in my room there was now a clear, empty space, and it remained that way. Sometimes thin ropes of light streamed into the area from the top of the garage door or from the rafters, and sometimes I saw the dust illuminated—like floating planets, I thought, like tiny aquatic life—and then I would vanquish the thought, I would dismiss the fancy metaphors, the tricks. Still, I marked off the space from the rest of the room. I made sure the space was swept clean. I assigned it secret names, my own coded language, Rickaroo, Rickereeni, Ricko-Micko, Ricky Ticky Tick-Tock, silly things, fluttering sounds I had never thought of saying before. Later, in a few weeks, I got a little high, nothing serious, and when I was ready, when it was quiet outside, I stuck my hand into all that space, into a million miles of nothing, and I made a little tapping motion. I stuck out my hand, shoulder-high, into all that burning, wicked nothing, and I made my tapping motion and nodded curtly, and I said Hey. Hey, man. Hey.

What's Yours, What's Mine

A REUNION of The Boat People Club—at least that's what Thomas's letter called the group—had been planned for that June, on the east coast of Malaysia, and Maureen was just now hearing about it. Rueben had held on to the letter for a couple of days, checking flight schedules and costs, then poured them some wine at dinner. A reunion, he said out of the blue: wouldn't that be something? It had been more than a quarter of a century ago, after all, that everyone in the Club had gone to Malaysia to work with Vietnamese boat people, and as Rueben sometimes said over drinks, when you've worked in a refugee camp you're pretty much guaranteed a long memory. "Oh, Miss Maureen," he said then, plucking Thomas's letter from his pocket and waving it over his head. "Miss Maureen, Miss Maureen." That was what the refugees called her when they wanted something. He placed the letter on the table and stood behind her as she read. "What do you think?" he whispered. Once again into the breach? Or wait until they each had one crotchety foot in the grave?

Maureen almost burst out laughing. He sounded like a teenager lobbying her into bed, and she couldn't resist turning around sharply and letting loose with a mocking "Who *are* you?" which she immediately regretted upon seeing his serious and unflinching expression. He was sensitive to criticisms, and he sometimes picked up on implied ones to an alarming degree, but, more importantly, both of them had long ago agreed that courtesy was not something to be demonstrated only in front of strangers. In fact, Maureen held, courtesy was an underrated marital virtue and when looked at over the long haul, yes, she'd say it, a substantial and perhaps even transcendent act of love (maybe Presbyterian love, Rueben joked, but still he, too, practiced it daily). So as her husband pressed forward with his case she listened attentively, and even before he was finished she knew she would say yes. If he wanted to go so badly, then she would give herself every chance to want to go as well. He would have done the same for her.

She had to admit, too, and with some surprise, that what he was saying seemed to ignite some long-cold ember of her travel passion, which she believed had ages ago burnt itself into a perfect ring of ash. Imagine, he said to her, imagine returning to the country where they had first met each other all those years ago. Imagine seeing their UN comrades-in-arms again—The Musketeers, The Marco Polos, The Faces You Would See from Your Deathbed. How had the group ever fallen out of touch? Wouldn't it be something, he wondered aloud, to see Thomas and Kathy and Kevin again? "And let's not forget Stella and Tony," he added, grinning.

"All right," said Maureen, "them, too." She paused. "Though they were more your friends."

"Oh, come on now," Rueben said. "They were second-stringers for me, too. I just knew them a little longer."

They had never been back to Malaysia—they had not, in fact, left the confines of Washington State for more than a decade—and though Maureen didn't say so, she felt an exotic adventure in June would be perfect for her husband. He had been teaching English to foreign students at the same language school for so long that his colleagues named the new breakroom after him. Just recently he had begun expressing disappointment over his career. Last month he asked her if she thought he was a lollygagger. Of course not, she told him, but later he asked her another question: okay, he said, how about a flunky? He would not be consoled. Last year he had stopped jogging, and now he spent his evenings on the Internet playing Texas Hold 'Em. During his breaks between teaching sessions he hardly seemed to know what to do with himself. More than once, she had found him holed up in the TV room, sleeping his day away.

They quickly dispensed with logistics and finances. She had just been promoted at Boeing—she was now a senior proposal writer—and had enough clout to swing a summer leave. ("My tutoring money?" Rueben said. "There's five bucks we'll just have to do without.") They could get the Morrison boy to housesit and look after the yard. They could put the bathroom renovation on hold until next year.

The matter was settled.

"Wow," Maureen exclaimed. "Did we just step into a time machine?" She twisted an imaginary dial and addressed the couch: "Boat-people refugee camp sighted, *Capitan.* Set the way-back for one million B.C."

"I must have a different machine," Rueben said. "Seems like yesterday to me."

— — —

In May the plan began to unravel—grand plans always did, Maureen asserted, they always pushed you off the sidewalk—and Maureen found herself second-guessing their decision. Thomas had came down with some unspecified but serious illness, and Kathy, now living in the French countryside, had to make expensive repairs on her collapsed roof; Kevin, never the effusive one, sent everyone a postcard from Buenos Aires with a curt *Sorry, maybe next year.*

That left only Stella and Tony.

But the dye was cast, and pulling out at such a late date would have been difficult. They had already purchased plane tickets and arranged to board their two dogs at Seattle's perpetually booked Canine Retreat. And Maureen's mother, who had originally hoped to meet up with her daughter and son-in-law in nearby Vancouver that summer, had given the trip her blessing. Going back, she told them, would be a kind of anniversary, wouldn't it? One needed to reflect on one's past, after all, to burnish it like a trophy, not store it like an urn. "Think how you might have ended up if you hadn't done relief work," her mother said. She shuddered theatrically at Maureen, and they all smiled. "You would have turned into a traffic sign," she added, after which no one laughed because the comment seemed a little cruel and because neither Maureen nor Rueben was completely sure what it meant. "You know," her mother explained. "Let's stop now. Let's yield here. Let's use caution."

Oh, ha ha ha, said Maureen.

Oh, ha ha ha, said Rueben.

Why, Maureen said to Rueben later, did even her mother not understand where the line was?

After overly loud phone calls to Stella and Tony—"How *are* you?" Rueben shouted into the receiver, both times. "It's been for*ever*"—Rueben mimed an orgasm by thrusting his hips forward and quivering. They laughed, then they reviewed their itinerary until Maureen put her hands over her ears and said she hoped they weren't putting too many eggs into this particular basket.

Rueben put the plane tickets down.

"Okay," Maureen said, "maybe it's not the basket. Maybe it's these particular eggs." She had tiny hands just beginning to spot and a reedy neck her husband still found appealing, especially when counterpointed against her long, dark hair. When agitated, she had a habit of jutting out her chin and pursing her lips, and she did so now.

"Well, look," Rueben said. "I'm disappointed about that, too. I wish everyone was going."

"I mean Stella and Tony are fine," Maureen said. "But I don't want to be the third wheel."

"Do I really have to say it?" Rueben asked mournfully, and he clasped her hand in his own. "I wasn't tight with them. You're my rudder. No you, no rudder. We'd all just sink to the bottom."

It was the kind of language she had grown accustomed to hearing from him, especially in times of stress. After the fall of Saigon in 1975, Vietnamese by the thousands crammed onto leaky clinker boats and set out into the South China Sea, and by the thousands they drowned. The lucky ones followed the Dutch oilrig lights to the refugee camp on Bidong Island, just off Malaysia's east coast, where they learned English and waited for the UN to deliver their fate.

"It's like I told you back then," Rueben said, yanking on the chest pocket of his t-shirt. He was tall and still bony. Lanky, he liked to say, and in a gesture Maureen recognized as contemplative, he lifted his glasses by one of the stems and scrunched up his nose as if repressing a sneeze. "We were just work buddies," he said, "but I didn't understand that. Then you showed up. And Thomas and Kathy and Kevin. You helped me understand."

She had lifted the veil from his eyes, he said once. He had been the first UN English teacher on the island, working cheek-to-jowl with Stella, a social worker, and Tony, an engineer. For six months they were the day-to-day UN presence, back in a time when, as Rueben put it, the Malaysians running the camp were as likely to put a gun to your head as say hello. Then the wire services printed some devastating stories, and along with bushels of money and supplies came Maureen, also an English teacher, and the other three principal members of the Club. Suddenly Stella and Tony were on the outside looking in.

"Yet here we are going," she said. "With Stella and Tony."

She could not keep the edge out of her voice. She had fallen head over heels for Rueben from the get-go, and he with her, and one of the first things he did after their first night together was to distance himself, politely, of course, and quietly, from Stella and Tony. They were presumptuous and pissy, he told her. They both had some kind of I-have-seen-the-abyss Lord Jim complex. What must his life have been like in the camp, Maureen used to wonder, before she was in the picture? Before Thomas and Kevin and Kathy declared their pairing an inspiration? The question had long ago dried up. Its answer had been without consequence for so long, she had simply stopped wondering.

Rueben reached over now and touched her arm. Weeks ago, they had agreed that the trip itself was the important thing. Who else was there wasn't supposed to be a deal breaker. "Help me understand," he said. "Where's this reluctance coming from?"

She had, in fact, been asking herself the same thing. The trip was all Rueben could talk about lately, and she had no intention of being the wet blanket. She knew, she said, how infantile it sounded, but remembering the old days and telling the old stories was one thing—she indulged in it herself at work, enjoying the admiration in her co-workers' eyes—but actually going back, with Thomas and Kathy and Kevin missing in action, was another thing entirely. When she imagined reuniting with the Club, laughing riotously, indulging their every whim, all she could picture was herself and her husband and the other three, sitting at a table with drinks in their hands.

But now, she told him, she couldn't get Stella and Tony out of her head. The more she thought about The Boat People Club, the more she suspected that if not for Thomas and Kathy and Kevin—all so witty, so kind, all so accepting—she probably wouldn't have hung out with the other two. Yet, she acknowledged, she could not even picture Stella or Tony anymore. She found herself accepting the fact of their physical existence as she did Bulgaria, as an article of faith. And that wasn't being fair, she knew—it was childish to linger on old, half-remembered slights—but in the camp she had been subject to their disapproval. What the source of the disapproval had been she couldn't recall, but she suspected it probably had a lot to do with the sort of girl she was back then, bookish and complicated in a gooney, perhaps trivial way. ("You weren't gooney," Rueben said. "You weren't trivial. Come on now.") She had been, she believed, uncommonly pliant and needy, and someone, she said, she doubted she'd even like anymore.

It was almost as if five people were going—them, Stella and Tony, and that damn ghost of herself. Crazy, wasn't it?

"No, it's not," Rueben said.

"I'm babbling."

"No, you're not," he said. "Talk it out."

All those old feelings, she told him: they were like some noxious vapor rising from the floorboards. They added a dimension of uncertainty to the trip, even dread, that she hadn't felt since going to live and work in the refugee camp in the first place. Back then, fresh out of college, she had signed on with a UN relief agency and raced headlong into a vast and terrifying unknown. She hadn't so much left for an adventure in Malaysia as she had escaped a life of exquisite narrowness in her mother's house. She had felt herself on the verge of disappearing. Back then she would have done anything to shuck off her own skin and leave behind all those ghastly organs, all those earnest, dumbshit bones—the whole smelly mess of her—on her mother's spectacular veranda.

How, she asked, shaking her head at the sheer wonder of it, how could your ancient insecurities just pull the rug out from under you sometimes, as if you were just along for the ride? How could you wake up one day and feel like you were going backwards?

"We can still cancel," Rueben said. He clutched the tickets in his fist and waved them around. "We'll lose some money, but that's okay. Really."

No. She would not hear of it. She was just having last-minute jitters, that was all. She was just finding it hard to accommodate memories from a lifetime ago. All that uncertainty, that lack of control. That horrible ignorance about what was really going on.

Her voice grew confident and firm. It never ceased to surprise her how saying certain things out loud sometimes seemed to make them true. She hadn't understood her misgivings in this way before, and in defining her anxiety, in giving it a shape and a clear, seamless contour, she felt it grow meek and small. She could manage this. Yes. That was the clarity of middle age, the power it gave you to see what would otherwise be an airy flutter out the corner of your eye.

— — —

This is also what she saw.

She saw that her husband's response had once again approximated hers, had the roles been reversed. He had pushed hard for her to go, yet he was prepared to cancel the journey if she found it unpalatable. That was his M.O.—their M.O., their signature behavior—and she took quiet pleasure in their refusal to lord it over each other. He was solicitous and gentle—how like a teenager she felt sometimes, thinking in terms such as *gentle*—and even now, on lazy Sunday mornings, she would wake up next to him and with her index finger trace little hearts across his bare back. Time, she wrote in her occasional journal, was both an enemy and a friend: she was graying, as was he, but now a life together was no longer an option among many other options. Now it had weight. It had *gravitas.*

Exactly. So she was not silly, was she?—no, she did not feel silly—she was not silly, then, to interpret their negotiations over the trip as yet another example of the pattern they had created. No law said that a woman on the cusp of fifty could not cultivate youthful, even magical, connections. No number of blacktop roads and telephone wires and concrete slabs could assert their primacy over an invisible realm. She still had her arguments with her husband, of course, and they both fell into periods of testiness and exhaustion, but those moments simply meant their blood was still pumping. Somewhere along the line, somewhere in the midst of their mistakes and false starts, they had developed what she liked to think of as a kind of ESP, and as was the case with all things invisible, the more she tried to understand it, the more it seemed to hover just beyond her grasp.

She sometimes tried to understand their connection by comparing it to things she did understand. But even the comparisons sounded silly—and, she had to admit, equally mysterious—so she kept her attempts at explanation to herself, scribbled into her journal in nearly incomprehensible handwriting, even to her own eyes.

The comparison she liked the best was from her childhood, when she was ten. Her mother had lived in Sacramento then, and the back yard spilled over into the yard of her best friend, Gloria. When the raked leaves from the neighborhood oaks grew so high the debris swallowed their legs, she and Gloria dared each other to leap backwards into the piles and pretend they were dead. It was a contest. Whoever got up first was the loser, so they filled each other's heads with stories of scorpions and flesh-eating moles nosing toward their privates. They stared into the spare, bright sky, and they let their bodies go limp and smelled the soil and leaves. They saw tiny stirrings in the pile, little quivers whose source they subjected to terrifying speculations. They heard rasping and grinding underneath, like paper tearing, and still they lay perfectly still for what felt like hours, and when the moisture finally leeched into Maureen's scalp and the cold began to burn her ears, she sometimes cried at the strangeness of the sensations and calmed herself by speaking to her friend in a loud and rapid pig latin.

With pig latin, you felt you had stumbled onto a secret code, one that worked not only for child words but for adult ones as well, and even for the words you made up and said only to yourself. That was what she had with Rueben: a secret, middle-aged code. It provided comfort and calm, and though it had never been put to the test, she indulged her fancy and assigned it talismanic powers. There was a mystery to the code, of course, just as there had been when she was a child. But the parameters of both were essentially the same. You didn't want to announce you were using a secret code any more than you wanted to explain your jokes, or to say why some things moved you to tears while others didn't. If you did, the magic was lost (just as saying certain things sometimes brought them into existence, she suspected that saying certain other things could make them disappear).

So the existence of the code, then as now, had to go unspoken. It had to be accepted as a gift. If she sat smartly at the table, her face smiley and receptive, and told Rueben their negotiations over the trip formed a pathway into a magical and delightful pattern, then their future exchanges might grow self-conscious. A certain falseness might creep into their words; a certain expectation, one that could not always be met, might develop. A certain magic might be lost.

They resumed checking their travel itinerary. Not everything thrived by being said. That was another thing middle age clarified for you: what should be said out loud, and what shouldn't.

— — —

They flew for two days, and over the Pacific, Maureen told her husband that all the time zone changes made you wonder if you were coming or going. Move the hand forward, move it back. Watches didn't make a lot of sense when you were traveling.

— — —

Stella and Tony were already in Malaysia, in the coastal city of Kuala Trengganu—the agreed-upon meeting site—and they had apparently marked their presence by telling the city's waiters about the imminent arrival of their friends. "You are Mister Rueben?" asked a plate-laden Chinese waiter, eavesdropping. It was still morning, and Maureen and Rueben sat drinking iced coffees in the open-air Han Sui Restaurant, trying to recall some forgotten detail about the camp. Rueben looked up from his glass and acknowledged he was indeed said Mister. "And this is my wife, Maureen," he said, nodding across the table. "Ah," the waiter answered, smiling hugely, but when his eyes roamed her face he cocked his head to the side as if presented with a question.

It had been a wonderful morning until the waiter's intrusion. Their bags were safely tucked away in their hotel. They were hungry and buoyant, and the sun hadn't yet turned so hot their scalps would itch. Over the horizon from the city was Bidong Island, thirty nautical miles out, and even from the confines of the Han Sui, well up the steep hill from the harbor, they smelled the dank water and the diesel soaking into the peeling green walls of the shopfronts. It was one of Maureen's sharpest memories of Kuala Trengganu—the oily, burning-rubber odor; the ruined exteriors of the open-air restaurants—and when she breathed the fragrance, she recalled the name of her favorite Chinese noodle shop, where they now sat and drank iced coffees.

Maureen leaned in. "So they mention you, but not me."

Rueben waved his hands around a bit and almost knocked over his drink. "Don't you think you might be jumping to conclusions?" he asked.

"Easy for you to say, Mister Rueben."

"Granted. But don't you think you might be putting a lot of weight on some waiter's expression?"

He was right, of course. She was being peevish—slap-me trolling, Rueben had once called it—hunting for insult until she found one. And that was a shame because she found the heavy tropical air and the colonial-style buildings and the languorous, lapping sounds of Malay in the restaurant intoxicating. She found herself delighting in the chicory-laced coffee and the ridiculous wall portraits of the state sultan and his wife, bedecked in medals and jowly as frogs. So she thanked her husband. In return, he nudged her under the table with his knee, and equilibrium was once again re-established.

The trip, she felt, had actually been going well. Surprisingly so. Had it just been two days ago that they arrived at Subang International and took a taxi into the capital? She wished they could have stayed in Kuala Lumpur longer, reliving their luxurious R & R leaves from the camp. She likened their itinerary to rushing down the basement stairs: the farther you went, the less certain your footing. They had stayed in Kuala Lumpur just long enough to book passage north. Now here they were in quiet Kuala Trengganu, recalling how they used to leap from the camp supply boat onto the city's harbor docks. Tomorrow, who knew? Stella and Tony were supposed to meet them in the morning down by the harbor. Then they'd all rent a boat and head on out to Bidong Island to see what was left.

She ordered another iced coffee. How odd: if she was heading down the basement stairs, then her husband seemed to be heading up. It was a curious feeling, bumping shoulders with him as they passed. But perhaps, she felt, she had allowed a lingering uncertainty to cloud her perceptions. Perhaps she hadn't given herself the chance to appreciate that now was no longer then.

In the capital, they had gone straight from the airport to the long-distance bus terminal and purchased tickets to Kuala Trengganu. Driving in, she couldn't stop looking out the window of the taxi. The old city, the city she remembered, had been replaced by an amusing tableau of ham-fisted ironies. Hawkers sold dried snakeskins in front of glass-plated high-rises. Women in tarp-like religious garb drove by in BMWs, mouthing rock songs ("Oh, hey," she said, "she's playing air guitar"). There was no litter on the streets now, she said, anywhere. How was that possible? She pointed: there, right there, can you believe it, a Baskin-Robbins?

Rueben had murmured agreement, though he seemed dismayed by the absence of certain ancient landmarks, certain oddball items that struck her as vaguely and unpleasantly charged with masculine fantasy. That was a side to him he hadn't expressed in a long time, and though she knew she should be encouraging, she also felt his revival and romanticizing of all things dead and gone to be—well, she'd tell him if he pressed—a tad perverse.

But perhaps, she felt, she was in some way partly to blame. Perhaps she hadn't paid enough attention to his recent bouts of withdrawal and self-loathing. Perhaps she hadn't lingered with him enough in the back yard, a glass of wine in her hand, interrogating him about Malaysia and the refugee camp, pre-her. Back when she hadn't been in the picture. Back in his *Ur* life, when it was just him and Tony and Stella and about a million boat people.

In the taxi she made a mental note to do more of that sort of thing, even though it was sometimes hard to endure the camp stories he told to anyone who asked. It was all she could do at those times not to interrupt him with news of the latest outrage from their mortgage company, or to soften the mood with a funny anecdote she had heard at work. When you thought about what shaped you, after all, didn't right now count for as much as way back when? Wasn't plain old yesterday as meaningful as yesterday plus twenty-five or more years? Surely lots of things, not just their exotic year in the camp, went into explaining her interest in soccer, or her expertise with Vietnamese *pho* and vermicelli noodles with duck sauce, or her liberal politics and confounding sense of *realpolitik,* or her refusal, even now, to show too much skin in public. For crying out loud, she said to him once, in a fit of pique: they weren't refugees. They just *worked* with refugees.

A few blocks from the buses, she caught her husband frowning. She prodded. After a rain back then, he told her, staring out the taxi window, the truck tires for some reason smelled like hothouse sex. So did the food. He couldn't even breathe in Kuala Lumpur years ago, he said, without thinking about open-heart surgery, or innards rotting in a pail. Malay women flirted outrageously with him, he said, leering at his wife and laughing. Giant spiders crawled into his shoes and left behind squirming egg sacs the texture of sponges. Mornings, old Chinese men with neck goiters walked the sidewalks, carrying hot spiced dumplings on poles strung across their shoulders. The city's finest hotels posted "No Spitting" signs in their lobbies. Wonderful, he mumbled. Erotic.

At the terminal, watching the driver unload their bags, Maureen asked him about what he had said. "Was that wistfulness speaking?"

Rueben snorted, then pointed to their idling bus. It was enormous and spanking new, with TV monitors hanging down from the overhead racks, as on an airplane. "*Look* at that thing," he said. He heaved his bag at the feet of the harried-looking bus driver, loading bulky items into the luggage bay. "Wistfulness," Rueben said then, searching the ceiling of the station. "That's a Heathcliff-on-the-moors word, isn't it? I'm still in the game, sweetcheeks." He grabbed her bag by the strap.

"Of course you are," she said.

"We are," he corrected.

"You bet we are."

His hand lingered on her luggage. "Would it be too obvious," he asked, "just to say a lot's changed around here?"

"A first kiss can happen only once," she said brightly.

Her comment did not go over well. He snatched up her bag a bit too insistently, she thought, a bit too rough. She didn't press the point.

They arrived in Kuala Trengganu around dawn, bleary-eyed despite the deep, comfortable seats and reasonable air-conditioning. She knew they had arrived when she looked past Rueben, out the coach window, and saw the giant tin-plated statue of a leatherback turtle along the ribbon of highway, a landmark that even way back when marked the city's southernmost approach.

"Tommy Turtle's still here," Rueben announced, pressing his face against the glass. She nodded, but said no more. Once, she had taken a night bus from the capital to Kuala Trengganu with Rueben and Tony, up the same highway. Tony had become indignant when they passed the landmark. He had started a loud diatribe, within earshot of their fellow passengers, about Malaysians caring more for the sea turtles that came ashore than for the boat people. Then Rueben had chimed in, equally indignant and loud. Embarrassed, she had curled up in her seat and pretended to nap, and perhaps in remembrance of that moment, she gave no reply to her husband and instead folded her arms across her chest.

Within minutes, Rueben was beaming. The city had changed much less than the capital. There had always been an outpost quality to Kuala Trengganu—the low-lying skyline, the grand blacktop roads leading to empty fields, men in sarongs and dusty *songkat* hats—and Rueben announced, with approval in his voice, that much of that remained. At the bus terminal they flagged down two trishaws to take them to the new South East Asia Concord, which, according to the brochures (she had put her foot down at the suggestion of backpacking it), was a four-star hotel with a swimming pool and indoor sauna.

They bounced over rubble and freshly painted walls, clutching their suitcases, passing so close to Indian laborers they could have reached out and wiped the construction dust from the men's arms. *"Matsalleh,"* Maureen heard. White person. The term was not friendly. Its source was a group of schoolboys on the corner, smoking and spitting. Some things are constants, Maureen thought, some things eternal, though she quickly admonished herself for the mean and small satisfaction the thought produced (the satisfaction, she concluded, was unacceptable: it implied a flattening of sensation, a kind of mummification, as if the boys had been placed under glass decades ago).

Up ahead, Rueben lifted his t-shirt and wiped his face on the material. He turned around in his seat, smiling, and pointed: to the right was the cobblestone road that led to the docks, where they'd meet up with Stella and Tony the next day. It was hard for her to imagine now, but the docks had been the scene of many emotional departures and arrivals. Back then, Bidong had been considered a hardship posting, and they all received lots of leave time—three weeks on, one week off. If you turned one way on the docks, toward the water, you boarded the camp supply boat that delivered you back into hardship. If you turned the other way, up the hill, you trishawed to the taxi stand, then piled into a roomy backseat and roared off to R & Rs of such pleasure she sometimes cried when they had to return.

Something about clutching her luggage, glimpsing from her seat the back of the driver's bare soles—they teased, playing peek-a-boo in his flip-flops—something about the jostling sensations made Maureen sure she had been on this very road many times years ago, in the back of a trishaw.

She pictured the trishaw rides clearly, more clearly, she realized, than she could picture her life in the camp. She would step off the boat with Rueben, haggard from three weeks on the island, and they'd both be bursting at the seams to indulge their every passion. There was a weight to their anticipation, and it was crisp and tingly: the heft of their backpacks, the citrusy smell of their clothes, the mercantile greetings from the bean-juice vendors—all seemed infused with special meanings and rewards. They'd trishaw to the taxi stand and head south, toward the capital, which sometimes meant chilidogs and Baked Alaska at the Continental, sometimes afternoons in the butterfly parks, or root-beer floats along Batu Road, or Bollywood films at the Lido. They ate flaming steaks at wainscoted colonial restaurants and planted their faces inches from rattling air-conditioners. At night they lay naked on a clean duck-feather bed and giggled and stroked each other's skin, and their hands and mouths melted into blurs, and when the motorcycle cowboys roared in the early morning down the wide, empty avenues, they awoke sticky with sex and fanned themselves with the sheets.

Where Tony and Stella went on leave, she was never sure. She had heard stories they slept together, even on Bidong. If the stories were true, then their behavior was tawdry, full of shrieking and grunting, offensive to Vietnamese sensibilities and, she had to admit, her own. Once you got past the librarian clichés, sex and propriety were not necessarily opposed, and the interplay of the two, in fact, created a sensual *yin-yang* effect, the existence of one always present in the other (even now, she followed certain unspoken protocols with her husband, certain fetishes of omission and commission that had over the years taken on a ceremonial flavor). Back then, she had insisted to Rueben that they not hold hands on Bidong. They were to appear as colleagues; they were not to invite gossip and spectacle. Pshaw, Rueben had replied, joshing, but he complied with her request.

An image came to her then: dozens of flip-flops sticking out of the mud, just outside Tony's quarters on Bidong. There was concertina wire around the relief workers' compound, and the flip-flops had appeared as if by magic one morning, on the refugee side of the wire. The footwear, one of the British doctors told her, must have belonged to the Vietnamese Pervert Patrol. He claimed that Vietnamese boys often sneaked in the middle of the night to the compound wire and listened to the white people in their bungalows. The mud was so thick, he said, it sucked the flip-flops right off their feet. "Picture this," he told her. "Tony and Stella in Tony's room. Humpy-humpy on the bed, loud as you please. I'll bet it was standing room only outside the wire."

What a thing to recall, Maureen thought, clutching her travel bag: a story about Tony and Stella going at it like wild beasts, a line of silent Vietnamese boys listening at the wire. Had the doctor been correct? The only part she knew was true, even now, was the aftermath. That Swedish social worker with the lilting English, what's her name, had begun crying, mysteriously, at the sight of all those flip-flops sticking out of the mud. *Too much death,* the Swede kept saying. *Too much. I cannot stand it.* A few days later the Swede got shipped off the island.

And turning a corner now, listening to the trishaw driver tinkle his little bell, Maureen suddenly straightened. The flip-flops must have reminded the Swede of little gravestones. That must have been what had set her off.

How could there ever have been a time, Maureen wondered, that she did not understand something so basic?

— — —

After iced coffees, Maureen and Rueben lingered for hours in the Han Sui, listening to Malay pop songs, then walked along Kuala Trengganu's main thoroughfares until they were sleepy. They still couldn't shake their jet lag, and the tropical air—that big ol' smothering paw, Rueben called it—was taking a toll. They took a long nap back in their hotel, then wandered around some more that night, finding themselves on some street they did not recognize. In the distance, the tide thumped against the giant harbor moorings. It was a moonless night, and all the streetside houses and shopfronts had been shuttered. Somewhere nearby, Maureen thought, Stella and Tony were probably drinking or walking around or doing only God knew what. She swore she could sense their presence. Were they perhaps sleeping together, even now? It was a ludicrous notion, she knew, but she could not let the image go. With Bidong Island just over the horizon, she felt as if she were nearing the basement floor, hearing throaty, scratchy noises off in the corner.

Earlier, during their midday nap, she had awakened and tried to broach the subject of Stella and Tony. On Bidong Island, she asked, had Stella and Tony actually slept together? How much had been rumor, and how much fact? Rueben told her he had heard the same stories she had. "No, seriously," she said. "You were there longer. You knew them better."

Then he shook his head and surprised her: Jesus, he told her, what *difference* could it make now? Stella and Tony had been good workers, right? Wasn't that enough? He looked at her dully, then closed his eyes and turned over in the bed.

But now they were holding hands, grateful for the breeze, careful not to trip in the darkness over rough patches of concrete. Behind them someone gunned a motorcycle, and at the same time the air turned foul and rotten, as if they had stepped through the envelope of some giant, gaseous bubble. Maureen cupped her hands over her nose. She looked for the source of the smell, and there, piled by a sewer grate, were pulpy, dark clods the size of bread loaves. "Who died?" she mumbled through her fingers. "P-U."

"Oh, that's bad," Rueben said, stepping into the street. He made a show of inhaling. He bent down to examine one of the clods. "Dead rats," he said, screwing up his face. "How about that," he said, inhaling again. "Just like Bidong, huh?" He leaned closer, squatting, and rocked on his heels, and the motorcycle suddenly roared forward—Maureen saw a wraparound helmet and a man with dark Malay coloring—and the driver veered his bike directly at her husband and hurtled toward him. Maureen watched intently, as if engrossed in some particularly dramatic movie scene. Rueben fell back on his hands, hard. The bike then swerved abruptly, away from her husband, and weaved slowly to the middle of the street. Rueben straightened, glaring now, wiping at something on his pants, and when the bike stopped, the driver turned his head, as if waiting for a response. "Hey," Rueben yelled. He charged the bike, and as he did, the driver shouted out something incomprehensible, a sharp, mocking bark, and roared down the street.

"Chickenshit," Rueben shouted after him. His hands were curled into fists. There was no movement: the storefronts remained shuttered; no one switched on a light. He might as well have been shouting at the ocean.

"That was deliberate," Maureen said. She could not get her feet to move. She pointed toward the bike. The driver must have been doing seventy.

"You better run, chickenshit," Rueben called out.

"Are you all right?" Maureen asked. Her voice was quavering, but she was now in control of her body and walked briskly to him. She touched his arm.

Rueben cocked his head, listening for the motorcycle's whine. "Chickenshit's turning left. Toward the roundabout."

"Are you all right?" she asked again.

"Chickenshit won't be if he comes back," Rueben said. He shook off her hand from his arm and stood with his legs wide apart, staring down the street.

"Could you just answer me, please?"

He grunted that he was fine, but his expression didn't soften. He didn't look at her. "Damn," he said, pounding his fist into his palm, then his voice seemed to explode. "That was sweet. *Sweet.*"

She looked to see if he was kidding, but he was staring beyond her, vigilant and alert.

— — —

In their hotel room they argued briefly. Maureen poured them both a scotch, her hands shaking, and when Rueben came back to the room with a bucket of ice, he said the ice was for her. He'd drink his straight, he said. And since when did he drink scotch straight? she asked.

"Since before we met," he said. "If that's okay."

He might as well have rolled his eyes. "That felt good back there?" she asked. "Is that what you said? 'Sweet'?"

"I might have," he said. "I don't know. It was kind of an intense moment. I wasn't keeping track."

"But it felt good. Honestly?"

"This is beginning to sound like disapproval," he said. "I sort of almost got killed."

"It's just you sounded weird."

"Did you hear what I just said? I almost got killed."

She looked at him a long time. He was standing at the foot of the bed, lifting his glasses by the stem and scrunching his nose. He seemed to be waiting. "What are we doing?" she asked.

"I don't know," he said evenly.

"I don't know, either."

"Then let's stop doing it."

"I agree," she said, nodding. "Let's." She held her arms out wide, and with pleasure she saw that Rueben understood her intention: they *faux*-ran in slow motion toward each other, feigning cartoonish expressions.

Of course everyone was a different person after a quarter of a century. The trick was to make your desires known to the person you used to be: stay away or please come in. You had to be clear on that. But as Maureen lifted first one leg, then the other, moving in aching, slow increments toward her husband, she could not help wondering if over the years she had interfered somehow with his conversations with himself. Even in the glacial calculus governing a life together, you were sometimes made privy to small, innocent-seeming errors you might have introduced years ago, errors that if unacknowledged might eventually invalidate the entire equation. A life together allowed such moments. It gave you the power sometimes to see right through yourself. Perhaps she had been graced with such a moment now. The lamps glowed seductively. Her skin felt on fire. Had she, she wondered, now touching her husband's fingers, now his hand, had she out of some tenacious flaw in herself encouraged him over the years to sever a connection too abruptly?

Or was the question too simple? When the motorcycle had veered toward him, she simply stood there, a worthless sentinel, while for all she knew her husband was about to die. Shameful. She could have at least shouted to him. She could have made her presence felt. Instead she had watched the whole thing unfold with a terrifying equanimity, with an almost serene resignation; then her whole body had tingled and gone soft, impervious to command, as if injected with syrup.

And now hugging Rueben tightly, now with purpose and force—"Let's make love," she said. "Okay? Now?"—she felt the return of an old fear: that she lacked a certain kind of fierceness, a capacity for entanglement and blood that others—Rueben, too, yes, most certainly him—that everyone she knew back then could plumb and summon, and thereby make themselves complete.

— — —

Maureen's first sight of Bidong Island had been through the rain-spattered cabin window of the UN supply boat, commanded, she still recalled, by a pot-bellied Malay who removed his flip-flops and piloted the craft with his bare feet. She had stood behind him in the dark cabin, out of the drizzle, not quite believing that a man vetted by a relief agency would actually steer such a large vessel by looping his toes around the spokes of the pilot wheel. Thomas, Kathy, and Kevin—the other new UN arrivals—stood outside under a canopy of goopy, engorged clouds, leaning against the railing at the edge of the prow. They began to whoop and point. Bidong had emerged from behind some fog and was now in view. Just like that, it seemed to Maureen, nothing else existed in the world, just the ocean and the sky and the small, green knuckle of land ahead. A volcanic cone formed the peak of the knuckle, jutting up the far side of the island in a dense carpet of vegetation (she could not help thinking of an old King Kong movie), then tapering to a deep orange gouge that stretched from the ridgeline down to the beach. The near side, rising slowly into a squat, round hill, was a blur. She saw faint ropes of smoke drifting up from a layer of scrub and palms, and hundreds of crisscrossing squares of color, like tiny regatta flags, mostly whites and blues, around which some giant dark mass seemed to wriggle.

The skipper turned his head. "You can see the people, yes?" he said in perfect English, indicating the wriggling mass; and when she stepped closer, squinting—yes, those *were* people, she confirmed—she saw blackened boat hulks sticking out of the sand and, off to the right, a deep cove shielded at either end by long peninsulas that ended in boulder-strewn fists angling sharply into the water. The cove was their destination. Arriving on Bidong, she had heard back in Kuala Trengganu, felt like the Charge of the Light Brigade. Cannon to the left. Cannon to the right. Cannon in front. Someone had spent a long time deciding on that description, she thought, and it had unnerved her. She made out a long, narrow dock stretching out to the middle of the cove, but everything behind it flickered into and out of focus. There were fires on the hillside, and smoke and fog obscured the trees and the lines of dark-haired people.

"Forty thousand boat people there," the skipper said, smiling. "How many are Communists, hey?" he added, his voice trailing off. It was a provocation, not a question. He squirmed in his chair, then clutched the armrest when the boat suddenly heaved.

Forty thousand refugees. She had heard sixty thousand earlier that day in Kuala Trengganu from some pompadoured Indian functionary in a safari suit. Did no one truly know how many Vietnamese were on the island? The Indian—"I am not from Indianapolis," he guffawed—had mentioned other numbers, too, figures numbing in their casual, rounded-off ease: the UN estimated, he said, that over a span of two years, two-hundred thousand Vietnamese had set out into the South China Sea. Of those, fifty- to one hundred thousand were estimated to have drowned or been murdered by pirates—or died of thirst, he added gravely, or of sunstroke, or of starvation. He then withdrew a document from a red folder. Someone had written *RPM*—Rape, Pillage, Murder—in large block letters at the top of the paper. That, he said, shaking the document over his head, was the most common code written onto refugee-history forms. Just to let you know, he said. Just so you won't blunder about.

There would be no slow introduction. Already the musty, wormwood odor of the cabin was thickening, and as the skipper twirled the wheel violently toward the cove—he leaned back, giving his feet room to maneuver—a current of sour, tangy air filled the cabin. She flinched, then leaned against the wall, across from the pilothouse doorway. The skipper pulled back on a lever, slowing the craft, and the waves strong-armed the hull, thumping the boat leeward, which caused him to swear and spin the wheel first one way with his left foot, then the other. Ocean spray spilled over the prow and onto her comrades. The bottoms of their pants were now dark and sopping, and even from the cabin she could see Kathy's bra strap outlined against her soaked t-shirt. They were still whooping. Kevin raised his fist and yelled.

Deep into the cove, a long, high-keeled boat bobbed alongside the dock, and on its deck dozens of men, all thin and dark-haired, all bare-chested, lifted boxes and green bundles onto their shoulders. Off to the right were barn-like wooden structures ringed with concertina wire. She let her gaze climb up the hillside, and there were the bits of color she had noticed before, all those tiny white-and-blue regatta flags, which she now understood to be laundry hanging from lengths of pink raffia and shelters of rusting sheet metal and tarpaulin. How could so many people live on such a tiny speck of land? The island, she had been told, was zero-point-eight miles, east to west, but that fact, so precise and for some reason so comforting, seemed at odds with the unending crowds of people, all milling about (were the women actually dressed in pajamas?), some pointing and shouting, some carrying plastic jugs or sewing machines or planks of wood. A circle of men seemed to be berating someone; one raised his arm and brought it down hard again and again, as if raining down blows.

On the beach to the left of the dock, a head-high wall of color smoldered in the rain. The camp garbage dump, the skipper shouted over the din, noting her attention. It stretched all the way to the far outcropping, and when some men with hook poles began tearing at the wall, she saw a solid crust of yellow-green pineapple husks and swirling brown cabbage, then twisted red Marlboro cartons and strips of cloth and blue tarp winding in and out like ribbons, and glistening, creamy pockets of white and yellow, all supported by foundations of crumbly gray and brown. Bluebottles shimmered over human and garbage alike, and above the constant yelling a loudspeaker squawked non-stop, a whiney *ching-chang, ching-chang,* which she now realized had to be spoken Vietnamese.

She waved to her comrades on the prow. She wanted to be seen. She needed Thomas or Kevin or Kathy to turn around and wave back, to return her smile and to make a face that said *Are we hallucinating?* But no one turned around. They were all shouting and hoisting up their travel bags and backpacks. Someone was now shouting hysterically through the loudspeakers, but the shouting seemed to have no effect on the crowd—no one began running, no one even stopped to listen—and as the skipper cut the engine and let the boat bob toward the dock, the water off to Maureen's left suddenly began to roil, and a great sheet of white foam chattered in all directions. Maureen dropped to the back bench. She wrapped her arms around herself. She heard a loud galloping sound rise from the water, and what looked at first to be a giant, thrashing beast she then realized was hundreds of flying fish, all leaping together; and as she watched them leap and disappear back into the water, she noticed a dark, clotted line out the corner of her eye, swaying back and forth with the tide, all along the edge of the wall of garbage. She saw the tails. Rats. The island was full of them, she heard later, and when they swarmed at night they were pressed by sheer numbers off the garbage and drowned in the foam.

The tangy smell in the cabin was so thick now she put her hand to her nose. They had arrived. The boat clunked loudly against the tires lashed to the pilings, and the skipper, still seated, leaned back and shouted something in Malay out the pilothouse door to someone on the dock. The dockside man squatted and shouted something back. He was dressed in military fatigues. Hanging from his belt was a long handgun in a black holster.

Bye-bye, the skipper said to her, so she hoisted her backpack upright and began to adjust the shoulder straps. She pulled the straps tighter, then she loosened them. She tightened them again. Nothing seemed more important now than making sure her straps were perfectly adjusted. She felt her heart race, and when she looked up she found herself overcome with a sudden fondness for the cabin's dark interior. There was a completeness to it, a harmony created by its compact fire extinguisher, strapped like an infant into a metal wall strap, and by its nicked tongue-in-grove paneling (like her mother's den, she realized), by its movie-theater odor, its shiny metal-trimmed instrument panel, its church-pew benches, its straight, sturdy lines, its generous and maneuverable space.

Outside there were only accusations. How, she wondered, could she climb the short metal ladder that had been lowered down onto the deck? She had never climbed such a ladder before. She had never stepped onto a metal rung from a boat. And the rough planks and pilings of the dock were oozing some kind of gooey substance into the water. What if she slipped? From the bench she could see the bare, hairless legs and feet of the Vietnamese men now swarming the deck. Then a cloud of diesel erupted from below the engine line, spitting black globs onto them all, even as the men streamed by the pilothouse door, half-naked, swinging giant tins of kerosene onto their shoulders.

The skipper twirled around in his seat and said something harsh-sounding to her, in Malay. He seemed to be appraising. "Maureen," shouted Thomas. He stuck his head into the doorway. Strands of hair were plastered to his forehead. "They want us on the dock, pronto."

She nodded. Grunting, she heaved her backpack onto the bench. She fiddled again with the straps, pulling the material first one way through the stop, then the other. Then she swore, a sharp, angry yelp, and began to rummage through one of the canvas pockets.

"Skedaddle time," Thomas shouted at her. He looked delirious. An air horn went off on shore, and he turned toward the source, then slapped the doorway trim hard and picked his way through a tangle of deck rope, toward the dock ladder. But still she remained on the bench, unzipping one of her backpack's side pockets, then zipping it up again. She sensed the skipper staring. She shook her head at the pocket, as if in exasperation, then untied the top flap and frowned. She stuck her right hand into her backpack, but she might as well have reached into someone's Halloween sack. She could not recognize the shapes or textures.

"Come on, come on, you gotta go." The accent was American. She looked up and saw a tall man in glasses who identified himself as Rueben. In her right hand, she realized, she was holding a red cotton blouse. She began to unfold it, first the right sleeve, then the left. One of the collar buttons was dangling, so she lifted it gently until the thread was taut. The stitching had failed. When could that have happened? That morning the shirt had been in perfect condition. She was sure of it.

But she sensed the tall man standing over her now. The pockets of his jeans were black with mud.

She looked up into his face. "I'm frozen," she said.

He cupped his hand to his ear. Some kind of engine was roaring to life at the end of the dock. "What?" he shouted.

She waved him closer. She whispered: "I just need to put my clothes away."

He began to sway, just inches from her face, and she heard him and the skipper exchange a few words in Malay. He took one end of the blouse in her hand and ran it through his fingers. For a moment, the noise outside seemed to subside, and she was certain she heard him humming. He looked down at her blankly, still running the material through his fingers, and it occurred to her that he was arriving at some kind of decision. "Here," he said then, "let's put your shirt back." She did as he said. She brought her end of the blouse up, and he folded the other end and let it rest in her hand. "Now let's just lay this on top," he said.

She did this, too, opening the flap and pressing the blouse down.

"My legs won't work," she said, looking at the floor.

"Okay," he said. He clasped her shoulders and, smiling now, lifted her to her feet. "You should be one of the longshoremen," he said. "They don't work, either." She understood the joke. She tried to laugh, but nothing came out. "Just put your arm around my shoulders," he said, and she did. But still she could not walk: her legs hung limply and her knees buckled. He helped her take a step, then whispered, "It's okay. This happens to everyone. It's not a big deal."

She knew he was lying. She knew nothing like this had ever happened to anyone. She knew it was a big deal, that it would mark her as irrelevant, perhaps as an object of derision. It might even get her shipped back to Kuala Trengganu on the next supply run, and if that happened, then the Indian in the safari suit would stick a plane ticket into her purse, and everyone would smile and shake her hand, and with much crocodile sympathy they would drive her to the airport and she would fly halfway around the world back to her mother in California, too ashamed for weeks on end to tell her why she was back in her living room, crying in front of the TV. But here was this man clamping one arm around her waist and dragging her backpack with the other. Here was this stranger choosing to forgive her. "No big deal," he kept whispering. "Don't sweat it." They made it to the door, where he turned to the skipper. "She's seasick," he shouted, and she was so grateful she nodded and stepped out the door with him and into the rain and the smell and the noise.

And now in the open-air Choong Tan restaurant, which offered an unfettered view of the Kuala Trengganu harbor, she was sitting in the morning glare with her husband and with Stella and Tony, neither of whom had known anything about her long-ago arrival on Bidong Island because Rueben had never said a word about it. Now here were Stella and Tony who were so excited to see them they had leaped from their chairs and stood at the restaurant entrance, waving like signalmen. Stella had shrieked, then buried them both in a swaying, moist hug. Tony kissed Maureen's cheek hard, holding her so tight she felt each finger pressing into her back.

They all pulled out chairs and sat at a table, immediately chattering away, laughing their heads off ("Look at us! Can you believe it? Can you?"). The welcome had been so enthusiastic that for a moment Maureen gave herself over wholly to the reunion. Stella, in fact, kept leaning over and touching her arm, as if they were long lost sisters. The morning sun had burned off the mist, Maureen blurted out then, and didn't that make the breeze smell like cornbread? It was a foolish thing to say, but Stella immediately inhaled with pleasure. "Oh, *doesn't* it?" Stella said. Then Tony joined in. "That's it *exactly,*" he exclaimed, and both he and Stella smiled with an eagerness that said she could blurt out anything—Can I punch your face? Are you a dog-faced baboon?—and they'd be okay with it. Yet even as Stella and Tony bent forward in their chairs, rocking and smiling, Maureen observed them scanning her face and body, their camera-shutter eyes shifting rapidly, jerking up and down, then across, the movements so fast and small they were probably not even aware their pupils betrayed them. What judgments, Maureen wondered, were being confirmed? What evaluations?

So perhaps out of resentment Maureen established that she, too, was holding part of herself in reserve. *Quid pro quo.* She was, she decided, using them as well as reuniting with them. They fulfilled a secret function for her: they gave her husband what she could not provide. She hadn't wanted to talk to him earlier that morning, beyond what was expected, and on the way down to the docks she chose to lag behind. He had been quiet, and it was clear their argument the night before was still fresh in his mind. *Give him some space,* she told herself, so she feigned interest in a batik sundress on display. She'd catch up, she told him, waving him on, and when he walked away, engrossed with the Chinese shopfronts and glimpses of the harbor, she observed him closely, looking where he looked, imagining the sights through his eyes. He stopped every now and then and stared at something unremarkable—a yellowed plaster building, a section of cobblestone, a paint-chipped railing—and sometimes he'd smile.

She knew he wasn't really recalling the past. He was measuring his sense of himself in the present against himself in the past. Could he leap the dock railings now? Could he still choke down a slice of smelly durian fruit? Could he walk for hours in the sun? And in looking at him, examining his expression when he turned his head toward the harbor, he appeared baffled, in pursuit, it seemed to her, of what was after all only a modest and homely satisfaction. He wanted only to know that he had not betrayed himself. For him, there was no need for red Ferraris, or skydiving lessons, or humiliating flirtations with waitresses (he had always been self-regulating in that way). He was not asking for the world; he was not forging other attachments by squashing what they had created together. She stuck out her arm in his direction, as if to touch his tiny image, then let her arm drop to her side. She would give him this. Completely. She would not make him self-conscious or ashamed.

With Tony and Stella sitting across the table, he seemed energized. He was waving his arms around, laughing, speaking louder and louder.

She would indulge him anything, yes. They all toasted each other, and they toasted the three missing members of the Club. They shouted out names—Mr. Duong, Miss Lai, little Chi; Roland, Nina from Norway, Johann the Shirtless—and the names led to other names, and though Maureen didn't always follow, all her husband and Stella and Tony had to do was raise a finger to conjure up stern Task Force chief Rahim, who always lectured, or puff up their cheeks to summon that fat Bible-thumper—what was his name?—who gobbled all the meat during meals. They couldn't get enough of looking into one another's faces.

"To Bidong Island," said Tony, raising his glass. "Where all the acid commandos went to party." Tony had years ago been handsome, but even with his curly black hair, cut short now, and his faded tattoo of a refugee boat on his right forearm, he could no longer hide his paunch or his sun-ravaged skin. His teeth, Maureen thought, looked smaller somehow—everything about him seemed worn and ground-down—though he had the same appealing broad smile.

"To The Boat People Club," said Stella, and they all raised their glasses again and clinked them together. Stella's long blond hair, which she had always loved to sweep back from her forehead, had gone white, though she hadn't changed her hairstyle. She looked to Maureen as though she had stepped out of a photograph from her refugee-camp days and simply strapped on a few sand packets around her waist and hips. Her thick, pug nose still leaned to the left, and Maureen swore she had worn the same white peasant blouse, with the same lace trim on the sleeves and bosom, for her going-away party on Bidong.

They all sipped their drinks noisily, and when they were finished, Tony asked them if they knew Bidong Island wasn't even on Malaysian maps nowadays. True, he said: he had bought more than a dozen maps just to make sure. The island's structures, its dock, the hospital, even the sewage canals—everything, he'd heard, had been torn down or plowed under. Supposedly there wasn't a trace left. The island was now owned, he found out, by some Chinese businessman ("Fucking Chinese," he said tersely. "Fucking Malaysians.") who was going to open it to tourists as part of a snorkeling adventure package.

Rueben slammed down his glass at the news. Maureen hesitated, then looked at her husband and slammed hers down, too.

— — —

They drank all day, first iced tea, then coffee, then bottles of Anchor beer, and by the time the starlings came out in the afternoon, darting between the eaves of the restaurant, Maureen was ready to leave. The other three were still going strong, laughing themselves silly one minute and speaking with somber intensity the next. They talked as though the past twenty-five years had been a fraud, a hologram life, as if nothing of substance had truly occurred, and though she understood that the extreme nature of their claims was a way of underscoring their delight, she could not help feeling insulted. Apparently keeping a steady job and rising through the ranks and rejoining society was not worthy of discussion. Apparently maintaining a long marriage and tending to the house you paid for with your own money counted for little. At one point Tony checked his watch and frowned. Maureen caught his eye, and his sheepish grin told her she was right: he was imagining them just returned from leave, ready to head on down to the docks to catch the final supply boat run to camp.

"Remember Mr. Quang?" said Tony. "The Zone F dude who kept stealing blackboards?"

"That coconut head," Rueben said, grinning.

"Seven years on Bidong," Tony said. "Even the Australians turned him down. That, my friends, was the original down, brown, and around guy."

"I can't believe we're talking like this," said Stella. "'Coconut head.' 'Down and brown.' I haven't talked like this since we all left."

Tony laughed. "Weren't you the one who said Bidong was the cure for white person's disease? Check your bullshit at the door and all that?"

Maureen spoke up suddenly. "I couldn't have lived there for seven years. One was hard enough."

Stella touched her arm and looked at her with what seemed to Maureen appalling sympathy. It was maddening, like being compared to a blade of grass peeking out from the sidewalk—so plucky and minor, so unabashedly fragile. Tony was no better. He continued talking as if she hadn't said a word. Stella laughed at something he said, then turned her attention back to him and Rueben.

Stella revealed that she was working on a doctorate in comparative literature and, as she put it, was between marriages. She was ready to pack up at a moment's notice, she said with what seemed to be pride: let the matrons obsess over their marigolds and copper-plated wall hangings. When Maureen talked about working as a proposal writer for Boeing, Stella had nothing to say. Neither did Tony, who announced with challenge in his voice that he had never left the refugee business. For the past decade he had been in and out of Africa, working to eradicate parasites from drinking water. Ever since Bidong, he said, waving his hand toward the harbor, he had been home only a few times. But he could tell you the name of every relief agency director in central Africa. All, he said, were wankers. "Zaire, Rwanda, Burundi, Tanzania," he said, "you name it. Those places are hardcore and you need ass-kickers in charge. Bidong was like a country club."

"Tony, you know that's not true," said Stella.

Tony smiled. "Okay, you may be right. I don't know. Maybe it's just I haven't talked about Bidong to anyone who's interested in way too long. Does anyone besides me feel like only other people like me—and that would be you guys—have even *heard* of the boat people?"

Stella said, "It was a quiet holocaust for the Viets, wasn't it? All those people drowning. That lousy camp."

"No one remembers," said Rueben.

"Just us chickens," Tony added.

"What's that line?" said Stella. "'When history is annihilated there can be no closure, only a hole, an emptiness, an intimation.'"

There was silence. "Ph.D. candidate Stella is very deepeth," said Tony, and he nudged Reuben's arm.

"Most deepeth," agreed Rueben.

"Yes, gentlemen?" Stella said. "Mockery?"

"That's a mighty high horse you're speaking from, Stella," said Tony.

Stella smiled genially, then looked at Maureen. "What about it, Maureen? Is my horse taller than yours?"

"Don't look at *me,*" said Maureen, laughing. "I never made any claims about Bidong. I was just the latecomer, remember?"

"My little hard-hearted Hannah," Rueben said, patting her arm.

Maureen looked at her husband. He was smiling, and after some hesitation she decided to return the smile.

"I joke, of course," he said to her.

"It's getting late, isn't it?" Maureen replied.

No one said anything. Tony took a sudden interest in his beer bottle and began peeling off the label. Stella waggled her head, as if listening to music, and Rueben lifted one his bottles and stared at its logo. "I'll tell you what," said Tony, looking up. "Everything's still open. How about Rueben and I go see what we can find out about tour boats to Bidong?"

"Maureen," said Stella. "Do you want to do a little batik shopping while the boys are away?"

"Sounds great," Maureen said. She scooted back in her chair.

"I need to stop by my room first and change," Stella said, turning to

Maureen. "That okay with you? I'm sweating through my clothes."

Maureen was already standing and counting out money for their beers.

— — —

When they rounded the corner, Maureen saw the *Ping's Anchorage and Hotel* sign and realized it was the same hotel where she and Rueben had spent their first night together. Back then, the hotel had been well-maintained, boasting cheap rooms and a lively rooftop bar where, after ducking under the lines of drying towels and linen, you could look out over the city in privacy. The building was in shambles. Some of the windows had been boarded over, and a pile of broken bricks lined both sides of the back exit. Even the hotel's sign was faded and stained, and next door, which had been an Indian restaurant, was now a billiards room with a darkened shopfront window.

"Did you and Rueben ever stay here?" Stella asked sweetly, and something about her tone told Maureen she knew very well they had. She was testing, Maureen knew, giving her the opportunity to act the part of the possessive shrew. There was, in fact, and this was something she had always freely acknowledged, the remote possibility that Rueben and Stella might have had some brief romantic relationship, pre-her. Anything was possible—but for God's sake, they were on their third decade together. They were still going strong. What did she care, she once said to her mother, if her husband, pre-her and thus not actually her husband, had ridden naked on the backs of giant tarantulas? She was not so arrogant as to claim his history as hers (nor, in her opinion, did white people have the right to claim the history of the boat people). When history is annihilated . . . what a clever-sounding load of nothing. Stella would have gotten along famously with her mother. "Sounds a bit chilly, dear," mother had said about her tarantula comment. "I mean, seriously? If it doesn't involve you then it doesn't matter?" And now here was Stella, fishing the same waters.

When Stella opened the door to her room, the first thing Maureen noticed was the exposed wires leading to the electrical box, all painted, like the walls, a hospital green. Decades ago she had found the insides of cheap Malaysian hotel rooms calming. Nothing was hidden. Nothing threatening lurked below the surface. But now she could not help thinking of the inside of a garage. The walls were nicked and peeling. There were no top sheets on the bed. The bare fluorescent ceiling light flickered when Stella clicked it on, and bookending the dirty window slats were torn and faded blue drapes. The sound of a running toilet issued from behind the bathroom door.

"So you're going Bohemian," Maureen said.

Stella laughed. "Well, originally I had planned on staying someplace more upscale. But as soon as I stepped foot in the city, I knew I wanted to feel certain things again. You know?"

Maureen assured her she did.

Stella hefted a suitcase onto her bed and began rooting through it. "Was I too high-falutin' back at the restaurant?" she asked, tossing aside a pair of jeans. "I seem to have struck a nerve with Tony and Rueben. They thought I was being pretentious."

"I apologize for Reuben's response," said Maureen.

"Well, you know what was going on, don't you? The unspoken rule in relief work is that you don't talk about the big picture to each other. That's for visitors and movie stars."

"I never heard of a rule like that," said Maureen.

"I just mean when you *truly* get your hands dirty you don't have much patience with all the blah-blah."

"And you think that applies even now?"

"Oh, sweetie," said Stella. "Even more now. Bidong was a central life event for all of us." She waved her hands around. "For some of us. For me. I'm just trying to see what we did from a broader perspective now, and if that involves some blah-blah, then so be it. But I've always thought if you don't remain loyal to what moves you, it disappears like everything else."

Maureen frowned. "Is that another rule?"

"I'm sorry. I think I've offended you. I just take certain things for granted. I probably shouldn't do that."

Maureen shrugged.

"Does he talk much about Bidong?" asked Stella.

"Rueben?"

"Yes. Does he ever bring up working there?"

"Occasionally," Maureen said.

"What sorts of things does he say?"

She looked at Stella quizzically.

"Oh, that must sound weird. Sorry. I think I'm still jazzed about being here. Motor mouth." She returned to her suitcase and pulled out a blue blouse made of gauzy material.

"What do you think?" Stella said, waving it like a flag.

"Ooh-la-la."

"You think I'm trying to impress Tony?"

Maureen said no.

"I had a thing for Tony back then, you know. Did you know that?"

"I might have heard rumors," Maureen said. "I don't know. I didn't care then and I don't care now. Not my business."

"Oh, dear," said Stella, laughing. "Okay. If you say so."

"I do."

"Fair enough," said Stella. She held up the blouse for inspection. "So you think this is too revealing? Like I'm trying to act twenty again?"

"I make no judgments," answered Maureen, holding up her hands.

Stella laid the blouse on the bed. "Maureen, you're just like I remember. It's like Nabokov says. Time doesn't exist."

Maureen shook her head. "I think it might if you choose to let it."

"*Touché,*" said Maureen, approvingly. "So look, does Rueben ever mention the Vietnamese camera guy? Mr. Tan? It was right before you arrived."

"I don't recall," said Maureen. "I don't think so."

"Really? Well, you might ask him. I'd be curious to know what he says. Not that I *care* care." Her smile, Maureen thought, was mocking. "Just for curiosity's sake."

— — —

The plan was for everyone to meet up again by the sidewalk food stalls off the harbor. Maureen and Stella had Rueben and Tony peek inside their department store bags and exclaim over the batik. Then Stella leaned back. On to the issue at hand, she said.

"Well," said Tony, "we went to all the tour-boat places."

"Five, wasn't it?" said Rueben.

"Right," Tony agreed. "You're not going to believe this. The cheapest price for a boat out to Bidong is four hundred U.S. What you get is an early drop-off and a pick-up around five."

"Four hundred," said Maureen. "I thought the plan was to see it, not buy it."

"That's what I told the guy," said Rueben. "They wanted four-fifty at the other places. One guy said four seventy-five."

"I told him make it an even five and I'd pick my own pocket," said Tony.

"There's more," said Rueben. "Most of them had to ask where Bidong was. One guy looked at his map and said it didn't exist. So Tony says, 'if Bidong doesn't exist, then I must not exist, either.' Then he does this little ghost noise. Hooo. Hooo. That shut the guy up."

"You could have just shown him your passport," Maureen said. "That's proof."

Everyone ignored her.

"They all said wait a year until the snorkeling trips begin," said Tony. "Like we're just tourists. What'd that one guy say? 'Nuttin' dere. Why you want to go?'"

"Know what I think?" said Rueben. "I think the Malaysian government wants to erase all signs they kept the Viets there. They don't want bad press. No 'whatever happened to?' stories in the paper."

"Too much refugee abuse," said Tony, shaking his head. "Too many skeletons in the closet."

"I still cry sometimes when I think about it," Stella remarked.

Maureen spoke: "Are we sure we want to spend all that money? To go where nothing's left?"

Stella looked at her sternly. "I for one am sure," she said. "That's a chapter of my life out there."

"Mine, too," said Tony. "It's like Genesis. Chapter One. 'And God created the refugees and set our asses down next to them.'"

Everyone seemed to be waiting. Rueben rubbed at something on the tabletop. He looked up and nodded. "And mine," he said.

"Okay then," said Maureen. She stuck her hand into her shopping bag and pressed the material down with more force than she intended. "Majority rule."

— — —

Tony and Stella left almost immediately to confirm the boat reservation for the following morning. Later that night, they all agreed, they'd drink lots of Anchor beer and snack on bowls of tiny rice-padi fish at an Indian place Tony had passed, just up from the harbor. Before Tony rose from the table, he turned to Rueben and said, "You two probably want some alone time, huh?" Stella made a humming noise that sounded like agreement.

Rueben gave no response, but Maureen could tell the comment did not sit well with him. He watched them walk away, all the way to the end of the block, and his mouth moved a little as if he were rehearsing snappy comebacks. She imagined what must have been running through his head: Stella and Tony gossiping about how he'd have to tip-toe around his sour wife; Stella and Tony winking at his domesticity.

In other circumstances, she would have caught his eye and shared a mocking joke, something about Tony and Stella revealing themselves as willful children. True, she *did* want a moment alone with her husband, but Tony's comment, apparently intended to demonstrate his insight into long-term unions, revealed no understanding of accommodation. It was the sort of comment she might have expected a quarter of a century ago, back when she and Rueben argued as much to influence other people's opinions of them as to influence each other.

There was Tony's collateral insult to consider, as well. The fact that he had dragged a caricature of her into his scenario (did he assign her image a matron cut, her longish hair clipped short and sensible?) required some kind of response, at the very least a show of irritation, which she now expressed by exhaling loudly. At the same time, she acknowledged a surge of resentment toward her husband. Granted, she could have been more enthusiastic about shelling out all that money for the boat. But he could have tried harder to support her in front of Stella and Tony. He should have. Else, he should have opened his mouth and actually said, out loud, that money and his wife's reservations meant nothing next to Bidong.

"They're still pissy, aren't they?" said Rueben. "All those assumptions." And then she understood something else. He was trying to mollify her. If he went on the boat alone, they'd think he had a sulky missus pouting back in the hotel, ready to give him what-for when he returned. It was all so juvenile on her husband's part, so dismissive of their actual patterns, that she experienced for an uncomfortable moment a flaring of conviction and, at the same time, a retreat of certain indulgences she had regarded as bedrock.

"Are you saying that to shut me up?" she asked. "You seem to be having a great old time with them."

He was telling her the truth, he told her, but then he had no more to say. He studied his beer bottle.

"Okay, I choose to believe you," she answered, though she did not believe him.

They sat a while longer, watching an old Malay man pour his coffee into a saucer and drink from it. She had forgotten that particular restaurant etiquette, and she was about to comment on its survival when she put together what had just transpired between her and her husband. They had just enacted as theater, as an echo of lived events, what they had once enacted as a matter of definition. On Bidong, he had sided with her over them. Now he seemed to be hedging his bet.

Back in their hotel, she got him talking.

"I had an odd conversation with Stella today," she said. "In her room."

"Oh?"

"She asked me what sort of things you talked about. About Bidong, I mean."

"What did you tell her?"

"I didn't."

"Loyalty," Rueben smiled. "I like that."

"No," she said. "It just seemed like such a proprietary question, you know?"

Rueben nodded.

"She asked me if you ever mentioned a Viet who had something to do with cameras. A Mr. Tan."

"On Bidong?"

"Of course on Bidong."

"Before you arrived?"

"Yes. Are you being obtuse?"

"Sorry," he said. "I'm just surprised she'd bring it up."

She put her hands on her hips. "Are you going to tell me?"

"Well," he said, "it's not something that stands out. I'm not even sure I can remember it right."

He did, in fact, remember it quite well. He told her that before she arrived, there had been a yellow line painted on the Bidong dock, and no refugee was to step over the line unless they had a special badge handed out by the Malaysians. Mr. Tan, he recalled, had bribed some of the guards to buy him an expensive camera and rolls of film on the mainland. He made a lot of money taking pictures of fellow refugees decked out in their finest. They all loved, in particular, to pose in front of the vessels that arrived weekly to take away the happy recipients of resettlement papers, and they proudly displayed their special badges. But to take the photos, Mr. Tan had to step over the yellow line. Normally it wasn't a problem. The guards got a cut of the profits. It was a tidy arrangement for everyone.

But one day some asshole Malaysian colonel visited the island, and when the colonel saw Mr. Tan step over the line, he demanded that the refugee be taught a lesson, then and there. The colonel knew what was going on. He knew discipline had broken down. So the guards shoved Mr. Tan back behind the line. They rough-talked him a little, then they just stood there, jabbering, until the colonel exploded and upped the ante: whack the Viet around right now, publicly, or he'd make sure the man's resettlement interviews got canceled.

So the guards whacked Mr. Tan around in front of the colonel and all the refugees crowding the beach. They pulled out rattans and blistered his head. They struck him on the back with the stocks of their rifles. They formed a circle and kicked him hard when he fell, and you could hear the thump of their boots all the way down to the relief workers' compound.

As Rueben was telling the story to Maureen, she noted that his voice was growing louder. He was moving his hands, as if pushing someone.

"Did you know him?" she asked.

"A little," he said. Then he frowned at her. "This isn't about standing up for a friend. It's bigger. And you know what?"

She waited.

"I came this close to stepping in and trying to stop it. I was on the steps leading down to the beach, and you know how it was. If I'd made a big enough stink, I might have been able to stop it."

He may have been right. Before she arrived, the relationship between the Malaysian guards and the relief workers had been complex and unpredictable. Both were backed by powerful, competing infrastructures, and sometimes the white skin of the relief workers trumped the automatic weapons of the guards. Sometimes it didn't. You never knew. But as Rueben had once observed, in public scenes the white people often held the advantage. In public scenes you could put on your powder blue UN t-shirt and say you were going to file a report over the shortwave, and if you were lucky you could shame people into obeying you.

"Okay," Maureen said. "But they probably would have kicked you off the island later. Where would that have left you?"

"That's not my point. Come on. I didn't really care about that stuff then. I ran to the top step, and I was just about to tell them to back off. Then I see Mr. Tan looking at me. His eyes are telling me no. And they're telling me yes, too."

She pictured Rueben charging forward, then stopping dead in his tracks. He would have understood the logic of the situation. If he tried to stop the beating, Mr. Tan would have languished even longer in the camp. If he didn't, Mr. Tan would end up in the camp hospital. Which could Mr. Tan stand more? It must have been a difficult decision.

"Can you imagine that?" said Rueben. He paused. "He about bored a hole through my head."

She threw up her hands as if in irritation, but she was not irritated. She was confused. "Why do you suppose Stella wanted me to ask you about this?"

"Hey," he said. He seemed flustered. "Maureen, I don't know. Do you hear what I'm saying? What would you have done?"

"Not a clue," she said.

He frowned at her. "I couldn't decide. I just stood there on the top step and watched the whole thing."

"Okay. I'm sorry to hear that."

He pulled off his shirt and walked toward the bathroom.

"What am I not getting?" she asked. "Why would Stella bring it up?"

He didn't have an answer for her. He pushed up his glasses and shook his head. He mopped his face with his shirt. "All I can tell you is it bugged me," he said. Then he was in the bathroom.

She called out to him. "What about the part where I arrived and everything was okay again?" But he had already turned on the water.

— — —

The Indian place turned out to be darker and noisier than expected—Tony asked the waiter to turn down the sound system, but the man only giggled—and they had to shout across the table or lean forward until they appeared to be kissing. After an hour or so, Maureen looked around and saw the dark, alien faces staring at their table, and she was momentarily embarrassed at being part of the commotion, shouting and drinking and calling out in Malay for more beer and snacks. Years ago she might have whispered "you guys" to her companions and waited for them to look where she was looking and quiet down. But now such niceties seemed beside the point. She was no longer the little ambassador, influencing foreign opinion one local at a time.

She was in fact enjoying a sense of abandon, clenching the neck of her bottle in her fist, the way she had drunk in college. She felt touchy and impatient. It was her husband's doing, and though she was aware of the source of her feeling, she could not help extending her mood to their companions. When the waiter stopped by, Stella for some reason felt the need to tell him that she hadn't drunk so much in years, and Tony called out for a round of whiskies. The waiter looked grim and disapproving, and when he collected their empties, he held the bottles at arm's length, as if carting away dead snakes.

"What?" Maureen said to Rueben then, leaning across the table. "What did you just call this place?"

They had arranged themselves into couples, Rueben squeezing in next to Tony, Stella nearly touching Maureen. Earlier, Stella had noted the pairings. Like brothers and sisters, she said. Like mirrors or doubles.

Rueben looked at Maureen blankly. "This place?" He pointed at the table.

"The city," she said. "You just called Kuala Trengganu the magic portal."

"What's wrong with that?" Rueben said.

"Nothing."

"Tony calls it that," Rueben said. "I don't." Tony had just jumped up to remind the waiter about the four whiskeys he had ordered.

"I just heard you say it," she said.

"Only because Tony was calling it that. And I *have* called it that before."

"I'm just surprised I've never heard you say it," Maureen said.

Rueben thought a moment. "I have."

"Not in my presence, then."

"Oh," he said.

Their conversation had been unsatisfactory for hours. What, she wanted to know, did the fanciful term mean? Her interest surprised her, but Reuben's refusal to expand on his Mr. Tan story (it was refusal, she was sure, not inability) had emboldened both her sense of entitlement and her sense of failure. She did not recall ever hearing the term in the camp, and because Rueben was now using it with Tony, its meaning took on the aspect of a secret. Was it one Stella knew, too? Her tablemate had risen to shout something at Tony—"more *ikan bilis,* Tony, a big plate"—and did not seem to notice her exchange with her husband. She decided against asking. She was being ridiculous, that was all there was to it, risking embarrassment over a trifle.

Stella, in fact, seemed to have no interest in bandying about secrets. She was giddy and a bit wild-eyed, and her drinking had turned her sloppy. She sat down and spilled some beer on the table, then pressed her mug against Maureen's arm, securing her attention. "Do you want to hear something?" she said.

She started talking crazy stuff.

People were a menagerie of past and present selves, Stella said, slurring her words, but not in the way we thought (*menagerie:* the word was so unexpected Maureen concluded Stella had book-borrowed her idea). Those selves lived at different metabolisms, and they had different goals. Consider a rock, Stella said, holding up her index finger.

"Yeah, baby," Tony shouted, upon his return. "But wrong finger."

Stella ignored him. The consciousness of a rock, she said, if indeed it had one, would be apparent to us only in geologic time, over the span of millions of years. Think about it, she said. Who was to say we understood what all our menagerie selves were thinking or doing? They didn't necessarily share our timeframe.

"Why oh why?" Rueben laughed. "What are you trying to say?"

Stella put down her drink and stuck her erect finger onto the sudsy tabletop, as if writing with chalk on a blackboard. She said, "My point is, we think our consciousness has only one metabolism. Who's to say our past selves aren't still pulling some levers, just at a different rpm?" Then she said something that struck Maureen as blatantly aggressive. Show her the person who scoffed at that, she declared, and she'd show you someone whose life was turning to junk and carnage.

Maureen wondered who Stella was addressing. And when, pray tell, did normal people ever talk like that? Stella had always been a bit on the dour side, always a closet curmudgeon, always self-important, but nothing like this. In the camp, Maureen recalled, Stella had an opinion about everything, and she always managed to sound like the voice of authority. Once, she had polished off half a bottle of something and held forth on a dialect issue she knew nothing about. The British still used *whilst* in everyday conversation, she had asserted, and she wouldn't be swayed even when Maureen read aloud from one of her English textbooks that claimed otherwise. Stella had simply closed her eyes and rattled off ludicrous examples. Whilst I was walking, Stella said, I saw a Vietnamese refugee. Whilst I am here, the boat people are, too. Whilst I eat, they do, too.

"Don't go ivory tower on us, Stella," said Tony. He had placed full shot glasses in front of everyone. "If you're going to dissertate, at least take your top off."

Stella laughed. "You still know how to sweep a girl off her feet," she said.

"You know what I mean."

"Oh, I know. Tony, Tony, Tony," Stella said. She swept back her hair—a girlish gesture, but there was genuine affection in her voice.

"I see what you're saying," said Rueben, and he scrunched up his glasses.

"Do you?" Maureen asked, but she didn't shout it out. Rueben appeared not to hear.

"Hey," shouted Tony to everyone. "Did I ever tell you I wanted to be a writer when I was on Bidong? How's that for a menagerie guy? I still know what he's thinking, Stella. Last year I entered a ten words or less novel contest, in his honor." He nearly fell back in his chair with laughter. "Here it is, beginning, middle, and end. I quote: 'Don't know. Don't care. Fuck you.'"

He laughed again. How was it? he asked. A winner, no? Thing was, he said, it didn't matter what rpm you played words like that. If you actually believed them, then you weren't cut out for relief work. And if you didn't understand them, then you had never done relief work. He *did* know and he *did* care, he always had—"but fuck you anyway," he said—and only people who had put their money where their mouth could follow that.

"You and your acid commando talk," said Stella.

"You and your huff 'n puff talk," said Tony.

Rueben joined in. "Peace, oh my nutso brothers and sisters," he said, raising his mug in blessing.

"So we're the opposite ends of a bell curve?" Stella exclaimed in mock outrage. "We're the narrow extremes?"

"We walked the walk, didn't we?" Tony said. "That gives us the right to be nuts." He turned to Rueben. "Are we or are we not the real deal?" he asked.

No deal was realer, Rueben answered. He clapped Tony hard on the shoulder.

"You, too, buddy," came Tony's spirited reply. The real deals, he said, were members of the Boat People Club. They were at this table.

Stella raised her hand as if she were in a classroom. "Real Deal, would that include Thomas and Kevin and Kathy?"

Tony smiled, then hunched forward, looking Stella straight in the eye. As if, it seemed to Maureen, she and Rueben were not at the table. As if only he and Stella might want to hear the answer. "Interesting question," Tony said. "I defer to the other two members of the Club."

Tony and Stella remained poised, locking eyes, their faces expectant and still. A techno version of some Donna Summers song boomed in the background, and Maureen was for the first time that night aware that none of them were talking. An escalation had just occurred. Tony and Stella were fishing, certainly, but more than that, they seemed to want some issue resolved, right here and now. They knew what she would say. They knew she would understand the challenge, the assumption that no matter how long she had been with Rueben she was still one of the late-comers and therefore suspect. What they wanted to hear now was what Rueben would say. They wanted him to choose: them or us? Desperate people did that, Maureen thought. Lost people. They'd raise a question they couldn't stop trying to answer, and they'd make it your question, too. She wondered then if whatever had driven Tony and Stella for so many years now drove them into meanness and spite.

Rueben glanced at her—just long enough, she thought, to gauge her expression. She was at first approving of his refusal to engage their tablemates on such a level. But she then understood that circumspection had nothing to do with his silence. He was waiting for her to speak. And if he would do that, if he would sit back and let her risk insult from these people, would he also then lean back afterward and deliver a more modulated response? Would he stoop to critiquing his wife's fondness for the three absent latecomers?

She would not allow the scenario to take form. Yet she recognized, too, the dilemma posed to her husband, and she was aware of her recognition as a welcome kind of vanity. She knew things about him. She understood the long view, and when you understood that, you could make allowances. You could afford generosity and largesse.

What, after all, *could* his answer be?

Her husband's situation was something, perhaps, that people like Tony and Stella, graying wanderers, people without solid and intimate moorings, could not fathom. When you had a life together, that life could survive small acts of cowardice and sabotage. That life could absorb small betrayals. (Why had Rueben not objected when she first started working on Boeing military proposals? Why had he nodded stupidly when her mother called her a dilettante?) It was when you had a life apart, when your ties were fragile, focused on a few basic connections, that some words here or there, a choice here or there, became weighted with consequence.

Answer one way, and he'd disappoint her; then they'd both recover and move on. Answer another way, and he'd disappoint them, and they might not ever let him back in. There was proportion to consider, and effect, and because of that, whatever answer he might have given would be tainted with qualifications and amendments. She knew how he felt, she knew he loved Thomas and Kevin and Kathy, and though she could and did fault him for not saying it out loud, right now, she could not claim that she would have been bold enough to say it out loud herself, had their situations been reversed.

"Who knows?" she said then. "Who knows? Who knows?" She punctuated her answer by raising her shot glass and staring into its contents.

"Good old Maureen," Stella smiled. "That's what I like. Consistency."

But Maureen would not allow Stella's provocation to draw her out. Rueben leaned into Stella. "I like my wife, too," he said, his face opening like a parasol. Maureen did not know how to parse the comment—how much was jokey? how much boozily affirmative?—but the fact that he had chosen to speak at all was encouraging. So he had not completely opted out. It had simply taken him a while to find his bearings.

Stella seemed at a loss for how to respond, and Tony raised his eyebrows. Maureen took her opportunity to steer the conversation. She turned to Tony. "Why do you call Kuala Trengganu the magic portal?" she asked.

Tony laughed. "If I didn't know better," he said, "I'd swear you were changing the topic."

"Okay, guilty." She flicked a hand dismissively into the air. "So what does it mean?"

It used to mean, Tony said—and he sounded dark and raspy when he spoke, unaware, Maureen felt, of the theatrical trappings—it used to mean that when you stepped from the supply boat onto the harbor docks, you walked around town like you were coming out from under one spell, and entering another. Back when Bidong was a tougher place. Back before she and the other three latecomers arrived. Before the camp had a hospital and steady supplies and guards who weren't necessarily psychotic. It was like you were an astronaut and had just returned from Mars. You were disoriented. You got to walk down an actual street and eat in an actual restaurant, then you stepped into a taxi and wherever you stopped you got drunk and hostile and whored around until your money ran out.

"Well," Rueben said, "it wasn't *quite* like that."

"Said the boy scout to his wife," Tony said.

Rueben frowned. "What's that supposed to mean?"

"Oh, come on."

"I'm serious."

"I'm just talking," Tony said.

"So am I. What did you mean by that?"

"Dude. Dude," said Tony, grinding his palm into the tabletop. "You mellowed. Don't worry about it."

Rueben jerked himself up from his chair, and even in the dim light, Maureen saw that his face had filled with blood. She recognized the look: his lips pressed tight, the pouches under his eyes wrinkly and distressed, his gaze directed toward some distant point. "Bathroom," he announced—too forcefully, she thought, too abruptly—and without another word he walked toward the men's room.

They all watched him go. Maureen was the first to speak. She would have been justified, she felt, in making a stink, in splashing Tony with her drink, perhaps, or banging her fists down on the table. "Tony," she said calmly. "No more, okay?"

He shrugged as if he didn't know what she was talking about. Then Stella leaned across the table and told him to knock it off. "That's your friend," she said.

"Apologies," Tony answered, and he raised his bottle at Maureen, as if toasting. He seemed to be searching for something to say. Then he found it. He said, "He would have turned out like us sorry fucks if it weren't for you."

He was lying about himself, of course. And about Stella. They reveled in who they were and what they had done. They felt noble and damaged, and their damage only enhanced their sense of nobility.

"I hope that's a compliment," Maureen said.

"What else would it be?" Tony asked.

"Of course it is, Maureen," Stella said.

More lies. But she knew she wouldn't call them on it. She felt a little sorry for them. All their drama, their hopeless passions. They had no way forward.

"There he is," she called out when Rueben reappeared. He seemed better, smiling and waggling his head to the music. He bounded to his seat. She wanted to slide her hand across his arm, to give him a reassuring wink, but that just would have made him feel bad all over again. Hi, she said. Hi, he said back.

"Buddy," shouted Tony, and Rueben made a show of turning his head and looking back over one shoulder, then the other. Everyone laughed.

— — —

Back in the hotel, Maureen cried in front of Rueben, and because the tears were humiliating she walked out to their veranda and turned her back to him.

"This is hard," she said.

"I've got a history with them," he said, but he kept his distance and spoke from the foot of the bed.

But weren't they second-stringers? Wasn't that what he had called them?

He held out his palms. What, he answered, did she want him to say? What could he tell her?

"Tell me you called them that to spare my feelings," she said. "Because you knew I didn't like them. That'd be the truth, wouldn't it?"

"We've always been careful of each other's feelings," he said. It was odd hearing his words come from behind, disembodied, like listening to the radio. "Is this a fault now?"

She didn't answer, but she did invite him out the veranda to watch the harbor lights twinkle on and off, and to talk about nothing at all. It was heartening to know there was no evasion from him, no pretense of innocence or surprise. They would communicate, she hoped, later that night in a dream (they did not, though the possibility held her to one scotch). She understood that if she came out and asked him to cancel the trip tomorrow he might refuse, and if he did then something completely avoidable would have been brought into existence, some hissing fissure would have been created where there had been no fissure before.

So she was grateful and assured—she kissed him hard—when Rueben said, Look, look, what do you think of this? After tomorrow, he said, after they got back from Bidong, they'd leave Stella and Tony to their own devices. He could tell them something had come up, some emergency back in Seattle, and then they'd quietly slip away, just the two of them, maybe up to Thailand or maybe down the coast to Johore Bharu or Singapore. They didn't need this strife. It was like a pressure in the back of his head. In both their heads, right? Then he brought his hands to his skull, screwed up his face, and pressed hard. What was the name, he said, for where a river met an ocean? Where it got so murky you couldn't see in front of your face? That was how he felt now.

Righto, righto, she said happily, and she placed her hand on top of his head and brought it slowly to her own, and made their heads touch. So it would be a matter of waiting them out. Stella and Tony would have their drama tomorrow, and they would probably hug and point out where things used to be, and maybe Stella would shed a few tears, and then it would be over. Rueben would clear his head. Then they could go lie around on some hotel beach, tanning, maybe rent some boogie boards and go bodysurfing. They'd have some seafood, do some people watching. They could whisper and cut up over the shave-headed French women (she could not help thinking of photos she had seen of Nazi collaborators), or the Australians who winked every time they said hello, or the British retirees who paraded around in black socks and crisp white shorts. They could tour the Batu Caves, ride an elephant up in Changmai, visit the Thai snake farms. They could be what they were. A couple of normal people on vacation.

— — —

The boat to Bidong was a converted fishing trawler with two huge outboards in back. Like the supply boat, Tony said, only in miniature. Tony seemed beside himself with excitement, and in his haste to arrive early at the harbor docks, he had forgotten to bring along his snorkel and fins. Stella had too. She had been in such a state of anticipation, she said, that she couldn't even finish her breakfast *roti.* All she'd thought to bring was bottled water and a change of clothes. Tony proudly displayed the contents of his daypack: water, a flashlight, some clothesline, two lighters, a knife, a first-aid kit, and a spare pair of running shorts.

Rueben laughed—"*I'm* the boy scout?" he roared—then victoriously pulled his snorkel and mask from a shoulder bag that also contained Maureen's snorkeling equipment and a paperback novel ("just in case," she had told him, but they both figured she'd be reading it).

It was still early, and the sky was a band of purple and pink that seemed to carry the sounds of morning from the shophouses to the harbor water. Someone was clattering metal pots up the hill, and boys in oversized flip-flops splashed buckets of water onto the dirty sidewalks; outside the dock gate, a Sikh night watchman was still asleep in his cot, snoring. The harbor was so empty you could hear the boat's engine tappets clicking one by one.

They boarded. Maureen gamely leaped from the dock and onto the bobbing craft, piloted by a small Malay man wearing a sarong and a t-shirt. He had brought along his little boy and girl, both of whom appeared to be around ten. Rueben and Tony chatted the man up in rusty but still passable Malay, then Stella joined in. How, Maureen marveled, did their language skills remain so good? She had never learned a word in the camp. Our job, she told her friends at Boeing, had been to help the refugees learn *our* language. But in fact no one had ever offered to teach her Malay or Vietnamese. No one had ever entered the relief worker compound to knock on her door.

They passed the giant moorings, the vegetable women in their small canoes, the crumbling seawall, and then the ocean was flat and open before them, and Rueben and Stella and Tony stood on the prow and whooped. Maureen joined them a few minutes later, after first settling onto the bench behind the captain's wheel, as she had done so many years ago. The pilothouse had been her favorite spot on the camp supply boat, away from the prying eyes of any refugees who might happen to be onboard.

Early on, she recalled, she had purchased a snow cone from one of the harbor vendors and eaten it in the enclosed passenger area, where a Vietnamese family sat smiling nervously. Stella had sidled up to her. "Eating here, Maureen?" Stella asked, and Maureen had understood that she was not to flaunt her money and freedom in front of the refugees. She had been made to feel shame. Later, she found out that Stella had gobbled down half a box of *Chips Ahoy!* in the privacy of the boat's stinking bathroom. Maureen had felt it then: the encroachment of an alien code. It was oppressive and unfair, and its rules seemed to change every day.

When she joined the other three she almost said something mocking to Stella and Tony. But that would have started something. There was no need to complicate matters.

— — —

"For some people," said Stella, "doing relief work is like doing cocaine."

"It's a rush, all right," Tony said. "I won't deny it. What say, Rueben?"

Rueben mulled over the question. "Sure it is," he said. "But doesn't that ignore the flip side? We did good."

"Bingo," said Maureen.

"Well, right," said Stella crossly. "That goes without saying. Yes, we did good." They all stood in a tight circle, and their hair kept blowing into their eyes. Bidong, the skipper had said, was ten minutes away. "I'm just saying when you look closely, Bidong was more complicated than that. It's like history has entrusted us with secrets."

"Oh, Lady Stella," Tony laughed. "No more. *No mas.*"

"Laugh if you must," said Stella, shushing him. "But how can you explain the connection with Bidong we still feel?" She swept her hand though her hair. "There's been no memorializing. There's no communal memory of what happened. We're the only ones who know the story. There's an obligation there, don't you think?"

"Remember how close the Malaysians came to a shoot-on-sight policy?" Rueben said suddenly. "Remember the Ranger battalion they moved into position?"

"'Mane of spray, swarm of bees,'" Tony said. "I still remember you saying that, Rueben. If the Rangers came, they'd buzz in on their speedboats." Tony glided his hand through the air, *bzzz bzzz bzzz,* a speedboat trailing a giant rooster tail and bristling with antennae and weapons.

"I remember," Rueben said, throwing back his head. He turned to Maureen and spoke softly to her. "The Malaysians wanted to round up the Viets and put them back out to sea." (They had come *this* close to doing it, he had told her once, holding out his forefinger and thumb. She hadn't believed him then.)

"I know," said Maureen. It was hard not to snap. She would have to tell him later how she hadn't appreciated him using her as fodder.

Stella turned to her. "Before your time," she said.

"Did I seem confused?" Maureen said with irritation.

"I'm just reading your expression, Maureen. Just trying to include you, that's all."

"I've heard all this," Maureen said.

"Okay, that's good to know. It's just when you new guys arrived, everything changed."

There was a long pause.

"As in, things got better for the refugees," Stella said. She looked to Maureen for a reaction, but Maureen did not react. "It's just Bidong almost felt like a *job*-job then," Stella continued. "After awhile, you could just hole up in your room and read *Newsweek* all day. Right? Rise and shine, wake up and smell the anesthesia. No more Lord of the Flies—not that that was a good thing."

"Well, thank you, I guess," said Maureen. "Is that what they call damning with faint praise?" She felt her cheeks burn. She had in fact spent much of her time in her bungalow, poring over the magazines that agencies on the mainland crammed into the UN mailbag. Outside of teaching classes and playing board games at night, she hadn't found all that much to do.

"My *good*ness," said Stella, smiling. "I was just using your arrival as a timeframe reference."

"That's fine," Maureen said in a friendly tone. She stood and looked around, preparing her escape.

Tony spoke up: "What would you have done? If the Rangers came, I mean?"

"That's a tough one," said Rueben.

"They had a helicopter ready to evacuate us, you know," said Stella.

"I wouldn't have gone peacefully," said Tony, with menace in his voice. "You, Rueben?"

Rueben glanced over at Maureen and caught her eye. "There was a time I might have joined you," he said. "I don't know. Depends what day you ask me."

"Mister Ambivalence," said Tony, nudging Rueben with his elbow. "But I hear you. Push comes to shove, I bet you would've done the right thing."

They weren't going to ask what she would have done, and for that Maureen was grateful. Such talk led nowhere, around and around, and she briefly entertained the notion of slapping her forehead and shouting out, "Why, golly, the personal *is* the political." Or perhaps some comment about VFW reunions might be more killing. The pot bellies, the looping recollections, the posturing: there was something tobacco-stained and garlicky about the reminiscing, an apportioning of futile, fatty remains.

Had time stopped since Bidong? Maureen wanted to shout.

She walked to the railing to watch the waves crinkle in the sunlight.

What if she went up to Stella and said that if history wanted to annihilate, then she knew two sad sacks who should be the first in line? Yet she was also dimly aware that the conversation was drifting closer to home. All the talk-talk was also a hand scudding along the bottom of a table, unseen, inching toward her husband.

You still feel it, don't you, Rueben? Wasn't that what they were getting at?

— — —

There was no dock, no line of structures up from the beach, no back-alley smell, and even the giant boulders that had marked either side of the approach inlet had disappeared. No one said anything. No one wanted to admit what they already knew.

Before they waded in—the boat would return in seven hours, the skipper said—Rueben pointed to the skipper's two children and asked if anyone minded company. Apparently the skipper had been impressed with his passengers' language skills and Malaysian past. Would the white people mind, he asked, if his children combed the island with them? They both had had seashell collections at home, and both had come prepared with matching little buckets and plastic trenching shovels. They all looked at the kids. The boy was in shorts and sandals; the girl, the taller of the two, wore jeans and a long, thick shirt that looked uncomfortable. They seemed pleasant and well-behaved.

The children had never been to Bidong, Rueben reported, and their father said this was probably their only chance to visit the place, at least until the following year, when there would be facilities for tourists. The island was private property now and officially off-limits. But, said the skipper, who cared what rules Chinese businessmen came up with? The island was in the middle of nowhere, airy as a dream, and though construction wasn't due to resume until the following month, the skipper said he wouldn't think of leaving his flesh and blood there, even for an afternoon, with regular white people. But he had felt kinship, he said approvingly, with his passengers. He could tell they were good people, understanding of Malay culture, former humanitarians, and since his children wanted seashells with *cache,* shells to impress their friends with, would they mind?

Stella and Tony thought it a fine idea, as did Rueben, and the children chattered to effect, loudly demonstrating their desire to walk the beaches and find treasure. Maureen was much less enthusiastic, though she didn't voice her reservations. To put so much faith in strangers, foreigners no less, to trust strangers with your family . . . wasn't that like trusting to magic? Like setting out as the boat people had done, piling onto tiny ships no one in their right mind would take around a lake, then into the teeth of towering waves? Behind that faith was another kind of faith, one that perhaps the skipper had acted upon impulsively: the belief that something good and beautiful exists beyond the horizon. Something you don't yet understand. Something transformative and new.

Insane. Like moths to the flame, Maureen concluded. And then: like white people to the camps.

She'd have to remember that one. In case things got heated, it would be a good, clean stroke.

Rueben held back a bit, helping her through the shoals, while Stella and Tony jumped from the boat and lifted the kids down. She despised the way her companions bantered with the children—their exaggerated excitement, their avuncular jokes, their cooing—but at the same time she envied them their ease. Were they aware, she wondered, of an echo? The Vietnamese kids had loved to follow the white people around, hanging on their every word, and whenever the kids had a chance, they'd crawl under the bungalows—all the structures had been built on stilts—and watch the relief workers between spaces in the floor slats.

Big white arms and tiny brown hands. Boat people by proxy. It was disturbing.

On the beach everyone watched the boat pull away. Then the kids took off, and after a short burst they squatted by a small lagoon. They held up shells to the light, quietly assembling their booty.

Stella came up behind her. "You guys never had kids," Stella said.

Maureen shook her head. "I read an article once that said relief workers tend not to," she said. She did not see recognition in Stella's eyes, so she elaborated. "Because their experiences make them hyper-aware about what can happen. They develop defense mechanisms."

"What article was that?" Stella said, moving in close. "I'd like to read it."

Maureen shrugged. "I don't know. Just something I read online. Passing the time at work."

Stella looked at her, she thought, with disgust.

"We never made copies of ourselves," Maureen said. "But that's only because I've never been into children. Not that other stuff."

Stella didn't say anything for a moment. Then she examined Maureen's face closely and said one infuriating word: "Interesting."

Maureen made no reply. Instead, she began jogging through the sand to catch up with her husband. *Interesting.* A roommate had said that to her once, sneering, back in college. She had been thought mulish, she knew, and the judgment had burrowed deep. Even her wildness was of the drawing-room variety. She developed a taste for party drugs—some pot, a few long nights of Ecstasy—but only if someone else got them for her, and only if someone vouched for their ingredients. She slept with men occasionally, but only if they kept it a secret and entered her silently (as if committing incest, she realized, and the notion so repulsed her she stopped having sex altogether for a year). She stole a street sign once, and in her final year of college she climbed on top of a car and removed the "o" from the "Hello" on a church signboard. When she laughed she sometimes snorted, then pretended the snort shocked everyone. And when on the freeway one night, the gray city skyline in sight, she lost control of her car and spun around and around, and stared at headlights bearing down upon her, she sat calmly with her hands on the steering wheel and gave in to a vacant resignation: *so now I will die.*

She kicked some sand onto Reuben's legs. "This really is the basement here," she said to him. He didn't understand. Forget it, she said. If she explained herself, she'd have to tell him that this was where the monsters were, the bogeymen, all hiding behind the boxes and mealy pallets. And that would have been disturbing to say, so she didn't.

— — —

The Chun Fatt Company had bulldozed the eastern side of Bidong, where most of the refugee shelters had been, and their giant yellow earthmovers and their random trench work now littered the island the way boat spines and rusting engines had way back when. All the old shit canals, cleared by men with hook poles, had been plowed under, and the base of the vast orange gouge that led down from the volcanic cone, where the refugees had felled trees, was now alive with white roots and sea beetles and butterflies that alighted on the deposits of lizards and small rodents.

They walked the beach slowly, peering at the rocks, at the slope of the land, inspecting, as if at any moment some wispy-haired Vietnamese man might stumble out of the foliage, the way Japanese soldiers still sometimes emerged from jungle caves. Tony and Stella took off their flip-flops, and their weight left holes in the sand that quickly filled with seawater bubbling up from beneath.

Soon they all spread out, walking singly, and the kids went their own way. They quietly regarded the seagulls and the occasional fallen coconut, and every once in a while they heard rustling in the treeline and stared with much anticipation into the foliage. But mostly their walking led them to more of the same, to other gullies, other glistening rocks, other arrangements of palm and scrub. Behind them, the small waves fell in a continuous sheet, breaking at one end of the beach, then traveling to the other, and each time the water withdrew, it filled their air with a hissing sound. Hundreds of tiny sand crabs rippled in senseless patterns, then burrowed into the beach, only to re-emerge when the water receded.

They walked around looking this way and that, barking something loud every few minutes, announcing some tree or slope that looked familiar, or maybe, when they thought about it, wasn't familiar but reminded them of a particular morning or afternoon. They put their hands on their hips. They pointed. They kicked over small rocks and stared at the trees and up into the rockface.

Her poor husband. And poor Stella and Tony, she amended. They were all Odysseus returned to Ithaca, now ruined, Penelope gone missing, her loom broken in a corner of the Great Hall. After so many years their memories had begun to feed on themselves, generating sandals and string and plastic wrappers, drawing a vial of blood from a woman selling pickled bats, filling the still, quiet nights with a clanking generator, adding a squeak to the planks by the guards' dockside pillhouse.

The shout, the echo, then nothing. Where, she wondered, could all their passion go? All their insistence?

Tony spoke up behind her. "Are you still in touch with any refugees?" he said. He sounded like he was ready to cry.

"Oh, you know how it is," she said, turning. "They want to get on with their lives."

He shrugged. "Okay," he said. He had no more to say, which made it clear to Maureen that his question had not been a real one. He shrugged again and took off jogging. Had he actually wanted to speak to her, or had he been trying to fill the silence, distracting himself from the disappearance of his island? There was another possibility, too. Had Rueben, perhaps, started rambling, talking nonsense, all to avoid acknowledging his own disappointment? Had he unwittingly told Tony the truth?

She had never received any letters from refugees.

It was something she could not say to Tony, especially since he and Stella had been wildly popular in the camp. During their going-away party—Stella and Tony left together, on the same morning—the Vietnamese played Tony's favorite song, Steppenwolf's "Magic Carpet Ride," over the loudspeakers. The night before, a delegation of them had stood outside the wire to the relief workers' compound and serenaded Stella. When Tony and Stella left the next day, a huge crowd jammed the beach to see them off. They presented Tony with a model refugee boat made of coconut husks and equipped with small pearl lights. Stella had received a white and green *ai-doa,* hand-sewn from silk smuggled in by black marketeers.

The morning she and Rueben left the island for good, she had boarded the supply boat empty-handed. The Viets didn't like her, she whispered to Rueben. She didn't mean anything to anyone. Only to him.

No one had come to see her off, and Rueben pretended that the model boat he had received was for the both of them. "They made it big because it's a two-fer," he said, and she accepted what she knew was a lie, a clumsy one at that, one he surely knew wouldn't fool her. But that was okay: they both agreed to it, and because of that the lie became less of a lie. Now the boat sat on top of Reuben's bookcase, and if anyone asked about it, they repeated what had now become the truth.

She kept walking, passing silently into what used to be Zone D, scanning, and then she started up the hillside, into brush and dense stands of palm. Rueben was nowhere to be found. They had all gone their separate ways. In the distance, the sea seemed to quiver, lit up by the sun into giant strips, and the wind carried small crackling sounds whose source she could not fathom. She climbed, pushing aside fronds and swollen vines scaly as snakeskin; she tripped over the knuckly roots and scratched herself on the brambles and jagged points of stripped trees. And then she was headed down, holding her arms out like a surfer, sliding across smooth boulders and mossy inclines. She began running, unable to slow her progress, and then she felt herself crash through a wall of foliage. There was dust everywhere, and Maureen, reaching now for branches to slow her descent, plunged her hand into something that felt like soft wax, then continued running and sliding, coming to rest only after grabbing hold of tree stump. She swiped insects from her arm.

She had to find Rueben. She had to give him solace.

There, sitting on a small bluff, were her husband and Tony. She approached them from behind, downwind, and in the breeze their words arrived clear and sharp, as if snipped from their tongues.

When you're up in Thailand, Tony said, we could meet you guys in Bangkok.

Good, Rueben said. See you there in two days. Just don't say anything, okay?

— — —

She imagined rushing forward and pointing an accusing finger in his face. She imagined slapping him, though she knew she never would. Instead, she turned away, replaying his words, trying to find some way for the words to not mean what she knew they meant.

She hit on something then: he was keeping Bidong alive, his Bidong, the only way he could.

But his betrayal had been large, not small, and something like panic crossed her face, only it wasn't panic, it was feverish and blinding and when she looked around and saw no one there she whispered, How could you? How could you? She began climbing again, pulling on sapling limbs, yanking herself up. She looked for footholds in the flat rocks, leaning forward and probing with her free hand for tree roots. She lost her balance. Her paperback slipped out from her hand, and she cursed under her breath as the pages flapped and tumbled down the slope, coming to rest in a dry streambed. Her skin stuck to her shirt. Her lungs hurt.

Later, when she saw Rueben again, he was walking out into the water. Strapped to his head was his snorkel. The sun had begun to drop, and the horizon had taken on a metallic, bluish hue. It was almost time for the boat to return.

"Are you going out there alone?" she asked.

He tugged on his mask. "Just out to the rocks," he said. "See some fishies, then back."

She said, "It's angerous-day i-bay yourself-ay."

He jerked the breathing tube from his mouth. "What?"

"I said, 'it's dangerous by yourself.'" She pointed to the water, as if gesturing would prove her point. The water was shallow and calm all the way to the outcropping.

Rueben shook his head. "Jesus, Maureen," he said evenly. He slipped the mask on again and turned, moving out into the water, and then he was wading. She watched him for awhile. He seemed to make a point of not looking at her.

She listened to the birds overhead, to the gravelly rumble of the waves, and she pictured the camp sinking. Zone by zone, she made the tarpaulin shelters disappear. She made the hospital fall, then she imagined the UN bungalows quaking and dropping into sinkholes the size of buses. The Buddhist temple lay under rubble. Out by the dock, circling men clacked over the still-trembling tiles of the Task Force barracks. The bluebottles, the wilting brown cabbage, the jars of fermented sea slugs and baby iguanas, the loudspeakers nailed high in the palms, the phosphorescent tree where suicides left their notes—all trembled and fell. She felt the whole camp sink, and as it sank she tilted her head this way and that, encouraging the sudden lurchings and the even more sudden collapses, watching as from an airplane the funneling of planks and rusted tin roofs and homely food stalls into vast cleavages of earth and water. And then it was over. The ocean was glassy and smooth; the land was dark with furrows, the horizon flat and clear, and a dry, chafing wind from the back of her mind whispered the camp's oblivion.

"Miss," she heard then. The voice was panicked. "Miss, please. Miss, miss." It was the girl. She was out of breath. Maureen bent down and asked her what was wrong, but the girl's eyes darted around, and she began speaking a rapid Malay.

"I don't understand," Maureen said. "English? You speak English?"

"No, no," the girl answered, then she said something incomprehensible. She grabbed Maureen's arm and turned, beckoning her to follow. Something was wrong. An emergency. Maureen jogged behind, unable to keep pace, but she followed the girl into the treeline and crashed through some underbrush, then walked over a log laid over a muddy rivulet. She heard Tony shouting something, then a child's wailing.

She arrived at a clearing, the girl panting beside her, and saw Tony and Stella fiddling with Tony's clothesline, then tossing a length of it down a hole obscured by loose scrub and palm. She knew immediately what had happened. The girl's brother had fallen down one of the island's ancient wells, dug by Vietnamese men before the water barge brought regular shipments. She found herself staring, as if she had a seat at some theater-in-the-round, and she experienced then a kind of removal, an awareness of her own small presence, one dwarfed by the scrub and palm and the drama being played out before her. At the same time she reproached herself for not rushing forward, for accommodating her own nature too willfully and completely.

What happened, happened without her. Pull, Tony shouted, pull, pull, and she could see the veins bulging on his neck. The clothesline was taut now, and Stella, in the front position, spoke in a loud and commanding voice into the hole. Maureen saw the boy's hand then, like something out of a horror movie, a corpse come to life, then his head. The boy emerged with the clothesline knotted tightly around his chest, cutting into his skin. He was crying, and there was some blood on his arm. She told herself he was just scared. Nothing serious. He seemed to be moving just fine.

Don't just *stand* there, Stella screamed, but Maureen only looked at her in response. She noted the bright green colors around the clearing, the spiky fronds, the dappled sunlight, the way the hole seemed so artificial and out of place. And then her head was filled with reasons for why she did not move. There was no danger to the boy, not anymore. She didn't know first aid. She couldn't speak Malay. What difference would another person make? But Tony and Stella, they loved every moment, didn't they? They loved losing themselves in something vast and public and dangerous. They were ghoulish, weren't they?

She heard a whistling then. The sound rattled through the brush, near her head, and when she saw Tony staring at her, she knew he had just thrown a stone. At her. He had thrown it hard. He patted his chest, up down, up down, as if his hand held a beating heart. "You got anything inside?" he shouted. "Are you alive?"

Sunlight laced through the branches, and for a moment she had the sense she was transparent. The light seemed to shine all the way through her. Did one simply go from dream to dream, unable to wake? Under that thought was another, and she clenched her fists when she acknowledged it. She had never laid claim to a larger life. And she knew then, with certainty, why Rueben had sided with her over them all those years ago.

She had not been a question he could not answer, a secret he could not fathom. Not like them. Not like Mr. Tan.

The girl was whimpering. She grabbed for Maureen's hand, and they touched briefly, Maureen and the girl, and then Maureen looked down at her in confusion. I should stroke her hair, she thought, though the thought was wooden, as if she were reading from a script someone had just thrust into her hand. It was too late. The girl had already surged forward to join her brother.

"Maureen, damn it," Stella said. She pointed in accusation. "Do something. Go get Rueben," she shouted. "Do something. *Anything*. Get your husband."

So she did. She picked her way back to the beach, stumbling, her mind racing, and when she reached the beach she began jogging. There was a yellow earthmover off to her right, buried up to its treads, and as she passed, she saw something. She stopped. On the other side of the machine, leading to the water, was a narrow, deep trench covered with weathered palm. Through spaces in the palm she saw a line of steel rods pointing straight up through the trench water. Camouflage. The trench was just wide enough to snare a trespasser's leg. Someone, perhaps the absent driver, had taken it upon himself to disguise the danger. Someone callous had decided to guard what was his against all comers.

Rueben was just around the outcropping. She was about to go to him, to yell for him to come quick, when she saw Tony running toward her. He was running so hard she could see the fury on his face. She knew what would happen. He'd run past her and straight to Rueben. He'd tell her husband what they thought of her. It would all come pouring out, all their contempt, and Rueben would fall silent or make a show of defending his wife or deflect the accusations with jokes. But something would have started, some fissure would have been created, and in the slow metabolism of a life together, the fissure would either remain a crack or the fissure would open into a dark and treacherous gap. He'd mull things over in his quiet and solicitous way, and in Bangkok Tony and Stella would talk and talk, and they'd make his head rumble with questions, and a month or a year or a decade down the line, the questions would either fade into nothing or grow louder and louder until all he could hear was the ground giving way.

Tony was running straight at her, along the treeline, so she moved toward the water, directly behind the trench. His trajectory followed. She stepped back a few yards and yelled for him to run faster. "This way," she shouted. "Follow me." She waved her arms over her head. "Run," she yelled, summoning what sounded like panic in her voice. She waved him on, and as he drew nearer she shouted for him to run even faster—"there's no time, fast, fast," she yelled—and Tony picked up his speed, churning his legs in the sand, and she began to jog now, too, sweeping her arm through the air, signaling for him to close the space. "There's no time," she shouted again. "No time. Run." He ran and then his feet did not touch the ground, and his right leg dropped into the trench while the rest of him tumbled forward. His head slammed down hard and mud spattered in all directions. There was no sound at first. Then Tony began screaming. He yelled so loud he drowned out the waves collapsing onto the rocks and sand.

Rueben was where she had had left him, floating in the water. His back was to the sky, and the black stem of the snorkel stuck straight up in an attitude of finality. He wasn't moving. The current pulled at his hair and a length of seaweed sprawled over his calf. She feared the worst, but just as she about to run in after him his whole body quivered. There was a splash then, and he kicked his legs up violently and went under. For a moment he was nearly vertical, like a boat going down. He disappeared for a long time. She hated standing there while Tony was crying out, but she knew that when her husband emerged he'd look to her with questions. She'd want him to know that Tony and Stella would be occupied with doctors and hospitals for awhile. She'd want to make sure he understood what had just happened.